PENGUIN BOOKS

BROKEN BISCUITS

Liz Kettle was born and bred in south-west London. She moved to Sheffield in 1990, and still lives there with her partner and two sons.

Broken Biscuits

LIZ KETTLE

PENGUIN BOOKS

PENGUIN BOOKS

Published by the Penguin Group
Penguin Books Ltd, 80 Strand, London WC2R 0RL, England
Penguin Group (USA) Inc., 375 Hudson Street, New York, New York 10014, USA
Penguin Group (Canada), 90 Eglinton Avenue East, Suite 700, Toronto, Ontario, Canada M4P 2Y3
(a division of Pearson Penguin Canada Inc.)
Penguin Ireland, 25 St Stephen's Green, Dublin 2, Ireland (a division of Penguin Books Ltd)
Penguin Group (Australia), 250 Camberwell Road, Camberwell, Victoria 3124, Australia
(a division of Pearson Australia Group Pty Ltd)
Penguin Books India Pvt Ltd, 11 Community Centre, Panchsheel Park, New Delhi – 110 017, India
Penguin Group (NZ), 67 Apollo Drive, Rosedale, North Shore 0632, New Zealand
(a division of Pearson New Zealand Ltd)
Penguin Books (South Africa) (Pty) Ltd, 24 Sturdee Avenue, Rosebank,
Johannesburg 2196, South Africa

Penguin Books Ltd, Registered Offices: 80 Strand, London WC2R 0RL, England

www.penguin.com

First published by Fig Tree 2006
Published in Penguin Books 2007

1

Typeset by Palimpsest Book Production Limited, Grangemouth, Stirlingshire
Printed in England by Clays Ltd, St Ives plc

ISBN: 978-0-141-02582-7

For Matt, love Sis

Mis-shapes, mistakes, misfits.
Raised on a diet of broken biscuits, oh, we don't look the same
as you,
We don't do the things you do but we live round here too.
Oh really

'Mis-shapes' by Pulp; lyrics by Jarvis Cocker

Can't Breathe

Can't breathe. Want sugar in the morning.
The girl is here. She is stroking me, on the bumpy bad places.
She is touching the mark from the fire.
Must get air. Pull it in.
It's cold on my face. She's singing. She came back.
My chest is burning, I can't breathe, I want to be still.
What happened to you? she whispers, *Why did you hurt yourself?*
I see her. She came back. Girlie. Rebecca. Oh Rebecca. I'm sorry.

January 17 – Non-verbal Leakage

Doctor Hassani says I'm not ill at the moment, I'm just lonely. I should go out more. Meet people. Make friends. Take up an activity. Have I ever thought of photography, or pottery, or learning French? What about flower arranging, Jodie?

Flower arranging? How old does he think I am? I may be knocking on a bit, but I've still got functioning ovaries, thank you very much.

Flower arranging.

Flower bloody arranging, for fuck's sake. I hate arranging anything, and I'm not that bothered about flowers really.

I suppose they're alright for a bit, something to look at if you're in hospital. If you've got family who come and visit you and bring a bunch. Then you have to go and get a vase from the nurses' room and they usually won't give you a glass one, and before a couple of days are out, the flowers are all dried out and dusty with the heat. Eighteen years of in and out of hospitals and I've learnt that much about flowers.

But flower arranging.

No, Doctor Hassani is confident that if I got out more, it would bring me out of myself. Do me the world of good, stop me brooding, give me something else to think about. Take my mind off things. He wrote me out my prescription and smiled.

Just one thing. People take one look at me and that's that. Glazed eyes, bit of a gulp, heads turning away. Non-verbal leakage, they call it. According to your most basic social skills training, non-verbal leakage is the thing to look out for. And in my case, it's always the same. Shut down, bail out, evacuate the building quick, it's a nutter.

To be fair, it's not everyone, of course not. You get your kind social worker types, with their excellent open body language, looking at you directly, opening their shoulders in a welcoming, non-threatening way, facing you with a neat smile at the mouth. Not the eyes, obviously, but at least they're trying. Then they go and ruin it all by talking, of course.

'Have you ever thought about how your appearance might say something about you?'

Doh.

Or better still:

'You could look so pretty if you took just a little bit more care with your clothes. Culottes can be so useful; do you have any mascara?'

And worst of all:

'Go on – crack a smile. It's amazing what a difference a smile can make!'

June actually said, 'I read somewhere, Jodie, that a really good smile can take the equivalent of two whole stone off your weight. It's been scientifically proved.'

Like.

But that's June for you, always looking for the positive. Being supportive. Being a really supportive support worker. There are no problems on Planet June, just challenges. Challenges or, if you're really lucky, opportunities for growth.

Oh really.

Anyway, it'd take more than a mere two stone to make me an acceptable piece of humanity. More than two stone, more than basic social skills training, more than a cheer-up-it-might-never-happen smile, more than bloody flower arranging, I can tell you. I do try, don't get me wrong, I really do. When I'm feeling up, I try probably, say, once a week. Sometimes, if I'm having a really good run, I have been known to try every day for a few days. Okay, so I can rely on the others at the day centre for a bit of company, but I want more.

So I'm sitting here. I'm trying. Nice pub, not too late, not too dark yet, not too full, but enough people that I'm in with a chance. I've left my parka at home and I'm wearing my lucky purple jacket. I've picked the table: in the middle of the room with two chairs and two stools. It is shiny, recently wiped and has an ashtray. Bonus. Good. I leave my photos, my bait, and get up to buy a drink. Just a half of lager. I smile at the barman. He even smiles back. There's two stone evaporated just like that.

I can talk about soaps, pretty much any of them. English ones are my speciality, but I can hold my own with the Australians too. And if I'm really really pushed I'll do the weather, although everyone knows weather is boring and polite and for funerals and tea parties. No, it's the getting talking in the first place, striking up a conversation, that's the hard bit. You need something, a prop or something, to get you going, don't you?

So: photos, three of them, I thought. One is small and square and faded to beige (beige not sepia, mind). Me, thin, early eighties, in the back garden at the old house, holding up my brown striped silkscreen design. Just got into art school, very proud. The world is my oyster (but the future's a clam, Paul Weller, 1979). The second photo is a more conventional rectangle, slightly garish colours. A snap of my final project – a section of a black-and-white piano smashed up, pinned to the wall and then splashed with dollops of lime green and orange. The third picture is the same shape, next size up. Me and Natalie sitting in front of the gas fire. It's not switched on, but we're both smiling and she's got her arm round me. I'm wearing that chunky cream cardigan with the belt. Did I feel safe then? I can't remember when things got scary: I think it's always been that way.

I shillyshally a bit at the bar, checking my change. I open my purse and sort the tens and twenties into their proper pockets. Housekeeper's purse, very useful, but I'm keeping my eyes on my table to see if I've got a bite. I run my thumb over the tip of each fingernail, pressing it in, one at a time, left hand then right. One two three four; one two three four. Still there, still jagged. I hum my song, but when the barman gives me a look I know that I'm humming too loud, so I do it really quietly so that only I can hear.

Voluntary work, June suggested. A no-lose situation, she said. Everyone benefits. If I just popped (everything is popping with June) down to my local VB, she was sure they'd be able to fix me up with something. It didn't help that I thought she said VD and started laughing. VB, Jodie, she said, stands for Volunteer Bureau, so that told me. She didn't think it was funny at all.

No one at the table yet. Ashtray still at the ready. I feel in my pocket, yes, fags still there. That's one of the most useful things they teach you in hospital. The art and craft of smoking. Your different smoking options. First off, you've got all your straight fags in a packet. Most people opt for strong fags that scrape your throat and give you something you can feel, over the low-fat variety. Whether to get ten or twenty or even a great big carton depends on money, obviously, or friends and relatives who've been to France and are kind enough to remember to visit the hypermarket for you. Then, of course, there is the big roll-up debate. The Professor (a little bald bloke with round glasses, never spoke, but looked intelligent), he used to actually put filters inside his rollies, which was some kind of compromise I suppose. Still had to pull tufts of baccy out of his mouth, though. Typical pose of a roll-up smoker: tiny bit of tongue slightly stuck out of the corner of the mouth, one eye screwed up and an index finger and thumb making small searching tugs for strands. Too much like having pubic hairs in your mouth – not for me thank you very much.

The barman reaches over and empties the ashtray in front of me. He produces a horrible limp smelly cloth from under the bar and wipes it round till the cloth is even darker grey. Then, joy of joy, he plops a little black folded book of matches inside the ashtray, and walks the length of the bar to do the others. I pocket them straight away. Matches or lighter is one of the other big questions. Matches are best, no doubt about it, more physical, less alienating, more in touch with the whole process of putting burning poisons down your throat. They also take more time and involve ritual, always a plus in an institution, or anywhere else for that matter.

And here's a tip: that lovely little black sulphuric wisp of smoke after you've blown (or shaken, if you prefer) out a match can be useful for covering the smell of shit if you are caught short in a public place. I learnt that from my mum. She didn't smoke, oh my goodness me no, but she always carried a box of matches in her handbag to work just in case the need to empty her bowels should come over her un-expectedly, which it never did.

She got a bit of a reputation for liking matches, and people used to give her souvenirs from all over the place. My nan once saved up nearly a hundred boxes, squirrelled away from cafés and hotels over the years, and gave them to her for her birthday. Her best box was a kind of halfway-house size between standard and kitchen, but covered with an appliquéd señorita in full, bright yellow flamenco dress. She didn't carry that one about in her bag; it had pride of place on her dressing table, although, thank God, she didn't go so far as lighting matches in the toilet at home. No, at home, plop plop Frish was the rule. Work: matches; home: green pine. When Toilet Duck first came out, my mother was a very happy woman. My dad said it was high time someone invented a toilet cleaner with a sense of humour.

'Desmond,' I can remember her saying, 'lavatorial hygiene is no laughing matter.'

I glance over at my table again. Strike a light, I think we have a bite. A couple, man and woman, first or second date perhaps, are hovering. They look down at my photos and the woman says something. One two three four, nails in thumb. I edge very slowly towards the table and just catch the tail end of her sentence.

'Absolute gift for a short story. There's a whole world, a whole narrative too, encapsulated in those images.' She is touching the snap of my piano with a long tanned finger. The man nods his head vigorously. Ground control, we have lift off. Yes. Yes. No.

They change direction and head for a nice intimate little table in a corner niche with a long soft buttoned bench instead of wooden chairs. I don't think they saw me coming, but I can't be sure. I'm trying, I'm certainly trying, no one can deny me that.

The door swings open, and the noise and smell of traffic shoots in with a blast of cold air. Three men stride in. One of them heads for the other end of the bar but the other two go straight for my table. I stop humming.

I'm smiling. I widen my eyes, just a smidge, not completely, not Gary Glitter-eyebrows wide, and tilt my head very very slightly to encourage conversation. It's only very very slightly. I pull my lucky sweatshirt down straight over my front and notice a red stain, tomato sauce, at the top of my right tit. Luckily I can easily and quickly chip it off with my thumb. Don't think anyone noticed.

The music is louder, I'm sure someone has turned it up.

It's *I Should Be So Lucky*.

Kylie's wishing me luck. Thanks, Kylie.

The day they took her into hospital she didn't want to go. She liked her flat. She was comfortable in her flat; it had everything a person could possibly need. She had it just the way she wanted it. She knew where everything was. When she remembered. Sometimes she forgot. But usually, she knew what was what, and what was where. Her drawers were her own. She put things in them, and that was where things went.

Her little low modern black-and-white chest in the warm fuggy lounge, four drawers high and six drawers wide, was so useful. The drawers themselves were matt white with round holes like, like . . . that was another one Agnes struggled with. Like those little windows you get on ocean liners. She wanted to look out through one at the grey sea and hard waves from her cabin on the cruise. Round, grey, metal with rivets. Stylish, typically nautical. Like . . . portholes, that was it. Round holes, like portholes, instead of drawer handles.

Each drawer had something different in it. She could practise map co-ordinates with them. So: two along, three down was: rubber bands, various, although mainly flabby thick brown ones dropped by the postman outside the front door. They became algae-green and brittle with age but were bound to come in handy for something because they were such a good size. Agnes had lashed out on a small crinkly packet of 100 tiny fresh brightly coloured elastic bands from the newsagents, and they sat there too, surrounded by the dull lifeless ones.

Four along, two down was sugar sachets. She'd learnt to open that drawer carefully, not poking her knuckled finger in too quickly, as her nails had once torn a hole in one, and a trail of sugar had drifted down, leaving the crimson carpet crunchy underfoot. There was enough sugar to keep her going for a while. Tate and Lyle were the finest; tidy white cushions with little blue cube men on. She'd also squirrelled away larger gravelly lumps of demerara in flecked beige packets from coffee shops and tearooms across town. There was a selection of old wrapped sugar cubes too, which you didn't see much any more these days.

Next to sugar, five along, and two down, were little milks and creams. A new idea, but again, very useful. Trains and supermarket cafés were good for them.

Twenty-four drawers, each with something worth keeping. Sometimes, late in the evenings before bedtime, after she'd put the porridge on to soak for the morning, she'd sit with a cup and saucer of cocoa, and test herself. She was nearly always right. Two along and two down: paper napkins, mostly standard shiny white, with the odd thicker, royal-blue or pastel floral-bordered one sandwiched in between and to be saved for special occasions. One along, two down: packs of playing cards, nearly all complete sets, kept together with elastic bands, of course.

Three along, four down was toenail clippings. Grey lumpy crescents tipped with pale yellow in a range of different sizes, and collected over a period of probably fourteen years. Guest soaps, usually wrapped and all with a lingering scent, were in five along and four down, next to the bottom corner drawer, six along, four down.

She kept the bodies of those little dead things in the bottom drawer. What were they called? They had a prehistoric look to them, like tiny armadillos. Lived under piles of wood, and had been very fond of Agnes's damp floorboards. Years ago she'd spent months scrubbing the skirting boards with carbolic soap but it had no effect whatsoever. Not as bad as cockroaches, though. In the end, after the council wouldn't help, she'd got Rentokil in to treat the whole place. For a very long time after, trails of wee carcasses appeared each morning to be swept into slag heaps, and then transferred to that bottom drawer. Segmented, they were, built like little tanks. A bit like ants, but much sturdier than ants. It'd come to her later.

She was sitting in the kitchen the afternoon they came for her. It had been a dazzling blue day and one entire side of the small glass office block opposite her flat was blinding orange as the sun set. She had just finished putting out food for Molly, her husband, Mister Pugh, and their only remaining child, Polly. Their bowls went in their usual places, one each on a seat of three of the four kitchen chairs under the table, but there was no sign of Mister Pugh. They had half a can of duck heart in jelly each, leaving half a can for Agnes to scoop onto her own Portmeirion china plate with the misty purple and green leaf decorations around the edges. Two gas rings were on, and a pan of water boiled ferociously, steam condensing against the window, walls, cupboard doors and yellow Formica table. She'd been thinking about what vegetables to cook, but then started feeding the cats instead.

Just as Agnes was polishing her fork with a gritty wad of Duraglit and getting ready to eat, there was a knock at the door. She looked around at the cats, to check it wasn't one of them. She noticed a white hair on the shoulder of her black velvet jacket and flicked it off. Then she spotted a large bluebottle buzzing against the window and picked up the useful yellow swatter from its hook. There was another knock, a bit louder this time, followed by the sound of the letter box open-ing and a woman coughing.

Agnes swiped at the fly, but it buzzed off very slowly towards the floor. She followed it and got it. It squashed against the plastic like a plump raisin that had been soaked in tea. Agnes put it next to a pile of other raisins on the sheets of yellow-ing *Mirror*s in the corner.

'Eight juicy brutes,' she said to Molly and Polly. 'Not seven, but eight juicy brutes.'

The letter box rattled again.

'Mrs McKay? Mrs McKay, are you in there? It's Yvonne here, Yvonne Jacques. And I've got someone else with me who'd like to meet you.'

Agnes put down her fork and sank creakily onto her hands and knees. The brown lino with outlines of tiles was soft with cat hairs. Her face was level with Molly on the chair.

'Sssh, now,' she whispered. 'Don't say a word.'

The letter box opened and closed three more times and Agnes could hear a muffled conversation outside, like an episode of *Heartbeat* that someone hadn't bothered to switch off.

She put her finger up to her lips and nodded to the cat. Molly jumped up onto the table and started to eat the food on the Portmeirion plate. Agnes put her hands flat on the ground and began the slow crawl out of the kitchen.

'Mrs McKay, are you alright?'

The letter box was held open, and from the small dark hall Agnes could see some shadowy bobbing movement behind it.

'We just want to see that you're feeling alright.'

Agnes grunted. The letter box flapped shut and she lumbered through to the lounge. The chest of drawers, six along, one down, top right, things to keep you safe. She put her finger through the porthole, pulled the drawer open and frantically shook her hand around inside. She hissed and sucked her teeth as something sharp cut deep into her thumb. Things to keep you safe were mainly made of metal: razor blades, Stanley knives, two worn chisels without their handles, and a collection of lacklustre surgical instruments, including a wee torch for shining down throats and ear canals. Roger had nabbed them from the hospital, and she'd nabbed them from him. A large rusty razor blade was wedged into her thumb. She pulled it out and dropped it into her pocket.

'Damn you, blast you, you damn . . . sharp metal thing,' she cried.

Agnes heard them going away, footsteps retreating down the stairs and the door to the street slamming shut. The star-shaped scar on her neck from the chimney fire at Mr Walker's was throbbing. It often did when she got worried or excited. Mr Walker, the Weasel. She slid down and leant her head back against the useful chest, patted her hair back into shape, wiped the tears from her face and then forgot what was going on.

They came back later, this time with a key. Agnes opened her eyes just a chink, and saw them creeping in. The woman was coughing and pulled a few pieces of kitchen towel off a cushioned roll that she had in the side pocket of her purple canvas rucksack. Behind her, a man was making strange chok-ing noises, and the woman handed him a piece of kitchen roll and they both covered the bottom halves of their faces.

'Don't worry, you'll get used to it,' the woman hissed at him brightly.

She had little round glasses and a fixed smile. Agnes was sure she had seen her somewhere before.

The man, she didn't know. He looked plump and full of

water, like a capon, and moved gently. His hair was ridged like Sid James's, and he'd combed it back off his forehead so firmly that she could see the furrows made by each of the comb's teeth. He was clutching a briefcase. He'd look well in a white purser's uniform, Agnes thought, with gloves and shiny brass buttons.

The woman was busy at the window now, rattling it, and eventually pulling it up its sashes in jerky stages. She stuck her head out and turned to look up and down the street.

'Now, that's better, isn't it? Blow away a few cobwebs,' she said, smiling at Agnes. 'The smell . . .' She puffed air through her thin lips and shot a look at the man, who was tugging at the zip of his windcheater, briefcase on the floor, still standing in the doorway.

'John, can you work out how to switch the fire off? I'd better check out the kitchen.'

The young man smiled a weak smile at Agnes and walked with deliberate steps over to the large blazing flame-effect gas fire. He crouched down on his podgy haunches and read the dial very seriously before turning it round with a click. The red flames died and the fire went a dark grey that Agnes couldn't recall ever seeing before.

'Hello, Mrs McKay. My name is Dr Kenny,' he said, straightening up and pulling his jacket down.

Agnes was still leaning against the chest of drawers. She started to slide herself upright, and as she did, caught sight of herself in the oval mirror hanging on its chain over the dead fireplace. Her white hair was still neat and clipped, but blotted with blood. She reminded herself of a sheep that had just been marked by a farmer. Two thick smears of brown ran across each cheek. She looked down at her hand and saw it was wadded with napkins, mainly white, but with the nice bright blue one there too, largely purple with blood. Her thumb throbbed as she lifted it.

The purser came over and held her elbow.

'Who are you? Where's the captain?' Agnes said in a croak.

'No need to worry, Agnes. I just want to ask you a few questions. Come and sit down, you'll be much more comfy. And I need to take a look at your hand.'

He steered her over to the blue tartan settee. Agnes's usual place was indented and empty, but there wasn't enough room for company. Letters regularly dripped onto her doormat, and she was very good at picking them up and taking them into the lounge, putting them on the settee to deal with later. Sometimes, one of the postman's rubber bands would plop through with them, which was always a bonus. The young man let go of her arm and started to shift the piles of folded-up clothes and towers of various-sized, unopened envelopes.

Underneath the paperwork was Agnes's cushion collection. They always started out big and bright and bouncy, but lost some oomph as time went by. So she'd carried on adding to them. Some cushions she'd made herself, and a few had been gifts. A rather small green tweedy one had come from her third husband, Ajit, for their second wedding anniversary. Animal fabrics had always been her favourites, though. Somewhere, she had a real mink one, made out of an old coat. The more glamorous the better: a touch of Hollywood in South London. She snorted at the thought, and the young man stopped what he was doing to look at her.

She didn't recall the fluffy tan and black cushion, snug in between the fun-fur Dalmatian spots and fake zebra stripes. The young man went back to his scooping, moving like a fleshy forklift truck.

All of a sudden he was breathing hard and throwing his hands up in the air.

'My God, oh my God,' he panted.

At the same time, the woman had come galloping in from the kitchen, her face damp and hands full of Agnes's dripping tea towels.

'Nightmare in there,' she said. 'Mrs McKay, did you know you had the cooker on? There's a pan boiled dry. Very dangerous.'

Agnes looked hard at the new cushion, curled up, but stiff, on the rag-rug in front of the settee. The man was wiping his hands up and down his hips and sniffing his fingers. The woman took off her glasses and rubbed her eyes.

'Alright, John. Calm down,' she said quietly. 'It's only a cat.'

Everything went dark in Agnes's head. She could feel the blood start to thump in her thumb again. The wad of napkins fell on the floor with a thud.

'Who are you?' she said, slowly at first, and then repeated it, quicker and quicker, louder and louder. She thought of something else. 'How did you get in? Have you come for tea? I don't care for tea, but I've got chocolate fingers in the cupboard. Real ones, Cadbury's.'

Agnes got up suddenly and went to fetch the tartan tin from the sideboard. But when she opened it there was not a speck of chocolate inside. She poked the custard cream lids and garibaldi halves about until her thumb was coated in crumbs sticking to the blood and putting her in mind of that funny-shaped fish Desmond liked to order on the rare occasions they ate out in a pub. Came with wee sachets of tartare sauce. She licked her fingertips, nodded and carried on poking.

'Now where are they, the damned things?' she frowned, and began to shake the tin.

The woman came and took her elbow and moved her back towards the settee.

The sailor chappy had stopped making the noises now and was getting some papers and an expensive-looking silver pen out of his briefcase.

'Come and sit down now, Mrs McKay, Agnes. Can you tell me where we are?'

'Phuuff. Damn stupid question. We're at home, of course.'

'And where is home?'

'Flat three, seventeen Hastings Road.'

'Good, very good.'

'Now, do you know what day it is?'

'It's Monday today, all day,' she giggled. The man wrote something down.

Agnes looked down and saw her fluffy old tabby in front of her feet, surrounded by clothes, cushions and envelopes.

'What have you done with Mister Pugh?'

'Aah, Mr Pugh . . . ?'

'Mister Pugh, Mister Pugh, he's gone.'

Agnes felt in her jacket pocket for the sharp metal thing. She wanted to hurt them. Coming in here, disturbing her supper. Damn little shiny glasses, and him in his uniform.

'Right, I see,' he carried on, silver pen scratching away, 'and Mr Pugh is . . . a friend, a neighbour, is he?'

She pulled it out and waved it in front of his face. 'Woodlice. Woodlice, that's it. It's woodlice,' she screamed as she tried to cut him.

She tripped over the dead cat and the woman grabbed her arm.

When things had calmed down a bit, they helped her down the stairs. Agnes looked around, trying to take in the details. A young red-haired policewoman had been waiting out on the quiet high-ceilinged landing. At regular intervals the lights went out, and the policewoman had taken it upon herself to just as regularly press the large round timer button to switch them on again immediately. Parked in his little red car was Desmond. He was leaning his head against the steering wheel. Such a good boy. In a flash of lucidity, Agnes realized how they'd got the key to her flat.

January 17 – Elvis Has Left the Building

I walk over to the table, lager glass in my hand, slowly enough not to be a surprise, but not too hesitant either. It's a balancing act. One two three four nail. One of the men is holding up the biggest photo. He says something to his mate, but I can't quite hear them till I get closer.

'Right state.'

He's holding up the picture of me and Natalie and he is half yellow, half pink. The colours of a Fruit Salad – those little wrapped chewy sweets. I always preferred Black Jacks because they made the inside of your mouth go dark and bitter. His hair is cropped and blond like a Hitler Youth toddler, but it is natural, I think, and his face is puce, sweaty and pink, several shades darker than his hair. It's not edge-of-a-heart-attack pink; he's either been exercising vigorously or overdone it on the sunbed. Big muscly arms glowing with tiny silver hairs; fingers like chipolatas clutching the photo; no tattoos. Body language: cock of the walk.

'Don't fancy yours much.' He's laughing with his mouth wide and thin, and it sounds like a snake. Ssss sssss. He looks up and sees me and stops hissing.

I keep smiling, keep tilting, keep moving towards the table. He looks at the picture again and does a cartoon double take. Down, up. Photo, me. Down, up.

I pull a cushioned stool out and sit down.

'Dead,' I say.

'Ay?' he says.

'My friend Natalie, she's dead now.'

Confusion, he doesn't know how to react. Flummoxed, he's flummoxed. I'm smiling still. He looks over at his mate, but he's no use to him. He's got his head down and is taking a fag out of a bulging new packet of Marlboro. Full strength, proper red and white pack. Zippo lighter. Enough said. Fruit Salad helps himself to one too. I can almost see the cogs whirring and spinning around inside his head, making his big bristly skull ripple. Which response to go for? On the one hand, it's a stranger, and a very strange stranger at that. But, on the other hand, it's a death situation, and death situations call for respect.

He takes a drag of his fag, looks over again at his mate and opts for: 'Oh, sorry to hear that.'

'Nineteen eighty-five,' I say, pulling the battered pack of Richmonds out of my pocket and lighting one with a match from my brand-new black glossy matchbox, which I casually drop on the table.

Marlboro Man finally looks up and nods. He is thin and wiry, with dark hair parted in the middle like stiff curtains. I think the look is supposed to be sleek and Hollywood, but really it is gelled so hard that he looks more like a bit part in a BBC Sunday night Charles Dickens. I smile some more at the thought. Mr Quig. Pickwick. One two three four nail. I catch them both glancing at my hand and put it in my pocket.

'Motorbike accident,' I explain, and a spark of interest flicks through their eyes.

'A bike, ay, Arnie,' the thin one says.

'Oh, yeh?' says Arnie, just as the third man arrives at the table, carrying three pints of lager in a triangle a good foot in front of his chest.

The third man is clearly top dog. Navy-blue Kangol beanie

hat, chunky gold chain bracelet, V-neck T-shirt, bulging shoulders and the most confident lolloping swagger I've seen in a long time.

'Who's your friend then, boys?' he says, lowering the drinks down without spilling even a drop. He looks at them both and they shrug. Arnie takes a big drink, emptying half his glass in one, and the skinny one shrugs again.

'They're her photos, Guy,' he says.

'Don't get you, Dave mate. What photos?' says Guy.

My turn, I think. Time to chip in, get the conversation going.

'I left them here on this table. By accident. And your friends picked them up,' I begin.

Guy smiles and raises his eyebrows. He's got a gold tooth.

'Photos, ay? Anything juicy?' He's laughing now with a dirty throaty grunt, and a nanosecond later, Dave and Arnie are laughing too. It's just like listening to a breakfast show DJ and his early morning crew. Yes men. Ha ha ha men. But they are laughing. That's good, isn't it? You can't beat humour as a tool for successful social interaction. I read somewhere, or maybe it was June that told me, that one joke does the job of up to twenty factual exchanges in terms of cementing, or it might have been oiling, social situations. Only one problem: I'm not too sure what the joke is. Guy stops laughing suddenly. Maybe he wants to catch the other two out, but they stop too, very quickly.

'So what have we got here, then?' he says, holding up the one of me in the back garden.

'That's me with some of my work. Ooh, early eighties. Outside in the garden. Number seventy-three, lovely house. I was happy there.'

I'm overdoing it and, even worse, I've got a horrible version of my mum's telephone voice on to impress. I can hear myself, but I can't stop.

'Yes, I remember how I did that. Browns, lots and lots of browns. Won that year's prize at art school for the most promising student. I nearly sold it. Lots of people liked that piece.'

Guy is staring at me. 'That's never you.'

'Oh, yes, it is. I was a student, you see, that's why I've got that spiky hair. Young, free and single, ha ha. Look at this one. This is one of my best pieces.'

I'm showing him my piano picture, holding it up close to his face. A deconstructed piano, strung up on the wall and dotted with tangerine and lime. Musical fruit. Smashed-up Joanna.

'*The Destruction of Tune*,' I say.

'Come again?' he says, and next to him Dave is sniggering.

'That's what I called it.'

'Aah,' says Guy, 'but is it Art?' Then he roars with laughter. The roaring calms down into a fit of loud grunts and guffaws. He carries on grunting whilst he is draining the last inch from his glass and sprays lager droplets over me and the other two as he looks round.

Arnie gets up for more drinks.

This is fine. This is good. Look, Doctor, look at me, Top of the World, Doc: socializing, having a nice quiet drink, discussing art with new friends. My hands are still but my mouth is in overdrive.

'Well, yes, art, abstract art, but art. I had a great future, could have really made it, been a prize winner.'

I feel a drop of spittle at the corner of my mouth. They see it and look the other way. I'm losing it. They're going off the boil. Got to get Guy's attention again or it'll all peter out completely. Bikes, try the motorbike again; the others liked bikes. First of all, though, there is the spit problem. I pretend to look at something on the floor, then move my head back up via my shoulder and wipe my mouth on it. Nice and dry again. I'm pretty sure they didn't notice.

'I had a motorbike.'

'Yeh, she had a bike,' chips in Dave, Pickwick hair gleaming as he pours more lager down his throat. I have this sudden vision of Charles Dickens sitting on a Harley-Davidson, wearing a crash helmet, and I giggle.

'What sort?' asks Guy, but his eyes have lost their glint now.

'MZ250.'

'Oh, yeh well.'

Blown it. Should have lied, should have said Triumph or a Triton. MZ equals no kudos. But I did have a MZ.

'Going on Saturday?' Guy turns to the others. But I'm in another place and time.

The sirens are blaring over and over and the blue light is on off on off on off. It's night-time, cold, damp and misty. It smells of petrol and metal. I can't tell what is bike and what is me.

Nee-naa nee-naa nee-naa nee-naaa.

Swooosh swoosh goes the traffic in the drizzle on the outside lane.

My leg is twisted, my head is wet and numb. I'm not in pain yet. But I can see, even at this distance, that Natalie is dead. Her black crash helmet is half on, half off, and back to front. Her right arm and right leg are poking out at unrealistic angles in her black leather jacket and trousers. Two of the ambulance men go to her, crouch down and feel for a pulse. One of them stands up but stays with her for a bit, and the other comes over to join the pleasant blonde ambulance woman who is both poking me about and stroking me. That's how I know for sure she is dead. The lorry in front has stopped. It's got a tiny dent in the back passenger side corner where it clipped my MZ. The driver is sitting on the grassy bank with his head in his hands.

They're looking at me. Nee-naa nee-naa nee-naa. I stop whispering as soon as I hear myself. Dave takes a drink. Arnie raises his eyebrows. Guy clears his throat in a very long lingering way.

'Yeh, what time?' says Dave.

'It was a good bike.' I'm talking too loud. Someone has cranked the music up another notch.

'About two or something.'

It's like I'm not there. I'm the invisible woman. I poke my thumbnail hard into my fingers to check I can still feel me. One two three four thumb. They all three down their pints and slam their glasses on the table almost at the same time. I've still got a sip of piss-flat lager at the bottom of my glass.

'Yeh, should be a good one,' says Guy. 'Your round, I believe, David, my son.' He holds his empty glass up and turns his back completely on me.

'I was in an accident,' I blurt, finishing my drink and holding my smudgy half-pint glass up too. But where Top Dog looks all manful with his pint, I'm like some needy toddler wanting a refill from Mummy.

Dave takes Arnie and Guy's glasses. He glances very quickly at mine and shakes his stiff head. He mutters something that I can't quite hear, but it includes the word accident, and the others laugh.

I follow him up to the bar. He gets served straight away, of course. He hardly has to speak words to the barman: it's all eyebrows and grunts and alright mate. Butch telepathy and a big flash note that he hardly looks at. I fanny about with my change and take ten times longer to get my little drink.

In my heart I know I should leave it here. I know. Leave them to their pints and jokes and hairy arms. But I'm trying. And it was going quite well for a while, wasn't it? My legs are itchy. I give them a good scratch through my leggings but stop myself from scratching the top off any of the scabs. Deep breathe, drink in hand, head tall, not tilting.

'Look, will you just fuck off, alright?' Guy's eyes are diamond hard. Right, even I can read the signs. I'll get my photos back and move on.

'My photos are . . .' My voice is phlegmy and unsure, and they're in there like a pack of hyenas before I can finish my sentence.

'Fuck your photos.'

I reach my arm out to pick them up, and knock Arnie's glass over. Nice full glass of lager.

That's it. Arnie and Dave are up, pushing their chairs over backwards. Guy stays sitting but leans back, holding his own drink carefully at the top of the glass and away from the table.

'My pint,' whispers Arnie. 'You've spilt my fucking pint.'

There's grunting and heavy breathing and eyeballs open wide. I step back. My stool falls away from under me and I'm on the floor, on my back, damp with a mix of spilt lager and sweat. Arnie and Dave stand over me and everything goes slow motion. They are about to lunge when all of a sudden they're standing back with their shoulders shrugged and hands up in front of them, surrender-pose.

'What's going on?' The barman is standing between me and the lads, breathless, with his sleeves rolled up. 'I don't want any trouble in here.'

'No trouble, Geoff,' smiles Guy, still sitting on his stool, pint half drunk now.

The barman kneels down and looks me over. He looks up at the others. 'It's a woman, for Christ's sake.' He puts his hand under my shoulder and tries to sit me up but I'm too heavy for him. He slides it out, looks at it and wipes it on his thigh. 'You okay?' he says, his eyebrows creased up like a Klingon.

I'm humming. I look up at the ceiling. I don't want to see his lumpy forehead any more.

'See what we mean?' says Guy.

'All the same,' says the barman.

'She spilt Arnie's pint,' Dave adds.

The barman looks back down at me, then up at them again. Another barman in an identical green polo shirt and black trousers walks over. One of his trainers squeaks, and I hear him coming before I look up and see him: squeak plod squeak plod.

'Come on, love, time to go home, I think.' The Klingon means business this time, as he thrusts both his hands under my armpit.

'Terry, give us a hand,' he says to the other barman.

They hoist me up to a sitting position, like a pair of proper physios. They're ready to handle me some more, but I shake my head and lean on the table. I'm jerky and wobbling, though, and the top of my arse is cold and exposed where my jacket and sweatshirt have ridden up, and my leggings have slid down. I manage to get myself standing up.

The music is still loud, but there's no talking. All eyes are on me. One two three four nail. I'm definitely still here: King Kong, Frankenstein's monster, The Fat Freak.

The barmen try to touch me again.

'Leave me alone,' I say, pulling my leggings up. I can't see out of my right eye because my fringe has stuck to it. I push it out of the way and pick my photos up from the table. They're wrinkled with lager. I begin the long slow limp to the big wood double doors with their shiny brass handles. People are starting to talk again.

The last thing I hear as the doors are swinging shut behind me is Guy shouting, above the hum drum hub bub.

'Elvis has left the building.'

Bastard. I clench everything. Hands, eye, jaw, arse. It hurts.

1986

The photograph in her new passport was not bad. She had had it taken in a photographer's studio in Balham. The photographer had worn a black turtle-neck sweater and told her to focus on a spot above his left shoulder for a gracious portrait. He said to call him Pete. Agnes liked the idea of looking gracious. She wore the pearls from Ernest, drop earrings from Ajit, and the velvet top that she'd bought just after the divorce from Roger. But she used her maiden name. McKay, plain old Agnes McKay.

Boarding time was quite early, so she stayed in a hotel in Thurrock the night before. The room was small and dark and smelt of new carpet. She laid her clothes out for the morning and switched on the bright light and whirring extractor fan in the bathroom. There were two wee bottles of bubbles and two shower caps in little plastic cases on the white shelf. She stashed one of each in her case, and poured a bottle into a deep steaming bath. She carefully arranged the shower hat over her newly set hair and climbed in. At first it was luxury, but after five minutes she felt bloated and the heat made her sick and giddy. She sat on the side of the bath with a towel wrapped around her, pink and gleaming as a piggy. She watched flecks of foam slide down her crimson legs like melting snow.

The bedroom was stifling. She opened the window and lay down on the queen-size bed with its shiny dark green Paisley quilt, and closed her eyes. She woke up with a start much later. There was a fox yowling somewhere in the distance and the room was cold. The towel was half unwrapped now, so she grabbed her sweater from the floor and pulled it over her head. It wasn't worth putting her new nightie on. She padded over to the dressing table and checked her clothes, jewellery and bag.

Keys cash comb.

All set to go. It was going to be queer having Christmas without a husband. She looked at the clock radio. It was nearly four o'clock. She pressed the button for the noise of voices. A trailer for news roundup of the year rattled out. Poisoned kiddies in Chernobyl, Mrs Thatcher battling on, and fuss over some Argentinian footballer. She tutted and turned the dial to find some nice music. She listened until it was time to get up.

The dockside was windy and grey. Agnes pulled her scarf tighter and looked at the hundreds of people milling around. She picked up her suitcase and tartan grip and headed for the queue. A porter in a neat blue blazer tapped her on the shoulder and loaded them onto a trolley. She walked up the gangplank holding her boarding card tight. A cold hard gust of wind caught her scarf and sent it up high into the sky. Agnes reached after it and then watched as it whirled round and round in the air, and flew back across the choppy slate water to the dockside. It blew down and caught on the barbed wire of a perimeter fence.

There was tinkly instrumental music playing on board, nothing like the brass band Agnes had hoped for. She made her way down to cabin 572. Her case and bag were waiting for her. The cabin was small with a square window and tiny balcony, and the floor rocked gently from side to side. No porthole. She'd wanted a nice round porthole. When she'd booked at the travel agents in the high street, she'd paid almost double for an outside cabin, thinking it would definitely have one. She walked past the two small dressing tables and single beds pushed together to make a double, and looked out of the window at the dark water. A flat black blob was moving on the outer pane, very fast on tiny legs like hairs. It was shaped like a drop of blood, and when it took off in a flurry of red and black wings, Agnes recognized it.

'"Ladybird, ladybird, fly away home",' she muttered. Then she noticed a large bluebottle on the inside windowsill. She had picked up the glossy *What's Onboard* booklet and rolled it up ready to swat, when there was a knock on the door.

Agnes peered through the spyhole. A tiny man in a white uniform was beaming up at her. She opened the door. There were excited old people's voices in the corridor, and the smell of floor wax and fried food.

'Good morning, madam. Welcome aboard,' the little man said. He spoke with a strong West African accent. 'My name is Isaac, and I am your steward for the voyage. Is everything to your satisfaction?'

Agnes looked back into the room and at the window. 'You wouldn't have a swatter, would you?' she asked.

Isaac hesitated, his smile fading very slightly. Agnes lifted up the rolled-up booklet and he took a step back.

'No, no, no,' she giggled, 'it's for the flies. There's a juicy brute on the window.'

Isaac nodded. 'I will see what I can do. I believe we have fly spray in the stores.'

'Ach, no, I don't like sprays, thank you. A fly swatter will do.'

After a brief pause, Isaac continued, 'I will see what I can find. I would like to tell you about the eating arrangements on board.'

Agnes wondered if the flickering in her stomach was hunger.

'Breakfast is buffet, but there are sittings for lunch and dinner. We have designated you a table with some other guests.'

Just then the ship lurched, and there were whoops and whistles from above. Agnes looked back at her window again and saw the dockside sliding along.

'Ah, we have set sail,' Isaac nodded sagely.

'I must go upstairs and see.' Agnes dropped the booklet on the floor and closed the door behind her.

On deck, people were bunched together, wearing big coats and scarves. It was sleeting now, and umbrellas were going up. People cheered and waved at the shore. Agnes held tight to the chipped white rail. Three long deep blasts from the horn vibrated through the floor and the cold metal. Her hands tingled and the cheering got louder. Seagulls flew in whirling circles, screeching like babies. The smell of salt and sewage filled her nose, and the clutching in her stomach was stronger as they pulled out of the docks towards the sea.

'Hungry, must be hungry,' she muttered to herself. She carefully clicked down the metal stairs in her heels to the cabin to freshen up.

She held in her tummy muscles and pulled her arse tight as she walked slowly over to her designated table. There were four people sitting down on chairs with velvet maroon padding. Two clean and shiny men in their forties sat close together drinking coffee. One had glossy corkscrew curls and flushed cheeks. The other had a tufty hairstyle and long sideburns.

The other couple were much older and white-haired. The woman was trim and picked neatly at her food, holding her knife and fork like pencils. The white-haired man was talking. Agnes pulled out an empty chair, and the man with the sideburns rushed over to help her.

'Second to none, they are usually,' the old man was saying as she sat down. 'And we've done a fair few, haven't we, Phyllis?'

A waiter appeared at Agnes's side. The menu had too many choices, and she'd left her glasses in her cabin.

'Why don't you go for the salmon en croûte?' whispered the younger man with curls. 'We did, and it was fine.' He glanced over at the old man, who was still talking, and then wiped his mouth with his napkin and raised his eyebrows at his friend. They pushed their chairs back at the same time and stood to leave the table.

The old man didn't stop. 'We started cruising in 1968 on P&O. But we've done the *Seawing*, *Sapphire*, *Emerald*, *Sundream*, *Arcadia*, *Aurora* – remember the *Aurora*, Phyllis?'

The neat woman didn't bother to look up from her plate.

The younger men both nodded vigorously, trying to butt in.

'Then there was the *Saga Rose*, *QE2*, not to mention numerous,' he said the word through his nose in a way that put Agnes in mind of Kenneth Williams, 'numerous short trips. Newcastle to Norway, Hull to . . .'

'Well, it's been lovely . . .' the man with the sideburns started, but the old man was concentrating on hacking away at his steak and chips.

'. . . Rotterdam and Zeebrugge, Portsmouth to Bilbao, Poole to Cherbourg . . .'

As Agnes opened her napkin, the two men waved goodbye and almost ran to the bar.

The woman laid her knife and fork at precise angles on her plate and smiled at Agnes. She leant over and said quietly, 'Hello, I'm Phyllis.' She had a gentle Scottish accent.

'Why, hello, I'm Agnes,' she hissed back, her Edinburgh burr stronger than usual.

'Not to mention the Greek Islands . . .' The man trailed off and looked up from his steak. 'Oh, have the others gone?'

'Yes,' sighed Phyllis, 'they have. Philip, this is Agnes.'

The man stood up and thrust his hand forward. 'Delighted to meet you. Philip, the name's Philip, and this is my good lady wife, Phyllis. And yes, the similarity has led to confusion in our time, we can tell you,' and he laughed a strange high wheezy laugh. It reminded Agnes of the wheezy coughs of her childhood.

'Due to medical conditions,' he continued, 'I have been recommended not to fly, so when we saw this Christmas and New Year Sunshine Cruise we literally jumped at the chance, didn't we, Phyllis?'

Phyllis smiled lamely. Philip sat down again. He coughed and wheezed into his napkin.

A young girl dressed in black with a ponytail hovered at Agnes's side. She handed her a green leather-bound folder.

'Good afternoon, madam, my name is Katie, and I'm your wine waitress. Would you like to order something to drink?'

Agnes opened the wine list. The print was too blurry to read. She glanced around the dining hall. The whole ship seemed to be on a tilt. The view out of the windows on one side was mostly murky sky; on the other, mostly murky sea. She glanced at the table. Phyllis and Philip were drinking sparkling water, but the two men had left the dregs of a bottle of red wine.

'I'll have a bottle of that,' she said, nodding at it.

'Pushing the boat out, are we, so to speak?' said Philip, and he spluttered at his own joke. The spluttering turned to wheez-ing and Phyllis put a glass of water in his hand. He tried to drink, but couldn't catch his breath.

'I think perhaps we should be heading back to the cabin,' Phyllis said softly. Philip closed his eyes briefly, but didn't speak. They got up slowly.

'Lovely to meet you, and see you at dinner time,' said Phyllis. Philip nodded at Agnes with his shoulders hunched and the two of them walked gingerly off towards the stairs.

Agnes examined the table. Next to the glass cruet set there was a white bowl full of sugar lumps. Double lumps, wrapped in paper. Her favourites. She checked no one was looking and swiftly nabbed a few. She dropped them into her handbag. The wine waitress appeared with the bottle of red, and poured a tiny drop into Agnes's glass. She stood waiting. Agnes looked at the glass and then looked up at her.

'Would you like to try it?' the girl explained.

Agnes gulped it back. It tasted dandy. She didn't know what to say. 'Oh, it's lovely, thank you,' she decided on, and the waitress filled her up.

Agnes sat back in her chair and felt the wine trickle down her throat. She put her hand up to her neck and looked around the dining hall. The chandeliers were swaying gently, and the crimson carpeted floor still looked tilted. She was glad to see that she'd got her clothes about right. There were a number of other women wearing fancy blouses or casual dresses. Most of the men wore blazers. Agnes approved. She also noted a fair few distinguished-looking gents sitting alone. By the time she'd ploughed through the four courses and most of the wine, she was fading. All she wanted was a little lie-down, and perhaps a go at getting that bluebottle.

*

She was awake and ready again for the eight o'clock dinner sitting. The place was different in the evening. There was a band dressed in dinner jackets, playing jazzy versions of show tunes. Agnes recognized most of them. The lights were lower; perfume and garlic were in the air, and a lot of the women were wearing ball gowns. The Captain's Table was at the other end of the hall, and full of laughing smart types. The two younger men from earlier were nowhere to be seen, and only Phyllis was at the table. She was looking through the menu and grinned when Agnes sat down.

'Evening,' she said, laying it flat on the table.

'Good evening,' said Agnes. 'Shall we wait for Philip?'

'Oh, we've had a bit of bad news.' She didn't stop smiling, though. 'He's been confined to quarters.'

Agnes raised her eyebrows. 'What happened?'

'We went to see the ship's doctor and he's got bronchial pneumonia. He gave him antibiotics, cough linctus and water tablets, but it's infectious, you see.'

'Oh dear,' Agnes said. She wondered how he would get on without anyone to talk to.

'The doctor's organized room service for his meals so he's well looked after,' Phyllis said. Her mouth was twitching and she picked up the wine list. 'Shall we have a wee dram?'

They had a fine evening. The food was rich and warm, and there were no awkward pauses in the conversation. Phyllis reminded Agnes of Lucy. She and Lucy used to laugh all the time when they were girls. They would pretend to be foreigners and talk in pretend German or Spanish on the tram.

Agnes looked up from her crème brûlée during a comfortable lull. The boat was rocking, but it wasn't tilted to one side any more. She'd noticed that when she'd woken up after her nap. Phyllis was quite rosy and began to talk in Philip's nasal London accent.

'Well, I've thought long and hard about the fifteen-degree list to port and my theory is that the foul water tanks were full on the port side and could not be discharged into the English Channel.'

Aggie laughed at the impression; it was very accurate.

'I think I might partake of a brandy now,' Phyllis continued with an exaggerated wheeze. 'Would you care to join me?'

By ten o'clock Agnes felt like she'd known Phyllis for years. It was so good to talk to someone, and Phyllis being from Leith was a bonus. They covered so much ground. Phyllis and Philip never had children: something to do with Phyllis's fallopian tubes. But Agnes told Phyllis about her boy, Desmond, and his kiddies; and about Rebecca, although she glossed over the fact that she hadn't seen her now for twenty-five years. She had even begun to talk about Ernest and the bad times, when she noticed that Phyllis was drooping. Her face was bluey white, and she raised her tissue to her mouth to burp.

'I'm sorry, Aggie, but I'm not feeling very well,' she said.

Agnes helped Phyllis up and they walked past the windows. The wind had whipped right up. The lights shone down on the water. It was rising up in choppy black chunks, glowing and tipped with white. Gusts of wind blew sheets of sea water against the glass. Agnes felt queasy too. They moved slowly towards the stairs.

Phyllis and Philip's cabin was two decks lower than Agnes's, and much smaller, but it did have a porthole. The smell of yeast and disinfectant reached her as she stood in the doorway. Philip had the bedside lamp on and was propped up in his narrow bed with big white pillows, his eyes closed. There were piles of packets and brown bottles of pills neatly stacked on his bedside table. His breathing was rattling away like an oversized cat purring and Agnes had a sudden flash of memory from when she was very small: cigar smoke, bedsprings and her papa coughing.

Phyllis stumbled in and lay on top of her bed. She curled herself up like a baby, facing away from Philip's bed.

It was quiet in the corridors, although it was still early. Agnes went back to her cabin and emptied a few more sugars into the dressing-table drawer. She changed into her peach satin nightie and picked up the rolled-up brochure. It was getting a bit ragged now. She checked all the walls and the curtains, but there were no live flies. The five corpses from earlier were still piled up on the windowsill. She'd have to ask Isaac again about a proper swatter tomorrow.

The next day was Christmas Eve. Phyllis was quiet and wan at lunch, and only a bit brighter by dinner. The ship was due to arrive in Gibraltar late that night. Agnes managed to persuade her to wait up in the lounge, but she would only drink cups of weak tea whilst Agnes knocked back brandies again. Agnes drummed her fingers and looked out at the lights getting closer and bigger. Blasts of rain and sea water smacked against the glass.

'Come on now, Phyl, we're nearly there. We can't miss this,' she said.

Phyllis put down her tea cup. 'Go on then,' she said, and they went to get their mackintoshes from their cabins.

A small gaggle of passengers followed some way behind them. The gangplank was slippery and the dock dark and blustery.

Not Christmassy at all. The wind blew Agnes's hair around, and Phyllis held tight on to her plastic rain hood. The rock loomed up in front of them. They could see hotels and buildings lit up in the distance, but there was not a taxi in sight. Agnes spotted a restaurant with a hopeful string of lights a hundred yards or so away, but when they got closer it was shuttered up. The other passengers were fumbling their way back towards the gangplank, and Phyllis began to shiver violently. Then, above the seagulls and the plunking of the rain, they heard church bells, and far-away cheering. The ship's hooter blasted.

'Well, a very merry Christmas to you, Phyllis,' said Agnes.

'And a very merry Christmas to you, Aggie.'

Phyllis put her arms on Agnes's shoulders and kissed her on the lips. Her mouth was dry and gentle, and her breath smelt of warm tea. Her rain hood had been blown off her head and coils of her silver hair stuck to her forehead. Agnes's throat felt tight and her eyes watered. It was good to have a friend. She kissed Phyllis back. They stood apart and looked at each other. Phyllis smiled. Agnes tried to smile back but felt tears running down her cheeks. She wiped them away with the back of her hand.

'Blasted rain,' she said. She turned back to look at the ship. 'The others have all gone back.'

The two women linked arms and walked back in perfect step.

Christmas Dinner the next day was a grand affair, although the turkey was rather tough and bland for Agnes's taste. The two young men from the first night joined Aggie and Phyllis, and between them they drank three bottles of red wine and a bottle of chilled bubbly. At two o'clock ('or fourteen hundred hours', as Phyllis chipped in with another impression of Philip), they departed for Casablanca. The rock looked half green and nowhere as doom-laden by day, and they had fine views as they sailed across the strait.

It was foggy in Casablanca. They braved the souk, and Agnes bought a large bowl for Desmond and Nanette, and a fez for Jodie. The next day it was cloudy in Lanzarote, but they made the trek up to see an egg being fried on top of Fire Mountain.

'Philip said he was literally gutted to miss this,' Phyllis whispered as the guide lifted his arm high and dropped the opaque gloop and yolk onto sizzling black rock.

'Not any better then?' said Agnes.

Phyllis raised her eyebrows and they giggled. The mountain was steamy and the frying egg smelt of sulphur.

There was still no sun in Gran Canaria or Tenerife. Agnes had planned to come back with a decent tan. She'd looked forward to lining her golden arm up next to Desmond and Nanette's pale wrists. So she set her hopes high for New Year in Madeira. The sun did shine briefly the next day, but it wasn't long before the gales. There was a heavy swell and shore trips to Funchal were cancelled.

Agnes had wanted a night out in a real casino on land. She sat next to Phyllis in the cabaret hall, stony-faced as Alfredo, the Bird Man of Magic, made a half-plucked pigeon jump through a weedy ring of fire. She wouldn't clap when he made bird shapes appear from rainbow-coloured bunting. Phyllis cheered as the strongman in his leopard-skin leotard flexed his muscles and lifted a very fat man from the audience over his head. She was keen for them to show their writing to the stage graphologist, but Agnes wouldn't budge.

Then the band struck up *King of the Road*, and a porky figure with a large black overhanging quiff leapt onto the stage.

'King of the Road, King of the Road? Never mind all that, stuck out here all at sea.'

Agnes shuffled up higher in her seat. There was something familiar about the man.

'Anyway, ladies and gents, it's my great pleasure to be here with you to while away the last couple of hours of 1986.' He tapped his watch, tutted and then laughed like a raven.

Agnes looked at him harder.

'By the way, I'm Liam "the King" Gilchrist. Talking of being all out at sea, did you hear the one about the sailor and the lady of, shall we say, easy virtue?'

He was sweating now, and tiny drips of black hair dye dribbled down the side of his face. She looked at his tight-fitting blazer.

Butlins, he was that Redcoat at Butlins. He'd put on a pound or two over the last ten years, but it was definitely him.

Agnes leant back in her seat, smiled at Phyllis and took a first sip from the gin and tonic she'd bought her earlier. The ice had melted, but there was still a nice zing of lemon. They sat and watched the King for nearly an hour. Then Phyllis went to the bar again and came back with more gin and two packets of peanuts. Agnes ripped her packet open with her teeth and chomped on the greasy nuts. Phyllis nudged her. 'You enjoying yourself now?'

'Ay, he's no bad, is he?'

'Probably a bit blue for Philip's taste, but I like him.'

Just then one of the crew reached up to the stage and handed the King a piece of paper.

'Uh-oh, ladies and gents, looks like I've been handed me notice,' he cawed again. But as he read, his forehead moved back. He looked up, pulled at the cuffs of his blazer and jerked his head like a chicken. 'Ladies and gents, I've got a message here for a Phyllis Duncan.'

Phyllis choked on her nuts. Agnes patted her on the back and handed her her glass.

'If there's a Phyllis Duncan here in the audience, please could you make your way to the purser's office.'

Agnes stood up and the other people in the audience all turned to look at her. Phyllis was still coughing and spluttering. Agnes put her arm around her. The man who'd given the message to the King weaved his way through the tables and led them upstairs. The purser's office was small. He ushered them in and gestured at two chairs against the wall.

'Please, Mrs Duncan, take a seat,' he said to Agnes.

His ridged, combed-back hair and large nose put her in mind of that chappy from the *Carry On* films, the one with the terrible laugh, but he had a kind look about him. They sat down.

'Mrs Duncan,' he began again, still looking at Agnes.

'No, no, no, this is Mrs Duncan,' she said, nodding at Phyllis, who was white as sleet.

He turned towards her. 'I've got some bad news, I'm afraid.'

Phyllis gasped and clutched Agnes's arm so tight she could feel her nails through her blouse.

'Is he dead?' She forced the words out between shallow breaths.

'No, but Dr Scott Brown says he has taken a turn for the worse. He's very worried about his breathing and we are arranging to have him airlifted to hospital.'

'Oh Jesus,' said Phyllis. Her grip on Agnes loosened slightly. 'Is he going to die?'

'He'll be in the best of hands, I can assure you,' the purser said, standing up. 'The helicopter should be here shortly. So I suggest you get yourself ready.'

Agnes stood up, but Phyllis stayed in her seat. Agnes put her hand under her arm and lifted her gently.

'Lloyd here will take you to the sickbay,' the purser continued, 'and then we'll go up on deck when the chopper comes.'

The man who'd brought them up stepped forward and smiled. 'Madam?' he said, offering Phyllis his arm. Agnes handed her over.

Agnes sat on her bed. She walked over to the window and looked out. The ship was lined up with half a dozen others in the harbour, all jerking up and down on the swell. On the side of the mountain there were scores of bonfires and weedy thin rockets shot up a little way into the big dark sky.

She looked down at the windowsill and ran her finger over the dead flies. Twenty-one of the brutes. They had shrunk as they'd dried out, and the movement knocked them over. Two floated to the floor. She bent down and struggled to pick them up. There was a knock at the door. Isaac was standing there with his hands behind his back.

'Have you got one?' she asked.

'Mrs McKay,' he said slowly, 'perhaps you should sit down.'

She tried peering over his shoulder to see if he was hiding something. He seemed to have paper, no sign of plastic.

'Did you get a swatter?' she said.

Isaac shook his head and walked slowly into the cabin, nodding for Agnes to sit in the chair. 'No, I have not. I have come with this.' He handed Agnes a sheet of paper.

She didn't understand. Was it from the ship's stores? Surely they could get her one before they got back home?

'It is a telegram. From your son.'

She sat down. 'Desmond,' she said. 'Is Desmond alright?' Her voice was shaky and her stomach was stony cold.

'Would you like me to read it to you?' Isaac was calm and slow. He's done this before, she thought, handing him back the paper. He paused between each word, and slowly Agnes understood.

'"Mum. Bad news. Aunt Lucy died this morning. Sorry. With love D."'

'But that can't be right,' she said, nodding her head over and over. 'She's the younger one. I'm the older one. She can't die first.'

'I am very sorry for you,' Isaac said. 'Is there anything I can get you? Would you like to see the chaplain?'

But Agnes didn't hear him. Her mind was full of ribbons and bows, haircuts and giggling wee girls.

Isaac stood up stiffly and made his way to the door. 'If there is anything we can do, please do not hesitate to ask,' he said, shutting the door quietly.

She sat still. Her jaw was clamped shut. She couldn't move her head. In the distance she could hear a strange chopping noise. It got louder and louder until the window began to vibrate. The noise became huge and hacking. It hurt her head. Red lights flashed in the air outside. She closed her eyes and put her hands up to her ears.

'No no no no no, I don't understand,' she whimpered.

The noise carried on for a few minutes and then the helicopter took off as loudly and quickly as it had arrived. Soon the racket was just a memory that left a ringing in her ears.

The cheering and the fireworks began in earnest at midnight. Enormous rockets and exploding stars took off from boats and shore. They shook the ship and screamed into the sky.

Agnes sat in the chair, shivering. She rocked with each massive blast. It reminded her of the Blitz.

She reached into her pocket and pulled out a sugar lump. She unwrapped the wee pointy folds of paper and let the granules dissolve on her tongue. Sugar in the morning. That's what Mama used to say every night after she kissed them all. Sugar in the morning.

'Mama,' she whispered as sweet saliva trickled down her throat.

It took three days at sea to get back to Tilbury. The sun finally shone on the last day. Desmond and Nanette were there to meet her at the docks. Jodie was waiting in the car. She didn't look well. She was pale and bloated and wouldn't look anyone in the eye. Back at their house, Nanette put the bowl from the souk on the sideboard, a forced smile on her face. Jodie said nothing when Agnes gave her the fez. She sat with it on her lap until Desmond plonked it on her head.

'Go on, say it, sweetheart,' he tried. He picked up her floppy hands and moved them up and down. 'Just like that, go on. Ah ha ha, just like that.'

Jodie ate another Penguin. The hat's tassel moved as she chewed.

Desmond helped Agnes find the flat. She could afford to pay for it outright with the rest of the Premium Bond win. Tooting was fine. People were funny about South London, but as far as she was concerned, it was all just London. Desmond insisted that she had the gas fires checked out, and when the man in the blue boiler suit condemned the one in the lounge, he paid for her to have a new one put in. She picked one with a warm realistic flame effect.

She had half the furniture from the flat she'd rented with Ajit, and a few nice pieces left over from Ernest and her father. She fancied the odd new bit too, but the Premium Bond wouldn't stretch that far. So she spent a Saturday trawling house clearance shops in Wandsworth. The chest of drawers was just what she wanted. Lots of useful drawers, twenty-four of them. Just right for sorting things out. She'd start as she meant to go on and get organized straight away.

When she saw the postcard in the pet shop window advertising tabby kittens, she couldn't resist.

'A house is not a home until pussy moves in,' lisped the woman in the shop, as she put the two fluffy pompoms in a cardboard box with handles.

Agnes didn't bother replying.

January 17–18 – Down the Little Red Lane

It's dark outside, but it's not too cold for the time of year. I'm still standing. I manage to walk to the crossroads and turn the corner down a side street. I usually only limp now when it's rainy, but the limp is back in full. The whole of my left side is aching. I'm gasping and rattling as I'm moving. I have to stop and lean against a wall in front of a very neat garden. Clipped hedges, spotless flowerbeds and a dirty big seagull strutting around the dinky square of lawn.

Bastards bastards bastards.

The wheelie bins are out in force. Friday tomorrow, bin day. I only wanted my pictures back. I only wanted to talk. Make friends. The bins smell. Rotten rich cheesy essence of bin. It may be neat here, but the bins stink the same as anywhere else. There's something sweet in the air too, like a Glade plug-in. Breathe in breathe in; good idea: calming breath, relaxation. I close my eyes and suck up the air through my nose just like June taught me. But my ears go pop and it hurts my chest and then my skull, breathing so hard. The bastards have hurt my head. The sweet smell is like wallflowers. Roger used to grow velvety red and yellow wallflowers in the front bed just under the wall. Call me Uncle Roger, he used to say.

Heels click quickly and I open my eyes. A woman in a long coat is running across the road, looking back at me and leaving the stink of flowery perfume behind her.

A chunk of light appears on the grass and the seagull flies

off, laughing loudly. Someone is looking out of the front room window.

Have a good look, eh?

Bastard. Bastards.

I kick the nearest wheelie bin till it totters. My leg hurts too much to kick it right over.

It's downhill to the sea, so I lumber down there slowly, stopping for a couple more rests and June-approved cleansing breaths on the way. The moon is shining on the sea, and there are people under the pier. They're laughing and drinking, but the pebbles hurt my feet and I don't feel safe. I move back to the prom and find a turquoise bench in a brick shelter. It smells of piss but I decide to sit there until I've got the energy to set off home. The sea is swishing in and out and I nod off for a few minutes, clutching my purse and my damp photos to my chest.

I wake up when my head flops down with a jolt. It feels heavy, like a lump of rock, and my neck aches. It's really cold, so I stir myself for the trudge through the sea mist and past the blurry streetlights back to number 194.

When I was a girl, my mum always kept the fridge spotless at home. Opening the door to that fridge was like going to a brand-new supermarket on its very first day. Nothing was out of place, nothing looked like it had been started. Food wasn't for eating, it was for keeping clean and tidy. There were always six eggs in the egg holes – never five, never ever none, God forbid. They were polished like little bald heads with Mum's special egg J-cloth; medium-sized, and never free-range.

'That's what hens are for, laying eggs. Why would they need to go outside? They're nice and warm inside, they'd only get dirty if they went outside,' she told Timmy when he went veggie and all ethical about his food.

Cheese was chopped with exact straight edges, wrapped up and filed away inside a clean Tupperware box labelled Cheese. There was always an unopened iceberg lettuce and full-length cucumber in one transparent drawer at the bottom, green vegetables in the other. We had the perfect balanced diet. It's just that everything tasted of bleach.

My fridge is my fridge. I call it Darth Vadar because it looms there in the corner of my room. I can hear it breathing when I go to sleep. I can't remember when I last cleaned it and I've never defrosted it. It is a bit mouldy inside, but I've not had food poisoning yet. And it's got its very own binge cycle. It's not consistently and evenly occupied like the fridge of my childhood. Mondays, when I get my DLA, I walk all the way to Lidl and load up. Cheese, chocolate, fromage frais, seven white sliced loaves, frozen pies, anything gloopy that's on offer. But by this point in the week, Darth is a shadow of his former self. His insides are nearly empty.

Normally I say 'Hello, Darth' or 'Hello, DV', depending on how I'm feeling, before I open the door. It's only polite. But my mouth hurts and I couldn't give a fuck about being polite just now. No, I want food. I need something to put in my mouth and anything in my stomach. It's like when money burns a hole in your pocket and you have to spend it. Anywhere will do: department store, pound shop, car boot sale. I've got an empty gob and I must fill it. I must have balls of food gulping down my throat. It's not about nutrition, or a perfectly balanced diet, it's about pushing greasy, lumpy chunks of anything in my face to block out the pain.

There's a small lump of Red Leicester, the remains of a packet of curled-up ham, half a pot of strawberry yoghurt, two dried-up carrots, chilli flavour HP sauce, piccalilli, and four pickled onions in cloudy vinegar. I pull out the cheese, ham and yoghurt and slam them on the counter by the sink. I need more. I start eating, squeezing the cheese through my teeth and drinking the yoghurt direct from the pot, whilst I'm opening the wall cupboard. Dairy is good, but most of all I need something solid and I know I've got no bread left. There's still half a pack of Happy Boy sugar puffs. True they're airy, but they're sweet and bulky enough to occupy my teeth and tongue, so I shovel them in. Down the little red lane: gulp gulp gulp.

I swing my hand around inside the cupboard. A can of spaghetti, a can of tuna, a can of rice pudding. Fuck the tuna, but the others will do. Down they come, out with the can opener, dig in. Take it in turns now, it's only fair. Spaghetti, rice pudding, spag, rice, spag rice, spag rice, till it's all gone. Good girl.

I'm absolutely certain that there are only crumbs in the biscuit tin, but, of course, I still reach up and open it, praying inside that somehow I've forgotten a packet of Boasters or Jesters or Jaffa Cakes. Or chocolate fingers, real Cadbury's chocolate fingers, just like my nan used to have. As if. As if I'd forget that I had biscuits. My, oh my, why, I did have a couple of garibaldis earlier with my bone-china cup of Earl Grey, but then I just popped them away in the cupboard for another time. As if.

God knows, anything would do: cream crackers or broken biscuits tasting of stale concrete would do. I open my eyes and look inside. There's a very paltry layer of crumbs. I had all the reasonable crumbs earlier, but I shake the tin about and pour the sand crumbs down my throat. They tickle and I cough.

By now I'm getting faster and faster, more and more frantic in my panic to eat. My eyes are closed and my mind is in a blank limbo as my mouth closes around anything that will go down down down. Finally it calms, my breathing slows down and I'm done. For the time being. The waistband of my leggings is digging into my belly, and there is a salty sweet taste in the back of my throat. I walk the four paces across from the kitchen cupboards and Darth, over to my armchair. I slump down and let out a huge sigh. Something on the floor catches my eye. My photos. I lean down to pick them up but I can't make it, so I shuffle them over towards me using my feet.

Natalie. Dead now for a long time. Getting on for twenty years now. Doesn't time fly? Look at that smile. She hated it, said she looked like Jimmy Tarbuck. I said a gap between your teeth was supposed to mean good luck. I sometimes wonder whether her teeth survived the crash, if they were intact when they cremated her.

I pass my eyes over the other two pictures and try to smooth them flat with the side of my hand. I breathe biscuit dust onto them, and blow it off. They're dry now but still bumpy and streaked with pale yellow. Must keep them safe. Never let that happen again. I force myself up and trudge over to the shelves above my bed in the corner. I pull down my six flip photo albums and throw them on top of the sleeping bag. It's Album Five I need: art school days. As I'm looking for it, Album Three falls open: Jodie Ledermann, the teenage wonder years. I slump down on the bed and look through the pictures.

I'm standing by a boating lake, scowling and wearing a zip-up navy-blue skinny rib cardigan with a huge turquoise letter J embossed on the front. It's got lapels the size of Dumbo's ears. My hair is no better: all flicky and stiff. I spent a good twenty minutes in front of the mirror in the mouldy chalet each morning, getting it like that, and squeezing spots. I was just beginning to get fat.

I remember that holiday so vividly. It was the only time we ever went to a holiday camp. God alone knows why my mum agreed to it: far too low class. Every spring, she would talk about touring and visiting a range of clean and refined places: Nice, Capri, Rimini. One February, she became completely fixated on the Cayman Islands. I blame Judith Chalmers with her permatan and her cocktails and her high life. In reality, of course, we hardly went away at all. But this particular summer in the seventies, my nan really wanted to go to Pwllheli. She'd been flicking through a copy of the *Daily Mirror* at the hairdressers, apparently, and seen a good deal. The whole lot of us went for a week for £70. All in, food included. Well, it was 1976. And it was Butlins.

The next photo is me and Timmy. He is so so skinny. A bunch of sticks, whacking big smile, cropped hair and a stripy T-shirt. If he had proper bumpers on his feet he'd look like an all-American boy, but the little black plimsolls from Woolworths let him down. We argued all day every day that holiday, but you wouldn't know it from the photo. Sibling rivalry, pah: we're frozen smiling in that moment, toasting each other with shiny blue and red cans of Diet Pepsi. I remember I'd wanted Tab, it was more sophisticated, but in the mid-seventies Pwllheli must have been beyond the reaches of some major soft drinks distributing networks.

We were singing the Diet Pepsi jingle over and over till it got stuck in our heads. We could do it, it could help. I'd just about stopped sulking about my Tab. My dad must have taken the photo. My mum and my nan are leaning right over the railings of the boating lake, arses sticking out and heads out of view, bent down towards the water. Looking for fishes, or at the manky ducks, maybe. More likely whispering and muttering about Him.

He didn't come on that holiday. My nan had finally given him the old heave-ho. Roger the Dodger. Uncle Roger. Call me Uncle Roger, he'd whisper. Sounded better than call me Step-granddad Roger, I suppose. He smoked thin little cigars, collected gnomes and coughed a lot. Gone but not forgotten. The thought of him makes me shiver and I look down to check the skirting board. Nothing there, safe. My nan was a goer, alright. South London's answer to Liz Taylor, that's what Timmy used to say in his camper moments. Three husbands, not a bad record. Three more than I'll ever have.

There was a lovely handsome Redcoat called Liam, and Alvin Stardust did the cabaret on the Saturday night, I can remember that. The real Alvin Stardust, not some tacky looka-likey. I was sure it was, whatever anyone said. Leather gloves, rings, sideburns: he pointed at me when he sang *My Coo-Ca-Choo*. Timmy was convinced it was him he was pointing at, but I know it was me. Timmy couldn't bear the truth and pulled my hair so hard that a clump came right out and made me cry. I ground half a packet of Smith's salt and vinegar crisps into his face and when he told Mum she smacked me. All under the alternating rosy, lime and sea-blue glow of the disco lights. Alvin didn't seem to notice.

Timmy's dead too. All that energy and dancing got him into trouble, and he's gone now as well. I'm tired. Tired and lonely. My eyes are shutting with swelling and soreness. I close Album Three, and slide my safe, beer-stained snaps back home into Album Five. No energy to put them back in their proper slots, though. My neck hasn't got any strength left in it and my head conks back on the wall with a small thud. This bit of wall is slightly slippery and smells comfortably of hair. My sleeping bag rustles as I pull it up over me, and the photo albums slowly thump down onto the floor one after another.

Five four three two one. There are five Russian Dolls all in a row, graded in order, teeny-weeny to freaky big and bulky. They start to move. The biggest one, with a face like Uncle Roger, whispers right in my ear, 'Do you like my wallflowers?'

Suddenly Nan is there. She is wearing a fez. She picks up the dolls and starts to fit them inside each other. She acts like Tommy Cooper, guffawing and holding her hands out. But she is rough, and they are squishy like Plasticine, and soon she is left with one large dollop of purple in between her hands. She rolls it out into lots of long fingers, and then lines them up inside her tartan biscuit tin, which has appeared from nowhere.

'Royal Stewart,' she says ominously, quickly followed up with, 'Would anyone care for a sausage?' A cat darts through a door and there are insects running all over the floor. Then Nan laughs. She laughs so much that she coughs and splutters and wheezes. The biscuit tin clatters to the floor and she groans. Wheeze, clatter groan, wheeze clatter groan.

Wheeze clatter groan. Wheeze clatter groan. I open my eyes. There's yellow light flashing on and off. Friday, bin day. The dustbin van is grinding up the road, wheelie bins cluttering up and down. It's stopped for a bit, and now the reverse beeps are going. I'm desperate for a wee, but I like it lying here, listening to the noise. My bladder is thumping. Friday. I could go down the day centre. My legs are hot and my scabs are itchy. I scratch them. I lie there thinking about my dream. Nan. I think I'll visit Nan.

1985

Desmond looked dreadful. He was the colour of the sheets on the girl's bed. Agnes hadn't seen him that pale since he was little. When he was a skinny seven-year-old, he went blue after swimming, even on a hot day. The girl was sleeping flat on her back with her leg in plaster and hooked up to the ceiling. She was a strapping lass, hardly a girl any more. Desmond was holding her hand and had his eyes shut. Agnes carried the bunch of strong peppery freesias close to her nose to drown out the smell of the hospital. Even now, the ether and disinfectant made her stomach lurch. She had walked around the block for forty-five minutes and then in circles on the pavement before finally making it through the swishing glass entrance doors.

She took a deep breath and walked over to the bedside cabinet. Her heels clicked on the floor. Desmond opened his eyes. Jodie let out a strange whinnying snore, shook her head from side to side and muttered something. He looked down at her in alarm, but she was still again.

'How is she?' Agnes whispered.

Desmond shrugged. 'Alive,' he said.

His eyes were tiny and sunken, with huge blue rings like bruises running underneath them. He looked strange without his glasses. He couldn't take his eyes off the girl.

'Her friend died, did you know?' he said, after a long pause.

'Oh,' said Agnes.

'Natalie – you wouldn't have met her.'

That was an understatement. Agnes hardly ever saw the girl, and certainly didn't know who her friends were. Agnes looked at Desmond again. The timing of the accident was cruel, coming so soon after Timmy. To lose one child was horrific. But to nearly lose another . . . Agnes sighed and Desmond noticed her looking at him. He stood up stiffly and gestured to the chair.

'No, thanks. I can't stop, I've got to get to work,' she said. Her stomach was on fire and the fluorescent lights were making her head thump.

'Here, you'll need a vase for these.' She handed the freesias to Desmond, then quickly pulled a piece of crumpled tissue from her sleeve. She held it under her nose and blew him a kiss. The girl's eyes were still shut as she clicked off across the ward.

When she got back to the maisonette after work, there were two brown envelopes on the doormat. The postman had dropped two rubber bands through the letter box with them, one thick, one thin. Always come in useful, Agnes thought. She picked them up and put them in her pocket. Bills, bills, bills. Life with Ajit had not turned out the way she'd expected. At first it had been all lovey-dovey, long weekends in bed and spicy lentil curries, but that had soon worn off. He was not to be trusted, it turned out. Agnes opened the first envelope. Water rates. Ajit was supposed to have sorted it out. And the rent – she bet he hadn't paid the rent again. She opened the second envelope, with the Lytham postmark. It was from the Premium Bonds.

She dropped the envelope, shrieked and danced a tango the entire length of the purple and pink Turkish rug, stopping each end on the parquet floor for a deep lunge and a sudden head turn. She was a fine figure of a woman still, no doubt about that. Most women in their sixties just let themselves go. She gently tapped the underside of her chin with the top of her hand before tipping her head down to look at the line of her body, smoothing both hands over her slightly rounded belly. She traced her finger over the star-shaped scar on her neck. Such a long time ago, the fire and Ernest.

A slight sweat had broken out on her upper lip. She bent down and picked up the envelope again. She read the figures and her mind swam. She lifted her right arm and sniffed at the red ribbed sweater; perhaps a bit more baked beans than soap powder just now, three days on. She'd change it tonight. Bugger that, she could chuck it in the bin and buy a whole drawerful of new sweaters. Cashmere, if she wanted. And her job, it suddenly dawned on her. Her two-bit part-time poky little job at the Hollies. She could tell them where to shove that now.

Twenty thousand pounds.

Her Premium Bond. Nothing to do with his nibs. She threw back her head and brought the letter down flat on top of her face, covering it with both hands so that all she could see and smell was paper and ink. Her kisses left a cluster of pink buds two-thirds of the way down the page.

Music, music, she wanted to dance some more. She rifled through her record collection but couldn't find a tango. She quickly pushed Ajit's few LPs out of the way, and plucked out a colourful cover with a triangular design in shades of orange on it. Desmond had given it to her. They'd played a snatch of it at Timmy's funeral, and he'd come over a fortnight later with the record, carefully gift-wrapped in thick, expensive paper. He'd not said a word, but given her one of those significant stares that she didn't understand.

He'd been such a funny little boy, Timmy. Her favourite grandson, she used to say to tease.

'But I'm your only grandson,' he'd moan, and she'd wink at him.

It was Timmy who encouraged her to enter the competition at Butlins, it was Timmy who dressed up in full kilt and sporran for her wedding with Ajit; and it was Timmy who giggled with her when Jodie looked through her as if she was a ghost. She put the record on but she didn't feel like dancing any more. It didn't seem to have any kind of rhythm and it was very loud.

He was a skittish teenager and then a witty young man. He'd got ill so suddenly. At first no one knew what it was. He was always skinny, but by the end, he was a skeleton covered in skin, freckles, purple lumps and bumps. Agnes had been afraid to touch him. He coughed all the time, and wore a big hat to cover his skully head. The last time she saw him he'd told her that eight of his friends had died.

'Eight funerals I've been to. That's not right, a fine young hunk of a man like me,' and he'd flexed his wasted arm like a muscle man.

She hadn't known what to say to comfort the poor wee boy.

The room felt chilly now she'd stopped dancing. She put the record away carefully, paused and looked down at the letter again. She went over to the gas fire and clicked on its living flame. That was better. She walked across the room to the glass-fronted drinks cabinet, a nice piece of Papa's, and looked for her little thistle-head glass, just right for a wee dram. A tot of whisky would be too small, so she took out two large crystal tumblers instead. She made herself a Whisky Mac in one, and poured flat pale American ginger ale in the other.

'Salud. Aspro Patos. Mazel tov. Bottoms up,' she grinned, bending her neck back much further than she needed to before chucking the drinks down her stretched-out throat.

Every morning she sat in front of the dressing-table mirror for at least fifteen minutes, doing her neck exercises. She'd met a girl in the Debenhams coffee shop, who had shown her how to do them. Called herself a beauty therapist and wore a white coat, but she'd overplucked her eyebrows and had such pockmarked skin that she didn't seem a very good advert for her profession, Agnes had thought. And when she said 'girl', she must have been in her early forties. They'd sat there drinking black coffee and not having cream cakes. Agnes had sneaked four wrapped packets of sugar cubes into her bag. The girl was on her tea break from the ground floor, but why she didn't go to the staff canteen, Agnes never asked.

They'd been chatting about how difficult it was to get hold of a decent herring, when she had suddenly put down her coffee cup, tipped her head back and looked right up at the ceiling with her mouth wide open, waited a moment and then shut it. At first Agnes thought she was impersonating a fish or else admiring the polystyrene tiles and sunken light fittings, but then the girl had made her do the same thing, describing all the various muscle groups and tissues improved by the action. They'd looked like a pair of guppies, but Agnes could definitely feel the benefit to her throat.

Agnes poured herself two more drinks, the same again. She could hear the fridge humming down in the kitchen. Outside a car slowed down to turn the corner. A small child was moaning and whining just below the window.

'Just shut up whingeing, for God's sake. You've got a bloody ice cream.'

More muffled moaning and the sound of a slap.

The screaming faded as they walked away down the street. It didn't change tone like an ambulance would, though. Downstairs in the hall, the phone rang and the answermachine clicked in after four rings.

Agnes pulled a chair over to the window, taking her drinks with her, and carrying the letter from Lytham in her teeth. It was Ajit's hometime. She always got back before him, being part time. She often came and sat here and looked out for him marching down the street, usually grim-faced, and almost always wearing his large sandy Detective Mac. Only once had he looked up and spotted her, his head tilting on to his shoulder. But that had been early on in their marriage. These days, as soon as she heard his key in the lock, she'd shift herself. Switch on the television, or pick up the phone and pretend to be listening to someone when he came in. She tried to remember when the 'I'm ho-ome, darling' and the hello kisses had stopped.

Another car approached the corner, this time without slowing. Brakes shrieked and there was an almighty crunch of metal and glass, followed by a long silence. The birds stopped singing, the kids stopped playing and the fridge stopped humming.

Agnes stood up, knocking the chair over behind her. She pulled open the window, leant out and looked up the street. About fifty yards away, where the street met the main road, a red car was half on the pavement, partly squashed into a lamppost. Cars were always crashing into that corner. Some of the neighbours had started a petition about it, but Agnes wouldn't sign it. She smoothed down her jumper and went downstairs to the kitchen to fetch her handbag. She put the letter from Lytham inside. The zip on her make-up bag was stuck again but she tugged it open. She wiped off the remnants of her pink lipstick with a piece of kitchen towel. Pink was for indoors, but Northern Violet, good and thick, would be better outside.

Out in the hall Agnes wiped a dot of lipstick off her front tooth in front of the mirror and pulled on her tight bolero jacket.

Keys cash comb.

The front door slammed shut behind her and Agnes changed pace. She ran her hand through her hair and trotted towards the car, holding her bolero across her waist. Her mules clicked on the pavement and she crossed the road without checking for traffic.

On the corner, a crowd was already around the car, and Agnes scanned the faces for anybody she knew. As she got closer, the thumping of some kind of music became thicker and louder.

'What's happened?' she asked a young woman with grey skin, and a mouth full of chewing gum.

'Been a crash.' She didn't turn around.

'Let me through, please. Can I get through?' Agnes elbowed her way behind a tall man in a navy suit.

'Excuse me, do you know what has happened?' she asked, tapping his shoulder and running her hand through her hair again.

'Well, there's been some kind of an accident. Car's just ploughed into a lamppost.'

'Is anyone hurt?'

'The driver's out, but the passenger can't open the door. Ambulance is on its way.'

A woman with a tight perm and folded arms twisted her head round. 'There's someone underneath it too. On the pavement.'

Agnes stopped jostling. Ajit's hometime.

'Who? Do you know who?'

'Well, how should I know?' tutted the woman, taking a packet of cigarettes and a lighter out of a carrier bag.

Agnes pulled herself up tall and closed her eyes. The man and the woman had turned round again.

Using her elbows like paddles, Agnes forced her way to the front, and then edged round nearer to the passenger door. The car was red and small, with two large aerials jutting over the roof. The music was booming out of the broken passenger window. It was all rhythm and no words.

A plump young man – couldn't have been much older than Jodie – in a green baseball hat was sitting on a garden wall, swinging his legs and smoking hard on a cigarette. Inside the garden, a Jack Russell with three legs was chained to the gate, yapping and growling without a break. The boy's face was white and shiny like an oyster, and his hand shook so hard that his cigarette wobbled in his mouth. An earth mother in a brown smock was talking to him gently. She reached out to put her hand on his shoulder, but he jerked away as though she was going to hit him. Inside the car, a girl with spiky bottle-blonde hair sat with her head leaning right back on the headrest, her unlined neck stretched taut. Pale again, but no blood. The thumping music stopped and a smarmy voice began prattling. The girl turned round suddenly and pushed and clawed at the door.

'Let me out of here. Fucking let me out. Somebody help me.' She began screaming a long thin scream, waving one hand out of the top of the broken window, clutching and opening and shutting it like a glove puppet.

Two more people were crouched next to the passenger door, and another woman was lying flat down on the pavement, her head and both arms stretched out under the crumpled chassis. Agnes pushed closer when a big fat man blocked her way. One of the neighbours, Mr Ostrowski, was still in his slippers. His bright yellow Castles of Spain T-shirt was too short to cover the lump of solid grey hairy belly that hung over the top of his tatty running bottoms. It was his dog and his wall.

'Come on now, Mrs Saund, they need space.'

'Who's under there, who is it?' Agnes barked. 'Let me see.'

She moved sideways, but he did too, his stomach wobbling at the sudden movement. She tried the other way, but he was there again, like a partner in a strange folk dance. The third time she managed to glance down and catch sight of something sandy-coloured just beneath the car.

This really was it. Not a game, not a dress rehearsal. He was under there. Her lungs deflated as the air rushed out of her mouth.

'Oh my God, it is Ajit,' she howled.

She was clawing at Mr Ostrowski. His big palms came down to stop her and she punched him in the groin, lunging down beneath the car as he bent over. She lost her left mule in the gutter as she pushed one of the crouching people over.

She knelt in something cold and slimy. A dollop of ice cream and strawberry sauce. Poking out from beneath the car: a sandy-coloured teddy bear.

'Mrs Saund, show some respect,' said Mr Ostrowski as he lifted her out by the armpits.

They'd married in a registry office in Balham. The registrar had insisted that they pose for photographs sitting at an oak table with the big leather book, and two ridiculously large quill pens. Ajit had looked at the swans' feathers in disbelief and Agnes knew that she'd made the right decision. Desmond took the pictures – another series outside on the small sandstone patio, cherry trees just out of blossom. But he'd had them standing in front of the sun, so when the photos came out, they were shadows surrounded by glaring white.

There was still no sign of him when she got home. She poured herself another drink and felt even more muzzy. When she'd thought it was him under the car she'd felt sick. But she'd also felt a huge auld surge of relief and elation. No more Ajit. She took another slurp. The sole of her left foot was dotted with gravel and her stocking had a hole in the heel. She hobbled over to the kitchen table and leant her forehead against the Formica. After a while she felt a bit clearer. She pulled the letter out of her handbag and stared at it for a couple of minutes. The lipstick marks had spread into greasy blobs on the paper. She wouldn't tell him. He could go to hell. She could go wherever the hell she wanted.

They had gone on holiday together for the first couple of years. Nothing very flashy. Agnes had hankered after city skylines and aeroplanes, but the Peak District had been pretty enough, and Ajit had a cousin they could stay with in Buxton. Once they took a daytrip to Calais.

'The arsehole of France,' Agnes had chirruped, and Ajit had laughed in delight and covered her face and neck in little kisses. But after a while it was clear they had different ways. She'd wanted them to go out to cocktail parties together; he bought her a telly. She'd wanted a cat; he bought her a cushion.

She trekked out into the hall, looking for her slippers. There was a red number one lit up on the answerphone. She slid the switch to play back the message.

'Hello. Hello. Are you there? Well, I'm going to be late. Something's cropped up.' Beep.

Agnes snorted and padded upstairs for a bath. Someone's cropped up. She was used to his slimy two-timing lies now.

It was ten past ten when he came back. His eyes were like pissholes in the snow. Agnes had seen this look before, plenty of times: slightly flushed with distinct round red blotches on his beige cheeks. He smelt of perfume. Not rose water, women's perfume. With his hooked nose, he reminded her of Mr Punch.

'Here you are,' he said, offering her a thin white carrier bag like a carefully chosen gift from one of those Mrs Tiggy-Winkle gift shops he said he adored for their kitschness. 'For you, my dear.'

'Oh, you shouldn't have.'

'Sausages, for tea,' he giggled. He was still wearing his mac, but the belt trailed onto the floor and his collar was half tucked in, half tucked out. His hair was sticking up like a schoolboy. It was nearly all grey now, with just a hint of the old black.

'What sort of sausages?'

'Beef.' He lifted his eyebrows suggestively, and made his chocolate-drop pupils twinkle, but he couldn't keep his hand quite still.

'Beef. You've been drinking.'

'Oh, you know, darling.'

'I know alright.'

'Come on . . .' Ajit cocked his head and smiled with half of his mouth.

He took the sausages out of the bag and held them in both hands, arms stretched out straight towards her. Agnes reached her hands forward. He gave them to her and she quickly pulled her hands away. They fell on the terracotta-tile lino;

pink-and-white-speckled meat burst out of the skins like lumpy turds.

'You really think I'm going to cook for you now?' she said with a snort.

'I'm hungry,' he whined, like a child.

She wondered what had happened to the tamarind, to the cumin and coriander seeds he used to fry. She would sit and watch, listening to him humming strange out-of-tune melodies.

'Well, bloody well cook them yourself,' she shouted. The crystal glasses lined up in the dresser pinged. Agnes's shoulders were rising, and the end of her fingertips twitched.

'Don't think I don't know where you've been.'

Ajit smiled again, this time using all his mouth, smoothing down his schoolboy short back and sides with his hand.

'Ah, don't be like that, Bebby.' Bebby. He used to call her Bebby in the early days.

Agnes snatched a large plate from the bottom dresser shelf, one of the few left from an entire set they'd bought when they visited Portmeirion, and raised it to shoulder height. Ajit put his hands up in front of his face and she threw. It caught his ear and the side of his jaw before smashing on the floor next to the sausage pulp. He yelped, and she reached for another one. Ajit turned quickly and ran for the front door.

'And don't bother coming back,' she shouted, chucking the plate at the door as it slammed shut.

Agnes woke very early the next morning. The house was lovely and quiet without all his gargling and humming and faffing about. She took a long bath and dressed slowly.

She went down to the kitchen and took Ajit's favourite frying pan out of the cupboard. She scraped the sausage meat, chips of crockery and crumbs off the floor and slopped them into the pan. When it got sizzling she sprinkled salt and pepper, paprika and turmeric over the lot. She reached in the drawer to find a fish slice to poke it about, and put her hand on the big black-handled kitchen scissors. Agnes stood still and ran her finger across the blade. Slowly she took them out and laid them on the table. She sat down and stared at them, her fingers itching. The sausage meat caught, and the kitchen began to fill with brown smoke.

Suddenly next door's dog set off barking. The letter box slammed shut and paper thudded on the doormat. The noise jolted her. She jumped up and switched off the cooker. She slammed the scissors back in the drawer and ran to the front door to get the post. It was only the free paper. She stood on the mat, turning the pages, scared to go back in the kitchen, to the scissors. Page three, she said to herself, something good will be on page three.

On page three, next to an article about a long-serving lollipop lady, there was a big display advert. 'Get away from it all with a luxury cruise.'

February 3 – Yes No Interlude

It is hard going outside. Okay, it's hard being inside, but there is something about going outside that is really hard. It's not just all that space and sky, although that doesn't help, not knowing where it all ends. No, it's the people. Must be weird being one of them. All safe and sound, all *All right mate, All right Jack.* They know what they're doing tum te tum and get on with it: no worries, pal. Sometimes I think: you Lucky Lucky Fuckers. Then an LLF spots me from the other side of the road and starts with the shouting and swearing. So outside is hard. Full of unpredictable shouting, scary people who get even the slightest whiff of me and go off into one.

I test myself every now and then, but today is going to be the biggest test for a long time. I know, I know, I should think of it as a challenge, an opportunity to seize and relish because it might make me grow. Welcome to *Opportunity Knocks*, and here's your host . . . June. She means it most sincerely, folks.

Well, it's only sixty miles to South London. Just a little jaunt to visit an elderly family member. No problem. I'm crapping myself.

The pier, that's a good testing ground. I was on the pier a few months ago, August Bank Holiday. Chock-a-block with people wearing sunglasses, even though it was very cloudy. The smell of doughnut fat and hot dog onions was making my stomach juices squirt, and Blondie was so tinny coming out of the speakers that my head was just starting to ache. I got stuck looking through the slats on the floor, staring at the olive-green sea whooshing away underneath. Couldn't tear my eyes away. I went giddy eventually and had to sit down on the floor. People just walked round me; one boy spat a lump of bubble gum on my head. Timmy once told me that if you want to hypnotize hens, all you have to do is hold a piece of chalk in front of their beaks until they notice it, then lower it slowly to the ground and draw a straight white line. Their chicken brains just can't cope with it, and they get stuck looking up and down the length of the line until you click your fingers or rub it out or say Colonel Sanders or some such nonsense. I was like a bloody big fat hen on the pier that day.

I made the mistake of telling June about it. Yes, Jodie, she said, quite right, it is a challenge, but a challenge can also be a bit of fun. So we had to go again, together, two weeks later. Bit of fun, my arse. She insisted on us having our photos taken with our heads poking out through the holes in a cartoon picture board. High larks, not. She laughed like a drain when she got her film processed and bandied the snaps around the day centre. June: muscle man, complete with waxed moustache, middle parting and red vest-and-pants gym kit. Me: voluptuous blonde in a sexy purple swimming costume, huge pointy tits and long legs topped off with high-heeled mules. Why anyone, even a cartoon, would want to wear high-heeled mules in the sea, I never fathomed.

Muscle-Man June is lifting up Voluptuous-Blonde Me. Real June's face is looking down at me, flushed and sparkly. I'm staring straight at the camera with dead fish eyes. I binned my copy.

Actually, the pier is full of people like me. When it started raining in earnest, me and June went and sheltered under an awning near the way out. We stood in a crush of people, and it smelt of digestive biscuits and stale fags. A nice comfortable familiar smell, better than the rest of the pier and the beer and chips and doughnuts. We were squashed between pac-a-macs and rain hoods and hundreds of well-used carrier bags. Bags bulging with things to keep their smelly plastic-coated owners safe. I always try to take at least two jumpers and two pairs of socks with me wherever I go, just in case. One old woman caught my eye. She was tiny with red raw eyes flitting madly in every direction. She was holding something up to her face. It was a glittery green toothbrush, and when she thought no one was looking, she began to quickly brush her teeth, moving her head from side to side and covering her mouth with her other hand. Maybe that'll be me in a few years.

The only good thing about the pier, as far as I'm concerned, is the exit. Up above you, as you trudge out with the drunkards and other misfits, there's this big long sign with a painting of a plump demented-looking teddy bear wearing a beret and a stripy T-shirt. Out of his lop-sided mouth is an enormously long speech bubble. I like to stand and read what it says, mouthing the different sounds. *Adios! Arrivederci! Auf Wiedersehen! Yassou! Adjo! Dag!* Then I try out the English phrases in funny accents that make me snigger. *Have a Nice Day! Don't Be a Stranger! See Ya Mate!* and *T'ra then Chuck!* I have to stop when people start staring, or when June or whoever I'm with says it's time to go.

But the pier is a piece of piss compared with the coach station. And today, I'm at the coach station. I've got two jumpers wrapped around my photo album and four pairs of socks, just in case, in my best big black and white folding laundry carrier. Plus a strong 10p carrier with two one-and-a-half-litre bottles of water, eight rounds of Marmite sandwiches and my biscuit tin, filled up with a nearly complete packet of Jesters and an unopened packet of coconut rings. It's got proper thick plastic handles attached to the top, not those silly holes you get in the free carriers. They're great, but they leave a big red stripe in the palm of my hand. The shopping meant a trip to Zeeta's on the corner first thing. Once I've paid for the coach ticket, I'll have used up the rest of my week's money, but a trip is a trip and you've got to have supplies. If I could afford a mobile phone, I'd have at least a couple of them stashed away in another carrier.

I need to put my bags down to rest my hands, so I'm trying to sit on the blue metal bars that are supposed to be seats, but it is very uncomfortable. I've got my parka on for travelling and in case it's cold, and my Russian hat, earflaps down, until the coach gets going. My legs shouldn't itch so much in my lightweight leggings with the holes around the seam for ventilation. They are itching a bit now, so I give them a good scratch that will hopefully last until we board. I get my new packet of Richmonds out of the right-hand pocket of my parka. My hands are still crunched up from carrying the bags, so I struggle with the Cellophane. I use my teeth and pull one out. I light it with my brand-new purple lighter, another treat for the journey. I left the shiny little black book of matches at home, in the pocket of my lucky purple summer jacket. Never know when I might need them.

Coach stations and train stations are always cold and damp. This one is grey and fumy and echoey. There's a man further down the queue looking at me. Oh God, he's winking. I reach down into my carrier for a Marmite sandwich and busy myself opening it up and examining it. When I look back again, he is still winking. He is also now pulling at his crotch with both hands. I pull the crust off the sandwich and sneak it into my mouth. A shadow makes the sandwich go grey and the man is standing right in front of me. He is very short, thin as a chip, and his head is shaved. He's got a pierced ear, a pierced lip and a pierced eyebrow. I wonder if he has a pierced dick, and if that was why he was pulling at himself. I narrow my eyes and look in between his legs, but all I can see is the bumps and wrinkles that could be anything.

'Alright?' he says. His voice is deep and almost posh, like an actor.

I finish off the sandwich in a couple of bites.

'Hungry?' he says.

The bread goes down in two big gulps and I wipe my mouth with the back of my sleeve.

He puts out his hand. It is a formal thing to do, but in keeping with the voice. I put up my earflaps, stand up and shake it. I am towering over him. He starts to laugh. It is a loud booming laugh and all his various bits of jewellery are rattling.

He carries on shaking my hand, making the shake bigger and more elaborate, up and down like barn dancing until it feels like he is going to pull my arm out of its socket.

The coach starts up with a lurch and a ground-breaking clatter. Saved by the fumes: thank God for that. I snatch my arm back from him, pick up my bags and lumber towards the coach door as it is opening. I can still hear him laughing. I'm the first person on board. The driver is engrossed with the buttons on his dashboard, but a woman in a maroon pillbox hat and a fitted jacket with epaulettes wrinkles her nose at me.

She puts her hand out. I stare at it. She doesn't move it. I'm not about to shake another hand so I carry on looking at her. She coughs loudly, and moves the hand around quickly. It's got long square fingernails shaped like shovels. They are very clean and shiny, like they've been bleached. People are pushing and jostling behind me. She has silver rings on the index and middle fingers.

'Ticket,' she says brightly, rolling her eyes to the people behind me. There is a dot of maroon lipstick on her left front tooth. 'You can't get on without a ticket.' She talks to me very slowly and loudly, like she is talking to a foreigner, and then laughs with a polite tinkle for the queue behind me.

I've got the ticket in the top inside pocket of my parka, with my purse for safekeeping. I put down my bags and tug at the long zip. The people behind me are getting restless. Someone tries to push past me, but there isn't enough room. The muttering and grumbling is getting louder, and the pushing and shoving begins in earnest.

Then I hear a loud actorly voice boom out from further back in the queue. It could be Kenneth Branagh himself. 'Desist from this jostling and per-lease allow the lady to get her ticket.'

Everything goes still. Lady. He can't be talking about me. My zip undoes with a long clear rasp. The jumped-up Gestapo hostess looks disappointed when I find my ticket. She snatches it off me and rips the top sheet out of it.

'Thank you so much,' I say quietly. Behind me I can hear a single clap and a whistle of victory. I try to muster up the dignity for a slow serene walk down the aisle, but trip over my bags. The lid of my biscuit tin falls off and there are coconut rings all over the little triangles on the thick dark carpet. A wave of impatience and cursing hits me from behind as I brush them into my bag as quickly as I can and lurch towards the safety of the back of the coach. I am soaked with sweat, but it is warm and dark back here and the smell of new uphol-stery, air freshener and mild sick is a great comfort. I pull my earflaps down, close my eyes and breath deeply through my nose, trying to remember some calming mantras. The preferred option of my relaxation tape is 'Peace, Tranquiiiillity, Serenity. Peace, Tranquiiiillity, Serenity' in a slow lingering voice. There is a lot of talk of golden rooms and inner sanctums, but it gets on my tits and I prefer saying 'Safe as houses, safe as houses, safe as houses,' over and over again.

My head is just beginning to stop spinning when I feel a plonk in the seat next to me. I open my eyes. It is the little thin chip man.

'Give us a biscuit,' he says in a voice like Kenneth Williams. 'I'm starving. That was why I held out my hand, back there. And then you went and shook it. What a hoot.'

I look at him blankly. I can't cope with this.

'I was after one of your sandwiches, and then you started shaking my hand. Made me giggle.'

I keep mouthing the mantra to myself. I'm pressing my fingertips into my nail thumb, left hand then right. One two three four nail.

'Safe as houses safe as houses safe as houses safe as houses safe as houses.' I mouth it to myself.

He cocks his left ear towards me to try and work out what I am saying. It is one long whispering noise that could mean something in another language.

'My name's Owen,' he tries, back in velvet-voice mode. 'Owen Lang. Are you from round here?'

'Safeashousessafeashousessafe,' I say. It sounds Spanish.

The coach is filling up. No one comes to sit near us.

'I live in the flats – just behind the big precinct. Do you know them?'

I carry on muttering in my very own language. He turns to look more closely at my face.

'What happened to your eye?' he asks.

I put my hand up and stroke the bruise. I'll pretend I'm Spanish.

'SafashousesQué?'

He raises an eyebrow and with slow perfect enunciation says, 'Your eye?'

I'm back in class 3N, sitting at the back of the school language labs, practising my Spanish oral.

'Mi ojo es safeashouses paella con tortilla safe as safe as. Muy bien,' I say in the most singsong accent I can manage.

He leans back against the dark bristly upholstery and folds his arms. The engine changes from its pregnant puttering to a fully blown take-off chug and we pull away from the coach station. The change from shadow to white sunshine is sudden, and people raise their hands to shield their eyes. I gasp. Outside, it is a gorgeous technicolour winter day. The screeching seagulls are a dazzling white in a perfect blue sky. The sea is shimmering and it is hard to see where the water ends and the sky begins. Inside, the coach is quiet except for the tinny shishing of a Walkman.

'Oooh, isn't that pretty?' he says.

'Yes, lovely.'

'Ah ha, got you.'

Damn, damn, damn. Caught out so easily like a game of the Yes No Interlude.

'I knew you spoke English. I don't know why you were bothering – I heard you earlier. What's your name?'

'Jodie.'

'And what did happen to your eye?'

'Fell over.'

'Why?'

I shrug. My scalp is itching underneath my Russian hat. I lift my flaps again, and my ears feel cold and naked.

'I know,' he says.

'You know what?'

'I know all about falling over and being pushed.'

'Are you a social worker?'

'No.'

'A CPN?'

'No.'

I look at him more closely. He raises his eyebrows at me.

'You're not a doctor, are you?'

'Good God, no.'

'Well, how do you know then?'

'I'm mad,' he says.

I don't know what to say so I look out of the window.

'In and out of hossie for years and years, up and down like a moody yoyo,' he carries on cheerfully. 'Had the lot, the whole shebang in my time. Lithium, Depakote, Stelazine, Thorazine, Haldol, Risperdal, Chlozaril, Prozac and early on I even had a spot of the old ECT.' He judders his arms out in front of me like he's having a fit, and giggles.

I turn back round to look at him.

'I'm currently also trying out a cocktail of St John's wort, glycerine, gingko biloba and omega-3 fatty acids.' He's using his index finger to count them off on the fingers of his other hand, screwing up his right eye to remember, like he's coming up with a shopping list. 'But you know what works best?' he suddenly whispers.

I shake my head.

'Just not being scared.'

My hands are still, and the sweating has stopped at last. We're chugging inland now, the English Channel and the seagulls are far behind, and the hills are like rolls of grey shagpile. I sneak another look at him, but he is rummaging in a green canvas rucksack. He pulls out two carriers – free flimsy stripy ones – stuffed full of paper, and tips his head down to read. He is humming a tune. I half recognize it, but I'm drifting off to sleep before I can put a name to it.

The coach is shaking as it stops. I wake up and close my mouth. My throat is dry and my chin is damp. We've stopped at a small coach station. It is very well kept with glass canopies, bright yellow tubing and even a couple of dried-out hanging baskets. Not London yet. Owen is standing up.

'That's me, just visiting,' he says, humping his rucksack onto his little pointy shoulders. He looks at me expectantly, but he doesn't touch his crotch.

'Here,' I say. I hand him a couple of rounds of damp sandwiches, straight from the bread bag.

He smiles. 'Much obliged, gracias.'

The coach door swings open like something out of *Close Encounters*, but with lots of hissing, and Owen tinkles away down the aisle. He looks tiny under his rucksack. I look at the window. There's a greasy patch where my head has been bumping, and lots of handprints on the glass. Suddenly, his grinning face pops up from below like a demented jack-in-the-box. He opens his mouth just as the coach starts up and I have no chance of hearing him. He lifts his arm and points at the seat next to me, then steps back and blows me a dramatic kiss with both hands as the coach pulls out.

Me, a kiss.

There's a piece of paper on his seat. It's half the size of a normal sheet and covered with writing that is so dense I can't read it even with my eyes screwed up. There's a purple line-drawing of a strait-jacket and above that, it says

GLAD TO BE MAD:
Survivors Speak Up
Meetings 7.30 every Tuesday,
Upstairs, the Dog and Partridge,
Station Road

I turn it over and there's a note in tiny blobby writing, like an invitation to a dinner party: 'Do try to come, it would be lovely to see you again.'

A tune is running around my head. It's been lurking there for the last ten minutes or so. A big anthem, a male voice choir. *Go West*, that's what it is. That's the tune that Owen was humming.

1976

The boating pond had a surprising number of birds on it. Gannets the size of small toddlers splashed and picked around for bloated chips and flabby crusts of bread. Mallards quacked and a moorhen made for the wee island in the middle with a line of black rocking chicks paddling behind. Not at all what she'd expected of Butlins.

She and Nanette leant over the green railings to get a better look at the chicks. One of them had gone the wrong way and was peeping violently. It paddled round and round, panicking amongst the crisp packets and empty Coke cans.

'How did you find out then?' said Nanette. She was wearing a white ribbed top with a polo neck but no sleeves, and her arms were like twigs.

'The woman in the paper shop. She keeps in with the people from the hospital,' said Agnes.

'Serves him right.' Nanette stood back suddenly from the railings and looked down at her top. She sucked her lips and tutted, then picked a tiny crusty flake of paint off with long pink fingernails.

Roger had found a richer, younger woman two years ago. Maria, another patient. The divorce had been swift and painless, papers completed in six months. He was now firmly ensconced with Maria, God help her, in her cushty detached house in Amersham, and Agnes was free. Last week she'd heard that he had lung cancer.

'Ach, Nanette, why that's a terrible thing to say,' she said, eyes wide and glaring. The two of them looked at each other for a few seconds and then snorted with laughter. Agnes even slapped her leg. They whooped so loud that the kiddies and Desmond stopped what they were doing to stare. Desmond lowered his camera and frowned.

'Good riddance to the bugger,' spluttered Agnes between the laughs. She was finding it hard to breathe, and felt giddy.

She hadn't known what to do with herself for ages after he'd gone. When she spotted an advert in the *Mirror*, she rang Desmond. It was Wales, it was still just about summer and it was cheap. Nanette wasn't best pleased at first, but she'd come round.

There was a sharp squawk. Jodie was punching Timmy. The girl was getting podgy, and the queer clumpy cardi she refused to take off didn't do her any favours. Timmy began to wail and Desmond pulled Jodie away, cuffing her around the backside.

'Ow, that hurt,' she screamed at Desmond.

'It was supposed to. Leave your brother alone.'

'He called me names,' she shouted.

'Did not, she's lying,' wailed Timmy.

'Did. You called me a stupid fat cow.'

'Well, you are.'

'Da-ad, Timmy called me a name.'

Desmond clouted Jodie again. She took a step back and then ran over to Nanette. She stood with her back to Agnes.

'Mum, Dad hit me, it's not fair.' She started sniffing.

'Now then, Jodie chick, come on now, calm down,' tried Agnes.

Jodie didn't look at her. She hadn't made eye contact the whole holiday. She pulled at Nanette's arm, and Nanette brushed her away. The sniffing got louder.

'Why don't you have a drink and stop crying?' said Nanette. She reached into her new string bag and pulled out a bottle of squash. Agnes had had a string bag years ago, and when Nanette had told her how much this one from a fashionable shop in the high street had cost, she'd spilt her tea.

'Don't want that.' The girl had spots dotted around her nostrils and on her chin. 'I want a can of Tab. Can I have a can of Tab, Mum?'

Nanette reached down again and pulled out a spotty toad-stool beaker. She poured some weak squash in and passed it to Jodie.

'Here, drink your Ribena, it'll make you feel better.'

The girl wouldn't take it. "That's got sugar in. I want Tab. Tab's good for you,' Jodie started sniffing again.

Agnes's bunions were aching. 'I'll get her a can of pop,' she said.

'Oh, for God's sake,' Nanette said, and she stormed over to Desmond and Timmy, leaving Agnes and Jodie alone together.

Jodie was jumpy. She looked down at the ground, sharply, as if she was checking for something. Agnes opened her hand-bag and got out her housekeeper's purse.

'Here, chick, I'll treat you to a drink,' she said, handing Jodie a 10p piece. The girl still had her back to her, and she folded her arms. Agnes shuffled round to her and held out the coin. 'Come on, you can get one for your brother too.'

Jodie tutted between the sniffs. She still wouldn't look Agnes in the eye. Agnes rifled in her purse and pulled out a 50p.

'Here, girlie,' she tried again. After a pause Jodie unfolded her arms and snatched the money. She said nothing but headed off towards the dining hall.

'Don't forget your brother,' Agnes called after her. Timmy

looked over and Agnes pointed. He trotted after his big sister like a wee doggy.

When they came back out they were laughing and singing. Some ditty about calories. Timmy jumped up on the bench and did an elaborate dance routine that involved swivelling his hips and flinging his right arm in the air. Put Agnes in mind of Lionel Blair. But they were talking again, that was something.

Over in the middle of the road, Nanette was hissing at Desmond. He was red and flustered. Nanette pointed over to the children, and at Agnes. Desmond zipped up his wind-cheater and jutted out his chin. He'd done that ever since he was a wee boy. She used to tease him and call him Mr Chinnywig. There was a sudden toot and they all looked round. The Puffing Billy road train chugged towards them. Nanette and Desmond shifted to the pavement, and it ground to a halt just beside them.

Five fat elderly women and one elderly gent with white hair got off. All the women were wearing blue pac-a-macs and they had chips, dotted with tomato sauce. The biggest of the women tripped on the kerb and dropped her chips, and the little man tottered forward to stop her fall. Before he could get there, out of the blue, a Redcoat appeared and caught her by the elbow. The women gasped and cackled in unison, and the old man stood back with his jaw open. The sun came out from behind the clouds and Agnes smelt vinegar and lard. Behind her a duck quacked loudly.

'Alright there, missus? Aw dear, dropped your chips – still, better than dropping a clanger, ay?' He laughed like a raven cawing and then bent down, making a big play of pretending to eat the chips off the ground. The women cackled and cackled, but the old man's eyes shone hard. The Redcoat's

curly black hair was slick with oil and combed into a large
overhanging quiff. It looked old-fashioned, even to Agnes. He
stood up, pulled at the cuffs of his blazer and jerked his neck
like a chicken.

Nanette and Desmond were arguing again. Agnes and Jodie
and Timmy watched. Desmond's voice was loud and angry.
'And she is so rude to my mother . . .'

'Well, what do you expect: she learnt off the maestro.'

'Now then, now then!' the Redcoat leapt across the road
and jumped between the two of them. 'We'll have none of
that here. You're on your jollies,' he chirruped. 'You can save
all that till you get home!' He took hold of Nanette's little
finger. 'What's your name then, mademoiselle?'

Nanette stared at him.

'Cat got your tongue, ay?' He dropped her hand and in an
exaggerated whisper from the side of his mouth said to
Desmond, 'We can all dream, ay?' He turned quickly back to
Nanette. 'Nar, only messing, mademoiselle. Go on, what's
your name?'

'Nanette.'

'A beautiful elegant name for a beautiful elegant lady,' he
said, and he kissed her hand and held her little finger again.
Timmy nudged Agnes and Jodie, then stuck his finger down
his throat and made retching noises.

'Shoosh, you,' said Jodie.

The Redcoat turned to Desmond and took his hand. 'And
you, sir?' He clicked his heels together like a soldier.

Desmond pulled his hand back. 'If you don't mind.'

'Oh, no no no, he's gone and got the wrong impression!'
He turned to Agnes and the kiddies for an audience. 'He only
thinks I'm one of them!' The Redcoat put one hand on his
hip and flipped his other hand down, limp-wristed. 'Ooh,

Betty,' he said, and then roared with raven laughter. 'Nar, bear with me, sir. I can promise you I'm a full-bloodied Englishman.' And he winked at Agnes and Jodie in turn before taking Desmond's hand again. 'Sir? Your name?'

'Desmond.'

'Right then, Nanette and Desmond, I want you to hook your little fingers together and repeat after Liam . . . make up, make up, never do it agaaaaain, if we do it'll be a shaaaaame. That's it, come on now . . .'

They both stared at him. Timmy made more sick noises, and Agnes shushed him.

The girl hissed, 'Yes, shut up. I think he's really nice.'

Desmond and Nanette muttered a few words, still not look-ing at each other.

'That's it, all pals again now. Brilliant,' said Liam. 'Now let's get the whole gang together.' He steered them over to Agnes and the kiddies.

Timmy tried to run away, but Agnes pulled him back. She held him close to her chest and could feel his pulse racing. He was like a bundle of kindling wood, and smelt of sherbet and baked beans. The girl stood solidly still.

'So, you lot,' said Liam, 'what you got on today?'

Timmy tugged harder to get away, but Agnes's arm was strong. She kept her face smiling.

'What about you, lovely lady?' Liam asked Jodie.

She filled up with pink. 'Dunno.'

'Well,' he rubbed his hands together, 'there's loads on, let me tell you. First off, for you, young man,' he threw a couple of play punches at Timmy, 'there's the Boy with the Best Physique competition later this morning.'

Everyone laughed except Timmy. He stuck his tongue out and finally tugged away from Agnes. He skulked over to the bench and sat down, with his skinny arms folded across his tiny chest.

'And for you, sir,' Liam saluted Desmond, 'we've got the Shiniest Bald Spot competition on. I think it's, yes, Tuesday.'

Nanette whinnied very loudly. Desmond rubbed his head sheepishly.

'But the big one, of course, is tailor-made for you, modom.' Nanette smiled and looked down at her feet, but Liam knelt down in front of Agnes. 'Tomorrow night, in the main theatre, we've got the world-famous Glamorous Grandmother competition.' He tootled a fanfare, using his hands as a trombone.

Agnes could hear a train hoot in the distance, and children shrieking from the roller-skating rink. Her skin prickled.

'Ach no, it's not for me,' she finally said.

'Don't be daft. It's right up your street. Gor blimey – you've seen the competition.' Liam pointed back at the chips in the gutter. 'This is the big one – the *Glamorous* Gran contest. You'll walk it. Won't she?' he nodded to the others.

Desmond smiled weakly and nobody said anything. Agnes looked down at her peep-toe sandals and stockings. She'd had her hair done before they came away, but she wasn't convinced. Was he taking the mickey?

'No, no, it's not for me.'

'Listen, love, Sir Billy started these after he'd met the lovely Marlene Dietrich back in the fifties. He just couldn't believe how a gorgeous bird like her could be a nan. And now I come to think about it, you've got a bit of a look of her, hasn't she?'

Again, no one said anything. Agnes shivered. Overhead a seagull cried. She thought she could hear the sea, waves coming in and out. How did he know about her and Marlene?

'Go on, what you got to lose? You can sign up over in reception block.'

Agnes looked over at Timmy. He gave her a wee thumbs-up.

'Well, maybe I'll think about it,' she said.

The cabaret hall was awash with platinum blonde. Not a paca-mac in sight. Agnes had spent over two hours in the damp mouldy chalet getting ready. There'd been three juicy brutes by the window, but she'd got them with a rolled-up newspaper. She'd done her eyebrows into careful thin arches, and powdered her face just so. No matter how much she'd fiddled with her hair, it wouldn't come right, and in the end she pulled her black beret out of the suitcase and pinned it at a jaunty angle that covered the difficult curls. She had wanted to be audacious, like Marlene, and wished she had wide stylish pants. But the best she had brought with her was her tight black wool skirt, and the velvet top with the scoop neck. Her cleavage had surprised her, though. It was still round and smooth, and with the string of pearls from Ernest, she almost looked, well, glamorous.

But that was in the chalet with its blurry spotted mirror. Backstage in the hall, Agnes felt ridiculous. There were about a hundred of them, and Agnes was easily one of the oldest. She was just about old enough to be the mother of some of them. The place was stuffed with strawberry blondes, sleek black pageboys and big golden bouffants; clicky heels and satin dresses. She suddenly remembered the airing courts at the hospital. That was the last time she'd been in a crowd of women.

The compere was toweringly tall and lanky. He took a tiny tortoiseshell comb out of his pocket and combed his thin black hair in a swoop across the top of his long forehead. He had large square glasses, a dinner jacket, ruffled shirt and floppy bow tie. The panel of judges sat below the stage, behind a table draped in a long white cloth. There were three men, all with widow's peaks and bow ties, and a posh-looking woman in a lilac ball gown. The woman drummed her fingers.

The hall was laid out with small round tables, dressed in diamond-shaped tablecloths and each with a wee fringed lamp. A layer of blue smoke hung in a haze and the air was full of beer and perfume. Agnes couldn't see Desmond or Nanette, but they'd promised they'd be there. The kiddies had gone to the discotheque, to see a singer they liked. The band struck up a jazzy number, and the compere pranced across the stage, throwing the microphone from hand to hand.

'Ladies and Gentlemen, it is my very great pleasure to welcome you to this, the 1976, Butlins Pwllheli . . . Big Boobs Wet T-shirt competition.'

The drummer did a drum roll topped up with a bang on the cymbals and the audience shrieked with laughter. Behind the wings, the women giggled and titivated themselves. Agnes chewed the inside of her mouth, hoping she hadn't smeared her lipstick. The compere bent over with silent laughter, slapped the front of his thighs, and wiped invisible tears from his eyes.

'No, not really, only kidding. But seriously,' and his voice went deep and treacly, 'it really does give me the most enormous pleasure to present this week's Butlins Pwllheli Glamorous Grandmother competition.'

The audience clapped respectfully, and the band played the first few bars of *Isn't She Lovely*.

'Now before we get the lovely ladies out here on stage tonight, I just want to remind you about the prizes.'

The drummer did his drum roll again, and Agnes ground her teeth.

'The lucky winner tonight will get the chance to join our area finalists to have a go at the one-thousand-pound – yes, that's one-thousand-pound –' he paused to wait for another drum roll – 'top prize for the overall 1976 Butlins Most Glamorous Grandmother of Great Britain.' He held his hands up to clap and nodded to the audience to applaud.

'Now the judges will be marking the ladies in four categories: grace, charm and deportment; dress sense; grooming; and personality. So without further ado, let's welcome this week's beauties . . .'

The women jostled against each other in a surge towards the stage. In a moment they transformed from a massive huddle of clashing and bumping into a serene line of smiles. The band played the chorus of the song again. Agnes was swept along with the flow onto the stage. Bright lights shone into her eyes, and all she could see was the back of the compere. Even the dandruff on his shoulders was illuminated. She looked again for Desmond and Nanette, but it was impossible to see into the dark smoky hall.

The rest of the competition was a blur. She remembered afterwards that the judges had seemed particularly taken with the fact that she was from Edinburgh. They seemed to think that she'd made a special journey all the way to Wales, and everyone had laughed and misunderstood when she tried explaining she hadn't lived there for nearly forty years. She hadn't tripped over, that was the main thing, or made a fool of herself like the tall busty woman from Sutton Coldfield.

They gave Agnes a single red rose wrapped in Cellophane, and a certificate because she made it into the top ten. Afterwards, she found an empty table in the hall and sat looking at them, waiting for Desmond and Nanette. A thirty-six-year-old woman from Coventry with jet-black hair and a deep tan had won, but Agnes wasn't bothered.

'Life in the old bird yet,' she muttered to herself, rubbing her finger against the glossy dark green thorn on the rose stem.

'May I buy you a drink?' A man with a look of Dirk Bogarde was talking to her. 'I couldn't help but see you up on stage earlier, and would be honoured if you would allow me to get you a drink to celebrate.' He pronounced the h in honoured. He couldn't have been more than late forties, and his breath smelt of peppermints.

'Well, that's most kind of you,' Agnes said, tipping her head to the side. 'I'll have a gin and tonic.'

'I'll just be a tick,' he said, and headed off for the bar.

Agnes watched him, shifting her bottom in her chair so that she could pull down her skirt some more. It really was a wee bit tight.

Just then she saw Desmond, Nanette and the kiddies at the other end of the hall. Timmy was crying again, and rubbing his eyes. Nanette had a face like a bag of spanners, and the girl was lagging behind. Agnes tried looking the other way and raised her hand to hide her face, but Desmond spotted her and they all trooped over.

There weren't enough chairs for all of them, so Jodie stayed standing. There'd been a row at the discotheque, and somehow the boy had ended up with potato crisps in his eyes. The girl wouldn't utter a word. The dishy tanned man made his way back through the crowd, holding a whisky tumbler and Agnes's gin. He smiled at Agnes, handed her the glass, put his fist to his mouth and made a tiny coughing noise.

Desmond looked at Agnes and then at the man. 'Who the

hell are you?' he said. His face was red and sweaty. Agnes didn't know what had happened to his manners.

'Allow me to introduce myself . . .' the man began. But before he could get any further, Desmond pushed his chair back and stood up.

'Look, we are here on a family holiday, and we really don't need your sort hanging about,' he blustered.

'My eyes, my eyes.' Timmy was crying again. Nanette tried wiping them with a tatty grey tissue but it made him worse.

'I'm so sorry, I can see I am interrupting,' the man said. He turned to Agnes. 'It was delightful to meet you and congratulations again.'

'Oh, we forgot,' squealed Nanette. 'How did you get on? You didn't win, did you?'

The man nodded at Agnes and moved away to another table. She smiled down at her rose and showed them her certificate.

When she got home she began looking for work. Money was tight and she was bored at home. The novelty of being alone was over. She bought the local paper each week, ringed any possible jobs – secretarial mainly – and posted her neat letters, written in blue ink, first class. Eventually the woman in the paper shop told her that they were looking for a part-time receptionist at the Hollies surgery. Dr Greaves had mentioned it when he popped in for his *Times*.

Agnes put on her lucky black wool skirt, did her eyebrows and went down to see him. The job involved a bit of filing too, and when they found out that she had done bookkeeping when she was young, they asked if she could start straight away.

The surgery smelt clean and piney. She loved the work,

being at the front desk and answering the phone in her best voice. She liked filing the records, and reading the notes when no one was looking. But best of all, she liked looking at the patients and trying to work out what was wrong with them, which ones suffered with their nerves and which ones were malingering.

The autumn after she started, Dr Greaves caught shingles and was off for months. They had to get a locum in. His name was Dr Saund and he was from Kenya. Agnes couldn't understand why he was Asian, but he explained it all to her in the staff room over camomile tea. He always came to the surgery wearing a tan-coloured and belted raincoat. Agnes grew to like his grey and black hair and looked forward to his smell of rose water and surgical spirit. He was fifty-seven and he lived alone.

February 3 – 23.35 in Tokyo

The rest of the journey is uneventful. Eva Braun trots up and down the aisle in her pillbox hat offering coffee and crisps to all and sundry. She steers clear of the back row, but that suits me – I just want to keep my head down. I haven't got the money for the tat on that trolley anyway. Shrink-wrapped doughnuts and mangy little muesli bars at two quid each. No, I'm happy with my Marmite sandwiches, rich in the vitamin B group, and it's okay, nobody's really bothered me once that grinny-gog Owen got off.

It's clouded over by the time we get into London, and I'm glad of my hat and parka when I get off the coach. It was warm and fuggy in there with the engine rumbling and all the people breathing, but outside the sky is white, and the exhaust fumes make me sneeze. The traffic is so noisy it makes my ears ring, right through my hood and flaps. One small mercy: I know the route to South London without having to check a map or anything. It's burnt into the circuits of my brain from childhood. All the same, my heart is pounding like a pneumatic drill when I go down to the tube. I close my eyes on the old steep escalator and cause a bit of a pile-up at the bottom when I don't get off swiftly enough and trip over my carrier bags. I have to change for the Northern Line. The longest deepest line of them all and so filthy that your bogies always go black with soot after just a couple of stops.

But I made it. I'm here. A wide quiet road somewhere off the South Circular. I put down my bags and rub my hands back to life. The red ridges made by the handles are shiny and flat, but the rest of the inside of my palms is like yellow batter, soggy with sweat. I shake them around and do a few minutes of wrist-turning exercises to get them back to life.

Mildred Mayfield House Residential Unit looks new. Custom-made out of maroon bricks, with sandy ones around the windows and doors. It's very square and toytown. The patch of grass in front is so green and thick that it must have been force-fed some kind of daytime TV wonder fertilizer as advertised by Frank Windsor in the middle of *Countdown*. Either that or it's AstroTurf. No weeds, no moss, no daisies, just hard green cocktail sticks of grass. Never had anyone sitting on it, having a picnic or drinking cans of beer, that's for sure. Probably gets hoovered.

I shake my hands some more and bend right down to check the grass. Yup, real. Then I try to look in the windows. At this distance all I can see are some lumpy grey outlines that don't seem to move at all. I think I can make out the back of a chair, but then again it could be a head. There's a palm tree in there, I swear, a bloody palm tree. I'll wait a bit for my eyes to adapt. It feels like when you first go into a dark room, or someone switches off the light on a moonless night, and it's so black that your heart hurts and you think you've gone blind. You blink your eyes like mad and think you'll never see anything again, but gradually very dark grey squares start to emerge, and after about ten minutes you're home and dry, and wandering about without banging into anything. So I'll give it five minutes. I'll stop here on the scratchy grass opening and closing my eyes for five minutes to acclimatize myself.

I twist my head around three times in each direction to loosen my neck, like Simon at the day centre always recommends before any kind of activity. It makes a horrible clicking noise that makes me feel a bit sick. Knots in my shoulders, tension, definitely tension.

Someone is looking out of the window, very close up. No hair and a pink shiny face, and he's moving slowly. He's wearing a big bow tie or something red around his neck, and he's doing some kind of Indian dance. He's holding his hands up to his shoulders and twisting his wrists about, and then bending over and now he's turning his head around in different directions. Oh Christ, he's copying me. But he's graceful and quite nimble, and nimble is a word not usually associated with me. A pale blue figure comes up next to him and they both move away from the window. Then Pale Blue is back, staring out at me. Very big yellow hair, Pale Blue has got.

I'd better make my presence known. I pick up my bags and walk up the concrete path to the big double doors. There's an intercom but I don't need to buzz it because something beige is looming up behind the safety glass and opening up.

'Hello, can I help you?' It's a very trim middle-aged woman with a huge banana smile.

'My nan, I mean grandmother, I just call her Nan, Agnes, she's here and I've come to see her,' I blurt.

She is staring up at me, and my ears and face are getting hot. I take a deep breath and step over the threshold. It is warm inside, and smells of new carpets and fish.

'Oh,' she says.

A nurse in a pale blue uniform and with blonde frizzy hair strides up the corridor towards us.

'Was that you outside?' she demands, nostrils flaring like a dragon. She looks at the receptionist. 'Was that her outside, Linda?'

I look behind me. No one else there.

'Yes.'

'Well you're disturbing the residents. Mr Jefferies has become quite overexcited and some of the others are getting very anxious.'

'I'm very sorry. I didn't mean to upset anyone. I was just looking,' I whisper through gulps. A drip of sweat slides down over my eyebrow.

'Well, perhaps you could just look somewhere else,' she says through her nostrils. I look at her bony flat chest and read the badge. Nurse Christine Bradfield.

There's a silence whilst the three of us take it in turns to look at each other.

The receptionist is first to cave in. She looks down at my bags and then back up to my hat. 'And you are?'

'Jodie Ledermann.' I pause to get it right. Say it slow, say it right. Another little June homily. I don't quite get it right, though. It sounds as though I'm putting a full stop between every other word. I dig my thumb into my index finger with each rest. 'I've come.' (thumb) 'To visit.' (thumb) 'My grand-mother.' (thumb). I try the next bit slightly faster, but it comes out breathless and odd instead. 'Shee iss staying heere.'

'We've got no Ledermanns here, sorry.' Quick as a flash, the receptionist moves to open the front door for me.

I take my hat off. 'She's not a Ledermann. She's a McKay.'

'Aah.'

'Well, why didn't you say so in the first place?' barks the nurse. 'Did you make an appointment?'

I look blank, digging my thumbnail across all my fingers quickly now. She's waiting for some response and I glance around the walls for a clue.

Above the reception desk is a huge gilt and pink frame. Inside a border of pink roses, there's some flouncy writing:

Mildred Mayfield House: Our Core Values

Privacy – we respect the right of individuals to be left alone and free from intrusion.

Dignity – we recognize the intrinsic value of people and respect each person's uniqueness.

Independence – we offer the opportunity to act and think without reference to another person.

Choices – we encourage . . .

Nurse Christine's voice cranks up and interrupts my reading.

'. . . until after four o'clock, as a general rule. It interferes with our afternoon activities.'

I look at my lucky green watch: 2.35 p.m. I flick through the time zones: 9.35 New York; 17.35 Moscow; 23.35 Tokyo.

I'm stalled. I can't look up from my watch. The numbers are going blurry as my eyes fill up with water, like looking through a swimming pool without goggles. I keep my head down, concentrating on them as they get paler and wobblier. I sniff. I'm not going to cry. Between them, Nurse Christine and the receptionist produce a series of snorts, restrained coughs and shuffles. But they don't say anything. They are waiting to see what I'll do.

Sometimes if I yawn, I can fend off tears, but I have to get the timing right. That's crucial. If I open my mouth as far as it will go too quickly, whilst my lungs are still inflating, then I have to abort the whole thing. That's when I want a dislocating jaw like a man-eating snake, so I can keep opening and opening wide enough to take in truckloads of oxygen and complete the yawn. It's a terrible frustrating feeling when your mouth has done all it can do, but your lungs are still working and gagging for air. Like a premature ejaculation, I should imagine, but of the jaw.

I need a proper yawn right now. Concentrate, don't let myself down. I open my mouth just halfway, like smiling, and then allow it to widen by increments of about half a centimetre. My lungs are filling up nicely and steadily. I can feel my sweatshirt tighten against my chest and my parka swelling in front of me. My shoulders are going up towards my ears. Breathe, open, breathe, open – it's jerky but it's going to work, I can tell. Yeesss. My lungs fill to capacity. I exhale quite loudly through my lips. They wobble gently as the warm air shoots out and I close my eyes. No more tears.

The digits are solid and dark on my watch again. I look up at the nurse and receptionist. The receptionist's smile is as solid as a beauty queen's. Her jaws must be aching. Nurse Christine pulls at her ear lobe. She speaks slowly.

'You're sure you're family, are you?'

I nod. She narrows her eyes, so I nod again, more vigorously, using my eyebrows and everything.

The phone rings, and the receptionist moves quickly behind the desk to sit down and answer it. The smile only wavers for the second before she picks up the receiver.

Nursey lingers with her look for a few more seconds and then turns around, jerking her head for me to follow. She tuts as she goes. It's only a tiny weeny tut, but a tut is a tut, no matter how quiet. She shimmies her way down the long corridor. It's dark, with thick brown carpet like padding. There are lots of manky doors and corridors leading off to God knows where. But she doesn't look back, the lovely Chrissie. She knows I am following her without looking, creepy mother-hen style.

'Aggie, it is then. She had a visitor last week,' she says, not turning round. 'Desmond, lovely man, very quiet. Comes quite regularly.'

'My dad,' I say.

She turns her head and looks me up and down, from my day-glo orange trainers and penguin socks to the top of my head. My hair is still flat from the hat and could do with a wash. She raises her plucked eyebrows and shrugs.

'I look more like my mum,' I say, trying to push my hair into some kind of shape.

She lets out a snigger as she trots, followed by an I'll-store-that-one-for-later snort.

'When did you last see her?' she asks, talking to the corridor again.

I think about my mother and her stick-thin arms and cleaning products, then realize she means my nan.

'Dunno,' I say.

We're standing outside a door with two metal handles and a round window. The smell of fish is stronger here, mixed with freesias and disinfectant. Last time I saw Nan, it was when she was still in the flat. Three years ago, four?

'Well, you may well find her changed,' says Nursey.

Of course she'll have changed. She's older. I'm older, we're all older. But it'll be Nan.

'And I'll thank you to try and keep nice and calm in the day room. Some of the residents get upset quite easily. They don't like anything too exciting. They like to know where they are. So no monkey business. Understand?'

Her nostrils are going ten to the dozen again.

The day room is very warm and there is a low buzzing noise, like a fridge, humming away in the background. Fifteen old people are sitting in high-backed chairs, breathing but not talking. Most of them have got their eyes closed. One of them, a large bald man, stands up when he sees us. He has a red plastic pelican bib around his neck. It is designed for a toddler and the scoop at the bottom knocks his chin as he moves his head.

He looks at me and breaks into a beaming smile. *Hey, Little Hen* – he's up and singing it, arms wide open and limping towards me.

Another nurse, dumpier than Chrissie Wissie, comes and steers him back to his seat in front of the window, next to the rubber plant. He sits quietly and she hands him a half-eaten cream cracker topped with something gloopy and pale. He takes it and holds it in front of his nose. A few flakes fall down into the bib.

I scan the faces again, but can't see Nan. There must be some mistake. Nurse Christine looks around the room smiling and then launches herself towards the window and the old man. Sitting next to him, with her head on her shoulder, a thin old woman is snoring. Her hair is white and wiry, and ochre pop socks are pulled up to the knees on her skinny legs. The red and white jumper I recognize, but the strange, fluffy bright turquoise slippers are not Nan's style at all. She's half the size she used to be.

Nurse Christine taps her quite gently on the shoulder.

'Aggie, Aggie. You've got a visitor.'

Nan opens one eye very quickly.

'They're green. Little round green things. Like marbles.'

'It's your granddaughter,' Nurse Christine says very slowly. 'Desmond's girl.'

Nan holds out her hand, flat, palm up, and draws the outline of a circle with the index finger of the other hand. She taps it five or six times to show she means business and then raises her eyebrows. 'On a plate.' She stretches her fingers back to flatten her hand even more and holds it still like a plate. She shakes it a couple of times and curls the fingers up at the end to make a beckoning gesture. 'You know. Aach. They're green.'

Her hands are all knuckles and wrinkles, and I decide to play along for a bit.

'Girlie, you know. Mmm?'

It's a long time since anyone called me a girl. Nurse Christine moves off and I sit down on the floor. Nan puts her thumb and finger together and raises them to her lips with a trembly chef's kiss. Her lips twitch and she smiles.

'They're very nice.'

I narrow my eyes and look serious. I know Nan's favourite vegetable. On the other side of the day room someone switches on a tinny radio. Three more old women are sitting in a line of the padded, high-backed chairs.

'Mary, Mary, Mary,' says Nan, nodding her head towards them in turn. The Three Marys.

A couple of empty chairs are lined up in front of the French windows. The sun's come out and is shining in, making everything look dusty and putting puddles of light and veiny shadows on the padded seating. Outside there's this massive sloping lawn with a funny old cedar tree slap-bang in the centre. It is weird and old-fashioned compared with the front of the building. Must be lovely in the summer.

There are loads more empty chairs sitting in the middle of the room in the shadows. Through the window, I can hear a van reversing, the engine revving and spluttering and drowning out the radio. Old people's day rooms are so flat and dead. At least the wards of the acutely disturbed have a bit of life to them. There's always somebody about to blow. Here, they're just waiting.

'Girlie. Girlie?'

She's getting red in the face. Her eyes are raw.

'Peas?' I say, although I know Nan was never very fond of peas. Peas were more my mother's line: evenly sized and predictable.

She rolls her eyes up so high that I can only see the yellow-whites. She crunches her shoulders up like the Cookie Monster and lets out an enormous sigh. 'No. They're like marbles. I said. Green. Nice.'

I look blank, extending the moment of suspense.

'You can have them with anything. They go lovely with a nice bit of chicken. You know.'

The van drives off. The radio plays a new tune and we both listen, and then Nan joins in.

'"Lonely rivers flow to the sea, to the sea . . . I'll be coming home, wait for me. Oh, my love, my dar-ar-ling, I've hungered for your touch, a long lonely time. Time goes by so slowly, and time can do so much. Are you still mi-hi-hi-hi-hi-hine?"' Her enunciation is perfect, but she sings it flat.

'You know all the words,' I say. She looks different. More vulnerable, more human.

'Oh, ay. I know all the words,' she says.

'Brussels sprouts,' I say very fast, putting her out of her misery.

'Oh, thank you thank you thank you thank you thank you,' she splutters with her eyes closed.

'Nan?' I say.

She doesn't move. I tap her on the shoulder, gentle as I can and she opens her eyes.

'Nan?'

She smiles.

'I was looking through some photos of us all at Butlins. Do you remember?'

She rolls her eyes up high, leaving a crescent of watery blue at the top of the eggy whites.

'We all went, long time ago, had a holiday. Remember?'

She moves her head away from me. The man with the red bib is humming and she is listening to him. Then she frowns.

'Butlins,' she says.

'Yes, that's right,' I say, but then her eyes lose focus and she's off again.

'He was on the boat with his quiff, I'm sure it was him,' she says.

I try again. I tap her on the shoulder.

'We all went. You, me, Timmy, Mum, Dad – Desmond, you know, Desmond, your boy?'

'Desmond,' she says without turning her head. 'Desmond, good boy. And Rebecca. Huh. She was no better than she should have been. Huh.'

I root down in my black and white laundry bag and pull Album Three out from between the jumpers.

'Look, Nan,' I say, opening it under her nose. 'Photos. See, remember?'

She's got tears in her eyes. 'So sorry, so sorry,' she is whispering. Then she stares down but nothing seems to register at first.

'We were feeding the ducks.'

She quacks and nods her head.

'You'd just divorced Roger, and we went on holiday. I used to come and see you and Roger when I was little. You gave me biscuits.'

Then she turns her head round slowly, like a ventriloquist's dummy, and looks at me properly for the first time. She raises a knuckly finger to a strand of my hair and moves it back off my face. 'Such pretty hair,' she says.

She stands up and lifts up her jumper. It is a chunky Val Doonican-style design, big white snowflakes on crimson. She pats her pale wrinkly stomach and it shakes.

'Fine figure of a woman, I am. Here, look, flat as a pancake.' She starts punching herself quite hard. 'You have to keep young and beautiful, don't you know. It's your duty to be beautiful. Exercise, that's the thing. Exercise. Keep yourself supple. Up, two, three, up, two, three.' She stretches her arms up and moves to bend down and touch her pompom slippers.

At the sight and sound of movement, Nurse Christine is upon us.

'Everything alright?' She stares directly at me.

I mumble a yes.

'Alright, Aggie, now, don't get yourself excited,' she says, straightening her up and lowering her into her chair again.

'Who's Aggie? I'm nae Aggie. Don't you call me Aggie, you're not to call me Aggie. She could call me Aggie, and Mama, but you can't call me Aggie.' She is talking quickly now, and trying to stand up again. 'But Lucy's gone, she's gone now. All buttons and bows. There were fireworks but she shouldn't have gone first. She was the younger one. She knew about the lido and the mischief. What larks we had.'

Nan is pulling at her arms and her neck. I look at my watch, it's a kind of reflex: 24.15 Tokyo time. She notices and pulls my arm, dragging me close to her.

'Don't go.' Her breath is hot.

'Yes, I think that's a very good idea,' says Nurse Christine, pushing Nan's arms into her lap. 'Visiting time is just about over anyway.'

I regain my balance and stuff the photo album back into my carrier. I stand up and put my hat on. Nan is smiling up at me, pleading with spaniel eyes. I bend down and kiss her dry cheek and head off for the door.

'Come back and see me soon, Jodie chick, there's a good girl.'

I stop in my tracks and shiver. Jodie chick. That's what she used to call me when I was little. I check the floor and get that shifting sand feeling in my stomach when nothing feels safe.

1968

She put the phone down and walked back into the sitting room.

'Who was that then, ringing at this time of night?' Roger was in his green armchair, head against the plastic sheeting that stopped hair oil staining the back. He was wearing his maroon cord slippers and crossed his feet on the pouffe, before looking over the top of *Amateur Photographer*.

'His nibs,' she said.

'What's he want now?'

Agnes snorted. 'Nanette can't cope with the two of them.'

'Needs to get himself a better wife, that boy of yours,' he said, turning a glossy page and scratching his crotch.

'So he's bringing the girlie round first thing, before he goes to work. Give Nanette a chance to catch up, just having the wee one around.'

'Catch up, my arse. Needs a good kick up the jacksie, that one.' He stubbed his Embassy out in the ashtray and reached down to pick up his glass from the occasional table. It was empty. He raised it right in front of his eyes for a better look, tipped it slightly and frowned. Agnes stood up and snatched it off him before he could start. It was best to stop him before he started.

'Fresh glass, mind,' he called as she headed for the kitchen.

Agnes got a Double Diamond from the crate beneath the yellow table. She pulled the top off with the lemon-shaped bottle opener that Rebecca had given her for her birthday years ago, opened it and poured it into the same glass.

'Peanuts,' he shouted from the other room, and she spat quietly into the glass and stirred it with her finger.

He had been as good as his word. He had tutored her alright, and told her exactly the right things to say to the doctors, then to the board. Within six months she was out. Within a year, they were married and living in a semi in Hendon. There were things that brought it all back, still, nearly twenty years later. Certain whiffs that would take her straight back to the wards. She couldn't drink tea now, always had coffee, and the smell of cabbage made her stomach jolt. Even now, when it came to washing his work clothes, she blocked her nostrils with tissue.

She licked the salt off her fingers. She sighed at the thought of Desmond's kiddies. Time was a queer thing. She could hardly believe that she was a grandmother, and remembered back to when Desmond was a child himself. He settled down well enough with Roger, and quickly too. He took the changes and his new daddy in his stride. Dezzy-boy, Roger called him, and bought him a new blue bicycle. Rebecca wasn't so easy. Prickly, that was what he said about her, and Agnes had to agree. 'Go on, crack us a smile, girl,' he'd say, but she wouldn't. By the time she left school she was spending more time round at Lucy and Toby's than at home.

Lucy still irritated the hell out of Aggie, all these years on. Just as fussy and flighty as she had been when they were little girls together, all powder and bows, but it didn't sit well on a dried-up auld prune knocking fifty. Rebecca thought the sun shone out of her porthole, though, and would never have a word said against her. It was always Auntie Lucy this, Auntie Lucy that, until Agnes felt her fingers twitching and pressure in her head again.

Nineteen sixty had been a real Auntie Lucy year. First her

Toby had the complications with his lungs and died, and then the corporation pulled down their prefab. Lucy had fallen on her feet, as per usual, and was offered a brand-new flat straight away. Not any old flat, oh no, it had to be a *home in the sky*. Shiny new bathroom with a whole wall of tiles, and out the front the balconies were wide enough for a milk float, so she'd told her.

It was about then that Rebecca had left home, and the trouble had begun. Agnes could count on one hand the number of times she'd seen her since. She kept her room for her, though, just in case, with its wee pink corner sink and the dressing table. She left the radiator on for Doctor Leicester, who loved to curl up on the bed, with his head under his tail. The name had been Roger's idea of a joke. Agnes hated being reminded of the hospital, but it made Roger chuckle to call his name and order him about. Rebecca had liked cats too. Ungrateful little madam. Not like Desmond. Agnes smiled as she put the bowl of greasy nuts and the glass through the serving hatch. Such a good boy; marriage hadn't changed him, he always kept in touch.

Roger rattled off a cough and hacked up some phlegm. She watched as he licked it out into his hankie and looked at it.

'By the way, I'll be back a bit late tomorrow,' he said, wiping his finger across the yellow bumps. 'Got a bit of business to attend to.' He picked up his *Amateur Photographer* and scratched his crotch again.

It was a lovely morning. The sky glowed blue through the steamed-up kitchen window. Aggie finished washing the breakfast things and leant forward to wipe a spyhole in the dripping glass. The garden was looking well. There were tiny chips of frost on the lawn, and the shrubs and bushes not still in shade steamed in the sunshine. It wouldn't be long before his wallflowers were up. The gate creaked and Desmond and the girlie walked through, hand in hand. Desmond's grey mackintosh was belted, ready for work, and the girlie had a short fluffy overcoat with an Eskimo hood. Knitted white mittens hung from string out of her sleeves, swaying behind her hands, which were pink with the cold. She ran straight to the shiny gnome with the fishing rod, Roger's newest and favourite. He'd named it Rod. She stroked its head, pointing and chortling to Desmond, and then spotted the others. Her fat little legs pumped fast down the path to the blue and red one smoking a bendy pipe, but she skidded on some ice and scraped her knees, making two holes in her ribbed navy tights. She let out a piercing yelp, and screamed until Desmond picked her up. By the time they reached the front door she was smiling again.

'Good morning, Mum,' said Desmond, shifting the child to one side to offer a kiss. 'Very good of you to do this at such short notice, much appreciated.'

'Morning, Desmond. Always pleased to oblige, you know me,' said Agnes, accepting the dry kiss on her cheek. She looked at the girl.

'Hello there, Nanny Aggie,' said Jodie. She had a trace of a lisp.

'Hello there, chick,' said Agnes. It was what her grand-mama had called her when she was small.

Jodie was wearing an orange and brown striped pinafore made out of corduroy. Up the middle ran an oversized zip with a large ring on the end. Agnes supposed it was modern. Nanette liked to buy modern clothes for her kiddies. The girl's hair was kept back with a wide tan elastic hairband, and her eyes were green and very sparkly. She put Agnes in mind of an overweight puppy dog. Not dissimilar to Rebecca at that age, now she thought about it.

'I've brought a bag of gubbins to keep her occupied,' said Desmond, putting a lumpy tartan duffel bag on the telephone table. 'Bits and bobs, drawing stuff, paints. You like your painting, don't you, Jodes?' he said in a singsong voice.

The girl looked up at him and smiled. He put her down on the lino.

'So, you be a good girl for Nanny, Jodes, yes?' he said.

'Oh yes,' she rasped quietly, looking down at her red rubber boots.

'Look, you can leave your wellies just here on the mat,' he said.

'That's right, Jodie chick, just there,' said Agnes.

The girl didn't move. She put her thumb in her mouth and began to suck.

'Right then, I'll be off,' Desmond said, leaning down and kissing Jodie on the top of her head. She sucked more furiously as he went out. He was a few paces up the path when he turned round. Agnes had half closed the door. 'You sure you're going to be alright?' He hesitated before he said it.

Jodie was still looking at her feet.

'Ach, of course we'll be fine. We'll be grand, won't we, Jodie chick?' said Agnes. 'Now let's get those wet auld boots off.' And she shut the door.

Tuesday was a busy day. Wash day for starters. After some time reading and playing with beads, Agnes set the girlie up at the kitchen table, opening up and laying flat sheets of the *Mirror* to keep the daffodil Formica clean. She had crayons and paper, and a queer colouring book. She dipped her soft plump paintbrush in a jar of clean water, and just slopped water over line drawings on thick yellow paper. Colours magically appeared. Suddenly the see-through donkey had a pale tan coat, and a lurid pink poppy behind his ear. The little boy's shorts and bib turned wishy-washy powder blue and his ice-cream cornet became an unlikely orange. Jodie poked the tip of her tongue out through her lips and nodded with satisfaction as each new colour materialized.

It kept her occupied for a while, and Agnes cracked on with Roger's work clothes. Before she braved the laundry basket, she nipped into the lavvy, and pulled four sheets of toilet paper off the roll. She carefully split them in two, and twisted the ends into points, until they looked like wee icing piping bags. She pushed them into her nostrils, right up, so they wouldn't drop out. She opened the lid of the wonky Ali Baba basket, reached in and pulled out a clump of shirts, trousers and his beige work coat. She kept her own dirty washing in a separate bag in the bedroom. She shut her nostrils tight against the toilet paper, and carried the bundle downstairs.

Jodie looked up from the magic painting as Agnes came through the door. She dropped her paintbrush and covered her mouth with her hand, giggling furiously. She pointed at Aggie's face.

'Nanny Aggie's got big white bogies. Bogies in your nose,' and she snorted and giggled again.

Agnes stood still and closed her eyes. She clenched her jaws, and her head hurt. She felt her fingers twitching and clutched the washing pile closer to her stomach.

'Alright, Jodie chick,' she said quietly and slowly, after a pause. 'That'll be quite enough of that.' She opened her eyes again. The girl was staring at her, smile wiped off her face. Nice and quiet for a while.

The new twin tub made things a lot easier, but there was

still a fair bit of humping about to do. After a bit of carpet sweeping in the sitting room, Agnes moved the first lot of clothes into the spinner. She popped the round rubber cover on top and closed the lid. She wiped a line of fine sweat from her upper lip and sighed.

The girl was watching her, paintbrush down on the table. She was still staring at the toilet paper up Agnes's nostrils.

The hospital smell was gone now. Agnes touched her nose. 'Are you all finished now, Jodie chick?' she asked.

Jodie nodded.

'What else have you got in the bag then?'

Agnes put the duffel bag on the table. Jodie didn't take her eyes off her face. Agnes pressed the top of the girl's head to look at the bag instead. She took her plump hands and wrapped her chipolata fingers around the thick ropes at the top of the bag to widen the opening. The girl got the idea and stuck her arm deep inside. Whilst she was rummaging, Agnes quickly covered her nose with one hand, pulled out the tissue plugs and put them up her sleeve.

The thud and rumble of the twin tub disturbed the girl, and she turned to look at it juddering.

'Ach, don't mind about that now. What have you got in there then?' said Agnes. Jodie pulled out a pair of large yellow-handled scissors.

'My cutting scissors,' she said, sticking her hand deep in again. 'And oh, oh,' she chirped, eyes wide, 'my real paints,' and she pulled out a rectangular tin with a brightly coloured fish on the front. She opened it and ran her finger across the blocks of colours, worn into circular dips in the middle. 'I like real painting. Can I do real painting, Nanny Aggie?'

Agnes looked at the table. The paper was still down, and she had the clean water already.

'What's the magic word, then, Jodie chick?'

'Please. Please can I do real painting, Nanny Aggie?'

Well, what harm could it do, thought Aggie as she smiled and nodded.

Jodie pulled out a much slimmer paintbrush from the middle of the tin and dipped it first into water, and then round and round in the hollow of the carmine red. The twin tub cranked up to full spin, and the kitchen floor vibrated.

At half-past twelve, Agnes made beetroot and cottage cheese sandwiches for lunch. The girlie was still engrossed in her painting. She had done Mummy, Daddy and Nanny Aggie, and Nanny Aggie's garden with the gnomes, but hadn't finished baby Timmy. Agnes opened the other leaf of the kitchen table and shifted the paints up to one end. Jodie wolfed down her sandwich.

'All gone, Nanny Aggie,' she smiled, and pushed her plate across the table.

'Good girl,' said Agnes, and she went over to the cupboard and brought down the red tartan biscuit tin. 'Would you like one of these for finishing so nicely?'

Jodie stuck her hand into the tin and pulled out a cigar-shaped biscuit.

'Choclit fingers, my favourite.' She held it tight and licked it like a lolly.

According to the *Radio Times*, *Watch with Mother* was on after lunch, and Agnes was looking forward to a bit of peace. When they'd finished eating, she settled the girl down on the sofa in the sitting room, opened the door to the television cabinet and switched on the set. The test card was still on, but Jodie seemed happy enough watching the girl playing noughts and crosses with the curious large clown.

'See, she's got my hairband,' she lisped. 'I don't like that clown, Nanny Aggie. Do you like the clown, Nanny Aggie? I don't like clowns.'

Agnes hoped she might fall asleep, although she was a wee bit old for afternoon naps.

Back in the kitchen, Agnes emptied the twin tub, shook out the washing and piled it in the laundry basket next to the kitchen table. She'd organize the clotheshorse in a while. She did the washing up and put the kettle on the ring for a cup of coffee, thinking about tea time. Sausages maybe.

Suddenly the kitchen door swung open and the girl came running in.

'Nanny Aggie, Nanny Aggie, Bizzy Lizzy, Bizzy Lizzy,' she shouted, skidding on the lino in her tights. Behind her the door hit the wall and rebounded shut again.

She looked like a wee clumsy ballroom dancer, like the women patients in hospital that managed to get to the Christmas social.

'And she's got a Little Mo, a Little Mo with a hood like my one. And the Little Mo, she's a Eskimo,' she lisped, sliding to a halt in front of the table. 'And Bizzy Lizzy, she's got a flower on her frock. On her pocket. And when, and when she touches it . . .' Jodie stretched her arms out wide. Her fist flew over the table. 'Everything goes true, what she wishes, everything.'

Jodie's hand knocked the jam jar sitting on the newspaper. Agnes watched as it wobbled from side to side. For a moment it looked as though it would straighten itself up, but then the girlie's fist whacked the jar again and it went flying. Pink water gushed down the side of the table, and slopped its way into the laundry basket. The jar followed, rolling its way into the deep crease of a clean white work shirt. The girl stopped talking to look. Agnes let out a cat's mew. Jodie pulled her arms back to her sides, like a toy soldier. On the cooker the kettle spluttered up to a whistle.

Agnes looked at the pink splashes on the clean white shirts. Her head felt tight and her fingers itched.

'Oh. The painty water,' said Jodie. 'Oh.'

The sides of Agnes's head felt like they were pulling inwards in jerks, and when she closed her eyes she could see Rebecca. Not this girlie, but her own girlie twenty years before. She could see Rebecca tap-dancing on the floor whilst she worked away at Ernest's blood on the settee. She could see her mouth opening and closing as she pushed her to the floor and scrubbed her. She could see her big green eyes staring at her from her grazed face when it was over. It couldn't happen again. Not again. Agnes opened her eyes and lifted her hands to the side of her face. She shifted her head so she wasn't facing the girl. The kettle was whistling louder and louder, and rattling on the ring.

Agnes put her hands around her own neck and squeezed until her throat felt like it was full of sticks. Her ears thumped and her face was purple hot. She held on as long as she could and breathed out in a gush. She saw the big yellow scissors on the table and grabbed them. She would not hurt another girl. She would hurt herself, not another wee girl. She grabbed the scissors and pulled down at her own hair, but the clumpy blades were blunt and they pulled, making her eyes water. She ripped at a few strands, but they still didn't cut properly, so she turned her arm and ripped some marks into the pale wobbly flesh above her wrist.

The girl sank to her bottom and shuffled under the kitchen table. She put her hands over her head and rocked backwards and forwards, humming a tune. The cutting was over and Agnes breathed out. She had to get the girl out, make her safe.

'Here, chick, come here,' she said, breathing heavily like a heifer and bending down with her arms stretching beneath the table. 'Come to Nanny Aggie.'

The girl shuffled away until she was backed up against the kitchen wall. Agnes reached down and grabbed her small shoulders. The girl shrieked. Agnes slid her out from under the table, and picked her up under her arm. The girl kicked and screamed. She bit her arm, but Agnes held tight and walked up the stairs and across the landing to Rebecca's old bedroom.

She pushed the white door open, and Doctor Leicester ran out. The girl stilled when she saw the cat. Agnes put her gently inside. There was a queer smell but it was nice and warm. On the rug was a sticky puddle dotted with black feathers, a pink claw and fragments of bone and beak. Doctor Leicester had been sick on a bird again. It put her in mind of stargazy pie, but she couldn't clear it up now. She closed the door, locked it and then walked slowly down the stairs again. She sang a tune to cover the crying and knocking on the door. An old Al Bowlly tune, one that she and Graham used to sing to each other. '"La la lala laaah, do do doo dudda duh . . ."'

The kitchen was full of steam and the kettle was rattling and whistling like a banshee. Agnes walked slowly over to the cooker and switched the ring off. She sat at the table and looked down at the laundry basket.

Two hours later the phone rang. Agnes looked up from the laundry and noticed the smears of blood and small clots on the inside of her arm. She picked up the beige Yorkshire Dales tea towel and wiped herself clean as she walked slowly to the hall.

'Hello, Mum?'

Agnes didn't recognize the thin voice.

'Mum?'

'Why, hello,' she tried.

'Is everything alright?'

It was Desmond. Such a good boy.

'Ay, fine and dandy.'

'Is Jodie behaving herself?'

Agnes couldn't remember. 'Ach, yes, good as gold, little lamb.'

'Oh, good. Mum, we were wondering . . .' his voice had gone wheedling; he often wheedled, Desmond, '. . . would it be alright if Jodie stopped the night with you and Roger?'

Agnes frowned. Then she remembered the girlie and the paint and the feelings. Better off keeping her here till things calmed down.

'Oh yes, that'd be fine.'

'It's just Nanette has just about caught up with herself and . . .'

'Oh yes, that'd be fine,' said Agnes.

By seven o'clock the temperature had dropped. Agnes put the sausages in the oven, low heat. She sorted out the laundry. It was very quiet in the house. Just after eight o'clock, Roger's keys rattled in the door and he strutted into the kitchen. He took his coat off and hung it on the back of the chair. The smell of the hospital filled the room. He picked up his knife and fork and banged them on the table.

'What's for tea then?'

He looked over at the cooker and sniffed the air deeply. Agnes put on the oven gloves and pulled out the sausages. They were deep brown and oily.

'Wa-hay, sossies,' he said, and he beat out a rhythm on the table using his knife and fork as drumsticks.

Agnes brought his plate over and he grabbed her arm.

'You been silly again?' he whispered, running his fingers over the scabs and scrapes. He looked up at her face for the first time and smirked.

'Got a new hairstyle then, have you, sweetie?'

Agnes patted her hair and pushed some of it behind her ears. 'Just eat your sausages,' she said.

'What did you say?'

'Nothing.'

She knew he was hungry and wanted his tea. He wouldn't start with a plate of bangers and mash in front of him.

'That's better,' he said, scraping his chair away from the table. It made a sudden loud noise, like a scratchy foghorn. He burped under his breath, leant back and undid his belt a couple of notches. He took his flat tin out of his coat pocket, pulled out his after-dinner panatella and lit it with his Zippo.

He stooped down to pick up a piece of paper that was lying on the floor under the table, held it up and laughed. It was Jodie's painting of the gnomes.

'That's good, that is. Look – it's Rod. Right little Picasso we've got on our hands.' He smiled to himself. 'How did it go with the nipper, then?'

'Ay?'

'The girl? Desmond's girl?'

Agnes stood still and listened, turning her head towards the stairs. There was a quiet thumping coming from Rebecca's room.

'She's staying the night.'

'Where is she then? Right little Picasso.' He laughed again until it turned into coughing. He didn't seem to hear the thumping.

'Gone to bed already. Rebecca's room.'

'She have her tea already then?'

Agnes said nothing.

Roger tutted and rolled his eyes. 'Get her a plate of sossies, you gormless cow. We've got to feed up our little Picasso.'

He thudded up the stairs, and Agnes followed him with the plate of lukewarm sausages. The knocking from the bedroom stopped. He unlocked the door and they went in.

There was a scurrying underfoot when he switched on the light. The room was very warm, but it smelt sour and mildewy. Agnes shivered. She should have cleared up the cat sick, and the little corner sink had a dripping tap that still needed mending. The girl was curled up on the red rug. Her left arm was stretched out with her hand in a fist. She was breathing heavily.

'Ah, bless, look she's asleep,' said Roger. 'Here, hold this.' He handed Agnes his cigar and then bent down and scooped the girl up.

'That's it, come to Uncle Roger.' The effort started him coughing again.

Agnes looked around the room: at the dust between the lino and the skirting board; at Rebecca's collection of dolls from different nations all lined up on the shelf that Roger made; at the kidney-shaped dressing table with the three smeared mirrors.

Rebecca never forgave her for hurting her. She left home as soon as she could, and that was when the trouble had started. Squats, drugs, hippy-dippy nonsense. Agnes hadn't heard from her for years: she'd be twenty-five now. Agnes felt a sudden pain in her chest. She wanted to see her. She wanted to say sorry.

'Oy,' Roger hissed. He was standing by the bed with its pale pink padded headboard. He looked down at the covers and jerked his head back. 'Come on, pull them back.'

Agnes put the plate of sausages on the bedside table and loosened the bri-nylon sheet and quilt. Roger laid Jodie in the bed. He walked over to the pink curtains and pulled at them. Agnes noticed black soot mould dotted at the bottom. One side caught on the pole and Roger pulled it hard until it came off its hooks at one end.

Agnes looked down at Jodie laid like a corpse beneath the purple bedspread. Her hairband had slipped down and looked like a queer beige bandage across her forehead. Jodie's eyes flicked open. She stared at Agnes, straight in the face, and then closed them again quickly.

Roger was huffing like an engine.

'Bollocks,' he said as he pulled over Rebecca's cushioned dressing-table stool. He stood on top, without taking his boots off, and hooked the curtain over the top of the rail. Agnes handed him back his cigar. They closed the door quietly and went downstairs.

Roger was rough in bed that night. He rubbed his arms against the cold and didn't take his vest off before he got in. He rolled on top of Agnes straight away. She was dry as sand, but that didn't stop him forcing his way in. She yelped loudly, like a cat, at the burning pain.

'Shut it,' he grunted between pushes, 'you'll wake the girl.'

February 14 – Chicken Dinner

The volunteer bureau smells like nowhere else on earth: lots of plastic, something chemical that I can't quite place, and an underlying hint of curry powder. And the décor, God, big geometric wallpaper and a carpet with huge stripes that lurch sideways when you look at them. It was a flagship in its heyday, apparently. Well, that's what June says and she knows about these things.

There's a murky feel to it too. The phlegmy green colour scheme makes it feel like walking into a bowl of asparagus soup. People wander by, reading brightly coloured sheets of paper and carrying files under their arms. They move slowly and gently. All the men have beards, and all the women have big earrings, usually shaped like teardrops.

I'm standing in the doorway looking in, planting my feet firmly on the ground. I try to feel each single toe press down through my socks and trainers, right through into the ground. I'm doing them one at a time but I can't seem to get the middle toes to work on their own. Three of them clump down together at the same time. No problem with the big toes and the little toes, but the middle ones are stuck together with superglue. It is very frustrating, but looking down at them and frowning doesn't help.

My posture needs attention. We do posture at yoga at the day centre every now and then. Once they made us pretend that there was a big thick piece of rope attached to the top of our heads. I didn't know where this exercise was going at first and was a bit concerned because earlier that month a lad called Philip, who used to come along, had hanged himself. Sometimes they spring these kind of debriefing therapy sessions on you, and I wondered whether this was some kind of insensitive role-play tribute to him.

But no, you had to imagine that someone ('think of a, like, spiritual puppet master,' Simon said, which didn't help those of us feeling paranoid that day) was pulling that string up and making you stand tall. It did seem to work, though. I looked around the hall and everyone was taller, even Lilian, and she was only about four foot tall and usually very bent. We were like some strange squadron of ramshackle soldiers on parade.

The other reason I liked this exercise was that it reminded me of a game that was all the rage at primary school. You had to shut your eyes and someone made you imagine that you had a great big gaping hole in your back, and out of that hole were lots of pieces of spaghetti. Long spaghetti, not tinned. The other person then pretended to pull and pull those pieces of spaghetti, and nine times out of ten, it made you sway and fall over backwards. For a couple of weeks, every playtime, the playground was full of lines of children rocking about and dropping onto the ground. Then one girl cracked open the back of her head on the asphalt, slap-bang in the middle of the red and green painted snake, and had to go to casualty. Mr Martin banned it. He announced in assembly that this voodoo must end, which made everyone giggle. The next month, there was a craze on voodoo dolls.

I close my eyes and jut my chin out. My lower back is aching from the walk here and my hands are damp and hot. When I raise my head and stand tall, my shoulders go back and my stomach pokes out like some fat Sergeant Major Shut-Up. I open my eyes and look down my nose. I let out a sigh, clench in my arse and walk. It's a silly stiff walk but I hold my head high, trying not to look down at the stripy carpet. Just inside the door is a desk. There is a woman sitting behind it, on the phone. As she watches me come in, her mouth falls slightly open and her eyes glass over.

I carry on clenching and standing tall. I had four cups of coffee before I set out this morning, and that with the hot adrenalin in my stomach is sending a warning tug to my lower intestines. I need a crap. I pull in my sphincter even tighter, which makes things worse. There are half a dozen tall royal-blue display boards in the room, so I go and stand behind one that is in front of a window, and pretend to look at the cards pinned on it. I let out a little humph noise to relax. Outside, the wind is whistling down the street. A carrier bag and a load of leaves and bits of paper fly past the window, and then disappear up into the sky. Every time the wind blows there's a huge draught inside and the doors breathe in and out. The posters on the wall look like they're shivering.

I fancied a job in a shop. A charity shop probably, because I already know the territory and I wouldn't have to wear a uniform. Well, when pushed that's what I told June. She was delighted and said Go For It, Jodie love, Go For It. June has just learnt this expression. She must have just seen some support workers' inspirational DVD or been on a seminar or something, because I've never heard her say it before and suddenly it's Go For It this and Go For It that. When I said I thought Go For It was a bit eighties, a bit passé, a bit Roy Castle, a bit *Record Breakers*, her forehead went back and she wrote something in her book.

To be fair, I could do with a job, something to do. Doctor Hassani would approve and it would get me out of the house. I look up at the cards on the display boards in front of me.

There are a lot of exclamation marks, and each card has got a symbol in the top right-hand corner – mainly smiley faces, with the occasional pink cartoon flower head. After a while I work it out. Smiley face is work with people; pink flower head is gardening. There are other symbols that I just can't get to grips with, and there's nothing obvious to stand for shop work.

Nearby, two women, both with tight perms, both wearing purple raincoats and both carrying tan handbags over the crooks of their right arms, are looking up and down at another one of the boards. As one of them looks up, the other looks down; as one of them looks right, the other looks left. Efficient scanning, or what. Twins, must be.

Apart from them, and the woman at the desk, the room is empty. I sidle over to the board in the furthest corner, holding my arse in tight. As I get there, a small hot fart escapes into my knickers. I shift round to the back of the board very quickly, but the smell comes with me. The twin women are a couple of yards away, but they are both sniffing the air, in opposite directions, testing for the source of the hot sulphur.

I swish my arm about behind my back in the smallest, slowest movements I can manage and head back for the young smiling woman at the desk. She is wearing a bright orange fleece, which clashes with her plum-coloured bob. A man with a beard and flecky grey jumper appears through an archway behind her and hands her a day-glo yellow Post-it note. She reads it and they both laugh.

'Trust Joan,' she says, rolling her eyes, and he goes out.

The smell has completely gone now, so I clench and move towards a chair.

'Hiya,' she says, big smile, open body language.

The wind outside is picking up. A powerful gust blows, and

a car alarm starts down the street. Somewhere in the building a wind chime is chiming.

'Have you come to find some voluntary work?' she asks.

I nod and look down at the chair in front of me. My posture
has gone to pot.

'Please,' she says, 'have a pew, take the weight off . . .' She
doesn't finish the sentence.

I sit down, the chair shifts sideways a little.

'My name is Maggie,' she says, holding her arm out straight.
By the time I realize she wants to shake my hand it is too late
and she is using her hand to tuck a purple lock of hair behind
her ear.

'I'm a volunteer here. Yes, funny, isn't it? You come here to
volunteer and the first person you meet is a volunteer. Kinda
ironic, hah?' She has put on a strange Cliff Richard accent for
some reason as she says this last phrase.

Then she moves her face into a smile and looks at me. 'So,
have you thought about what sort of thing you're interested
in?'

'Shops,' I say.

'Good, good. Now what we need to find out is what kind
of experience you have and, like anyone, you must have an
absolute wealth of experience. Okay, so it might not be what
the average person calls –' she stops and lifts both of her
hands just above her shoulders to make small double hooky
movements with her index and middle fingers – 'quote,
conventional, unquote, but experience comes in all shapes and
forms, and who is to say that a Ph.D. in nuclear physics is
worth more than knowing how to use a washing machine or
organizing things so the kids get to school on time and have
sandwiches for lunch and a hot meal every single evening?'

Her voice gets louder when she talks about the meals, and

pink dots are breaking out on her cheeks. I can see she is trying to be kind and open, she really is, so I smile. She takes a big breath and hands me a piece of paper.

'Have you thought about a city farm?' she says. 'We've just had some flyers in about helping in the café.'

I hadn't thought about a farm, and I sort of nod and shake my head at the same time, thinking about chickens and goats. Might be nice, but a bit beyond me.

She watches me patiently and then says slowly, 'Anyway, what we need you to do is to take a little time to look at this form. Well, when I say form, it's not like a proper –' she does the hooky finger move again – 'quote, application form, unquote. Think of it as just a piece of paper that we have to have to get to know you better. Imagine that this bit of paper is one of your mates, and you're going to have a chinwag with them about who you are and what you like doing. Do you see?'

I look down at the yellow sheet. At the top is a great big letter V shaped like a tick and the words 'Involving Local People'. Underneath this is a series of questions with dotted lines for the answers. I turn it over and there are more questions and blanks.

'Ta,' I say.

'What do you think then? Will you have a shot at filling it in? Have you got anyone who can give you a hand?'

'I'm sure I can cope,' I say, standing up.

Back home, I put the form on top of Tuesday's pile. The piles are getting out of hand; I've been neglecting them. The whole of the table next to my bed is covered, and several of the days are merging into each other. I start to flick through. I will be ruthless.

'Free delivery! Dando's – Simply the Best! Ten-pound meal

deal for two! Free garlic bread!' Could come in handy still. Keep.

Shiny fold-over Tesco brochure. Nah, some good loss leaders, but nah, I'm not going to fool myself that I'm going there: in the bin.

Small turquoise rectangle of card with a picture of a Malteser-shaped head and a bent arm cutting through wiggly waves. Half-price swimming offer. I stare and ruminate, moving my hand over the bin, back to the pile, over the bin, back to the pile. In the end I shift it to the Saturday pile.

Three sheets of A4 with type on – DLA paperwork. Not now. Move it to the business pile on the floor underneath the bed. Then I find something interesting and purple that I'd forgotten all about. The invitation that Owen gave me on the coach.

I take a deep breath and push the door to the Dog and Partridge. It opens quietly and slowly. Behind another door, men are drinking and burbling, and the smell of weak lager, testosterone and fags with an undercurrent of cigar seeps out towards me. I think about the last time I tried a pub. The inside of my thighs are weak and I feel sick. Outside, a train rumbles by. I stomp up the dark steep staircase and as I reach the top, a blast of warm air socks me in the face.

I go in and it's like a Magic Eye poster – about twenty-five people and so much activity I can't work out what is going on. Ant hill. This is nothing like a normal pub. There's a huddle around a bar stool with lots of giggling and a high-pitched humming noise coming from it. A tall woman in a beige baseball cap straightens up, holding a set of barber's clippers high above her head in a victory wave. The laughter gets louder briefly as a dumpy figure with a fluffy head – impossible to

tell if it's a man or woman – gets off the bar stool. Someone
with very long brown wavy hair sits down, and the tall woman
clicks the clippers on again.

The windows are covered by long purple swags-and-tails
curtains: it's warm, buzzy and womblike.

Owen is in the far corner. He is with two other men, leaning over a low table and writing something down. One of the
men has a scruffy white-haired dog, and it is turning round
and round on its soft green tartan cushion to make itself
comfortable. There is a saucer of beer and a few crisps on the
floor for it. The dog looks up as I come over. Owen looks to
see what the dog sees. His mouth widens to a huge smile and
he stands up so suddenly that the dog lets out a little bark.
The dog's owner strokes it on the top of its head with swift
soft strokes, and Owen stretches out his arms.

'You came.'

I gulp and nod.

He puts his hand on my elbow and rubs it for maybe two
seconds. I feel the crackle of static and look at his face. His
smile is wider, he's got a tooth missing right at the back of
his mouth, and the tiny pink tip of his tongue is poking out
of the front. His hair is even shorter than before. I'm smiling
and shivering at the same time.

'Like it?'

I nod again.

'Philippa over there did it. She'll do yours, if you want. Hair
artist extraordinaire, our Philippa. All you need do is ask.' He
says it like he's reciting Shakespeare.

We move over to the table and Owen makes a big deal of
getting another stool for me to sit on. It wobbles when I sit,
but nobody minds.

'Do you want a drink?' he whispers to me.

'No, I'm okay,' I whisper back.

'But what if it rains?' says a fat man with Friar Tuck hair, large glasses and tight tie-dye T-shirt.

'It won't matter. It'll be June. It won't be cold. People will get wet, but so what? No one ever got washed away by a few spots of rain, ay, Pooch?' says the man with the dog.

Owen coughs like a toastmaster.

'Everyone – this is Jodie.' He pauses before saying my name, very Peter Ustinov.

'Hello, Jodie.'

'Hiya. Alright?'

Even the dog looks up at me.

'Hello,' I say.

'What do you think about if it rains?' the Friar asks me, but before I can answer, dog man is in there again.

'We could get everyone an umbrella. Yes, that's it, every single person could have their own umbrella. We can have them all colour co-ordinated. We need a logo. Have we got a logo? Is the strait-jacket a logo? Then, then, then we could get a sponsor. Yes, they could pay for the umbrellas. They could pay for bikes for everyone, or scooters or rollerblades, with the logo on the side. We could get a car or a bus . . .' Friar Tuck puts his hand gently on the ranting shoulder.

'Yeh, okay, Bob. Slow down. Back to the date. What about mid-June, the fifteenth or something?'

Owen turns to me again. 'Crisps? Would you like some crisps?'

'Yes, please.'

'Come on then.'

We walk over to a dark corner of the room where there is a pile of cardboard boxes reaching the ceiling.

'What flavour?'

'Cheese and onion?'

'There's roast chicken, if you'd prefer,' he says, digging his hand into the open hole at the front of a box near the floor and pulling out an orange pack like a rabbit out of a hat.

'Roast chicken is my favourite flavour,' I say.

'Now how did I know it would be? Mine too – it's that peppery pseudo-stuffing tang that simply makes them the best. Don't you think? You can keep your cheese and onion, pah, common as muck. Paaah.'

He opens his mouth wide and hisses so hard that his throat growls and his eyebrow ring rattles.

I take the packet and open it carefully. I pick out one crisp at a time and eat it slowly and quietly, not taking my eyes off him. Owen snatches a packet and crushes it inside the palms of both hands. He rips it open and throws his head back, pouring the broken crisps down his gullet in one.

'Mmmm, chicken dinner. Excellent,' he sighs. 'You try it.'

Later that night he walks me home. He doesn't stop talking the whole way, trotting alongside me, a couple of little steps to each of my ordinary ones. The houses on my road are like rows of dentures: two long low Georgian terraces. Each house is small and lots of them are painted playschool colours. But by streetlight, they are just different shades of grey. As we walk past Mr and Mrs Williams' house next door, Owen suddenly hoots with laughter.

'How very twee, how very ridiculous,' he shouts.

A line of light appears between the curtains at the basement bay window. There's a flash of yellow light on Mr Williams' glasses.

'Shh,' I say. 'They're my neighbours.'

'Well, yes, but come on,' says Owen, pointing to the garden.

I've never really looked at it before. The wrought-iron fence with sharp points, fanning out to divide my place from theirs; the two matching yuccas in huge ornate green plastic pots; the ivy painted on the wheelie bin.

'I mean to say,' he says, by now bent double and shaking his finger at the name plate: 'Our Wee Cottage' in wrought iron.

'What's wrong with it?' I ask.

'Well, how smug is that?' he drawls.

The curtains open a bit wider and I drag him over towards my gate.

'They're alright.'

'Oh, yes, I bet.'

'They are.'

'Friendly?'

'They're OK.'

'Invite you round to tea on a regular basis?'

'Well, not really.'

'Ever, ever, ever?'

'Alright, no. But they could be worse. They've never had a go at me or anything.'

Owen stops laughing. He looks up at me and puts his hand on my chin so I'm looking him in the eye.

'I should bloody well think not,' he says.

'Could you just stop talking for a little bit?'

I look at his mouth, his pinky, tippy, studded, gappy-toothed little mouth. He nods. His lips are surprisingly soft and plump. Our kisses are small at first, with tiny popping noises. As they get longer, I feel the lip-ring against my mouth, and gently lick it. The inside of his mouth is narrow, but warm. I break off and sigh a loud sigh.

In the distance I can just hear the sea breathing in and out.

1949

The smell of the ward came in waves again, stronger this time. Sweat, boiled cabbage, floor polish, carbolic soap and paraldehyde. It was like coming up out of a deep dark underground cave. Her head, lungs and the inside of her mouth felt padded with wool, and she gasped and clawed for breath as she came bursting back up to the surface.

Sweat had hardened on her gown, making it even more like cardboard. She was still damp between her legs where she had wet herself. The side of her cheek was crusty with dried saliva, and the tube was in her nose. The needle was gone from her arm.

'That's a good girl now, Aggie, nice and still.' The nurse's voice was muzzy. She put her fingers across the bottom of Agnes's nose and upper lip and pulled the tube out steadily, scraping the inside of the nostril inch by inch. She used her thumb to wipe a drop of moisture from Aggie's top lip, before turning to the trolley and pouring beige liquid into a cup from a Thermos jug. This nurse was kind, gentler than the nurses on the back ward.

The radiators were blasting out heat, but Agnes shivered and shook like a wet cat. The nurse slipped her hand beneath her neck and raised her head. She looked into one eye and then the other, and smiled as she checked her fingertips one after the other.

'Alright there, ducky?'

Agnes's heart was beating fast and she didn't feel like

talking. Her tongue felt like sand and she looked round for the drink.

The nurse wrapped a rubber cuff around the top of her arm. It tightened as she squeezed the wee black pump. Agnes reached out for the cup.

'Now then, Aggie, you know the ropes. Blood pressure first.' She pushed Agnes down again, lightly.

On the next bed, someone was twitching. It was Mary; Agnes recognized the grey curls. It was Mary's last day this week too. Six days on, one day off. No food after suppertime, insulin jabs for breakfast, and then the dozing and muzziness before the unstoppable stampeding darkness and the burst into light. Needles, tubes, comas, aftershocks and sweet tea, over and over, day after day. The twitching became stronger, and Mary's legs and arms began to jump about like she was dancing. Dr Leicester went over and looked down at her. He was very tall with fancy hair – almost a Marcel wave – and he walked slowly like a waiter.

'Nurse Slater, trolley, please,' he called.

The nurse jerked the cuff, pump, tubes and gauge onto the trolley and pushed it away. One of the wheels needed oiling. Agnes listened as it squeaked almost in time with Mary's spasms. The blood thumped inside her arm where the cuff had been.

'My cup of tea,' she croaked.

Her voice was tiny and rough, and Nurse Slater was busy by Mary's bed, handing a needle to the doctor. Mary was slow-ing down now.

'My cup of tea.' Agnes's voice was coming back, and she called across to the other side of the ward. The double doors opened and a porter wheeled in a boy in striped pyjamas. The boy was chirruping quietly, like a budgie.

'Tea, my tea,' Agnes called.

The porter looked over.

'Keep your hair on, madam,' he said. Then as Agnes stared at him, he shifted his forehead up and down to make his black hair move and wiggle about like a wig. He finished the show off with a wink and then wheeled the budgie-boy over to the opposite wall, snatched up a cup of tea and brought it over. Agnes wondered for a moment if she was still in coma. She tipped her head up and drank slowly with her chin against her neck. Some liquid dripped down her front but it was almost cold. It tasted of sugar and salt, with just the distant memory of tannin and tea leaves.

Agnes leant back and closed her eyes again. The squeaking trolley got louder and she felt the shadow of the nurse fall across her face. Agnes squinted at the watch pinned to her uniform, but the numbers were all upside down and confusing. They'd taken her watch away early on, so she never knew how long she was under. Mary said it was only for half an hour, but it felt like days in the darkness.

'Alright there, Joyce?' The porter was still there, in his beige coat, cockney like a music-hall star. He put her in mind of Max Miller or Tommy Trinder.

'Will be in a mo. That one over there's just thrown a fit. But we're all ship-shape now,' said the nurse.

'Yeh, and Bristol fashion, I shouldn't wonder.'

Agnes opened her eyes to see him cupping his hands against his chest, and guffawing. The nurse was smirking and giving him a sidelong look.

'Oh, Roger Mitchell, you are terrible.' Her giggle sounded forced. She slapped him on the shoulder and then looked down at Agnes.

Agnes shut her eyes quick sharp. But she couldn't help a

twitch of a smile herself. She hadn't heard laughter for so long, it had made her feel quite giddy.

'What's this one in for then, Joyce?' said Roger the porter.

'The usual. Third week of insulin coma.'

'She's a looker, though, ain't she, despite it all?'

Agnes opened her eyes and looked up. His hair was dark and slick, and he was smiling a lop-sided smile.

'Uh-oh, wakey wakey, then,' he grinned. 'Rise and shine.'

He straightened up and looked at the nurse again. 'She can't have been that bad, Joyce. Look at her – butter wouldn't melt.'

'Yes, well, she's getting better now,' said the nurse, lining up all the bits and pieces on the trolley and glancing over at Dr Leicester with the wavy hair, who was fast approaching. She lowered her voice to a fast whisper. 'But then, when they certified her, oof. Seemingly, she was absolutely doolally. Ranting and raving and all sorts. Went for her little girl, she had. Her own daughter. Damn-near killed her, they said, poor lamb, and her little boy was watching.'

'It wasnae like that at all.' Agnes tried to speak but her throat had gone again.

'No,' gasped Roger. He was all agog. 'Who'd have thought?'

'Yes,' said the nurse, whispering even lower. 'And she's come from money, know what I mean? Husband was in the diamond trade. A Jew-boy, worth a bob or two . . .'

'Really,' he said, suddenly changing to a clean work voice as Dr Leicester reached them. 'Yes, miss, I'll take her straight back to the ward.'

The nurse took Agnes's half-full cup of tea away and pulled her blanket up to her neck.

'How's this one coming along, Nurse Slater?' barked the doctor.

'Blood pressure normal, rehydrated well,' she smiled.

'Jolly good, jolly good,' he said. 'Off she pops, then.'

The trolley wheeled smoothly through the double doors and down the corridor. The porter whistled as he pushed, a tune from a film. She recognized it, the quirky jaunty melody. It would come to her later. Her eyes were level with the dark green paintwork of the bottom half of the walls. She watched the scuffs and chips blur by until she dozed off for a little while and thought that she was lying in one of the wee row boats in the park where she and Lucy used to play.

The trolley trundled round the corner and stopped suddenly. The smell of floor polish was stronger at this bend.

'Toot toot, mate,' chirped Roger as another porter with another trolley speeded off in the direction of the treatment wing.

'Toot toot,' chirped the other man, already a way off in the distance.

Agnes jolted awake, hot and angry. It hadn't been like that at all. She'd not been ranting and raving. They made her sound like Mama, and she'd known exactly what she'd been doing, of course she had. It was the day after she'd found Ernest. There was such a lot to do. Rebecca had been running around, and she'd been told: keep out of the way, madam. She'd been told time and time again. Desmond had been good – he'd been fine. They were right about one thing, she supposed. It was a shame that Desmond had had to see it all. Such a good boy, Desmond. He would jut his Mr Chinnywig chin out, but he always did as he was told. Not like little madam.

The lounge had been such a mess. A terrible state, even after the police had been and cleared away. There was still blood and wee threads from Ernest's jacket and shirt over the settee and the carpet. She'd found a cuff link underneath the

Turkish rug. She wanted to get it all back to normal, but Rebecca kept running round and round, skipping, dancing and singing until Agnes's head had felt like it was splitting in half.

The police had been the day before, when she'd found him. She'd been out for the afternoon with the kiddies, visiting Lucy in her wee prefab. Lucy never had her own children, even though she and Toby had tried long and hard since the war. She loved having Rebecca and Desmond to visit. Six and nine were the best ages, Lucy said. Cherish them, Aggie, she said. Spoilt them rotten, in Aggie's opinion. Cakes and buns, never mind rationing.

They'd been to a matinée at the Gaumont too. Saw that film. Aggie had found it rather unsettling. It was dark and shadowy, but Lucy and the kiddies were full of it. When they got back, before the rock cakes, they'd marched dramatically around Toby's vegetable patch, taking it in turns to wear his big hat and coat, and using chopped-up beanpoles as pretend cigarettes. And singing that tune. What was it called, that film?

She'd known there was something wrong the minute the key was in the lock. Mister Bowlly and Fluff were mewing and scratching behind the kitchen door, and Ernest never shut them away. He adored the cats. Said at least they loved him, the two old tabby faithfuls. Sometimes she'd come back and find him with one on his lap and one round his neck. But that day he'd shut them out to do his business.

There was a strange smell, even in the hall. Like fresh meat and iron filings. And it was cold, even though all the doors and windows were closed. She never found out where he got the gun from, had no idea he might even have had such contacts. Maybe someone he'd met in the internment camp. He'd not been the same after that.

The police came straight away. Went on and on about the gun, and the fact that he was a German. Asked questions, lots and lots of muddling questions, and cleared away the crime scene, as they called it. But there was still so much to do. Desmond was playing quietly in the corner with his soldiers, but that girl, that girl was just in the way all the time.

Her head had hurt. Her arm had hurt from the scrubbing. She was concentrating on a bad stain on the sofa. The water was clearer now, like weak beetroot juice, but then Rebecca began tap-dancing again and kicked over the bucket. There were pale pink soapsuds all over the floor. Little madam. Little bastard. Little devil. Next thing she'd known she still had the carbolic soap and the hard bristle floor brush in her hands, but the little devil was on the floor: elbows, knees and cheeks grazed and raw, powder-blue cardigan ripped. Scrubbed clean, hair stiff and matted with soap. But nice and quiet now, with those big green eyes staring at her.

Desmond ran off to get his auntie, and that's when the trouble really started. They took Rebecca off to the hospital and then it was the police again, and doctors this time, and an ambulance. They weren't even his children, she tried telling them. Little bastards, little devils. Not his. He couldn't father anything, the state he'd been in with his little wee wee cigar. Always sniffling and moping about the house. And what about their real father? Graham, Graham the soldier, she'd told them urgently: ask Graham the soldier. Where was he when she needed him? He was a real man, a real man in the bushes alright, she tried to tell them. They still wouldn't listen, so she'd had to raise her voice again. But they just looked at her aghast and bundled her into the ambulance.

*

The trolley stopped in the shadows just outside the ward. The porter shifted round to the side, bent down and gripped both her breasts. He narrowed his eyes at her.

'Very nice,' he said. 'Very nice indeed.'

Then he moved back and began whistling again, but slower this time, and through his teeth so it sounded high and frilly, like a tin whistle. He wheeled her to the doors and wriggled a key from his belt to unlock them. He pushed her back over to her bed. A nurse came over, the smelly one with the wide damp hands, and they pushed her up onto the mattress.

The nurse went over to slap Irish Margaret, who was calling for her mammy, and the porter bent down and whispered so close into her ear that it buzzed.

'Shall I come and visit you later then?'

Sunday was the one rest day of the week from the treatment. After breakfast Agnes stood with the other women in a line in the middle of the ward. A right motley crew they made, together like this. Some tall, some short, lots of grey tangled hair and shaking and jerking. They were almost comical, like survivors from a shipwreck. Smelly nurse walked up the line, digging her finger just a bit too hard into each of their shoulders as she counted. The doors were unlocked and they were turned out to the airing court. The day was muggy and overcast, and there was a queer smell of tar in the air today, but it was a relief to be outside. There were scores of women out on the big, grey court. Most were weaving around the middle in a slow procession, but a few were scuttling around the edges with the wind in their tails. Olga, the musician, was standing on one leg, hands out playing the piano. A thin line of pee was running down into her shoe. In the opposite corner, near the hospital building, old Maddie was sitting with her dress up, playing with herself. Three nurses, young ones, on point duty, stood looking at their nails and chatting to each other.

Agnes looked away and walked slowly over to the edge of the court, next to the high iron railings. Her back and neck were aching but it was good to be moving, her mind felt lighter. A clutch of weeds was poking its way through crumbs of tarmac – two dandelions and three spikes of rosebay willowherb. A cabbage white butterfly landed on one of the spikes, and then took off through the railings towards the men's court. The men were inside today, apart from a work-gang that was busy shovelling out gooey puddles of tarmac onto the ground from steaming wheelbarrows. Aggie's mind cleared some more. She was definitely feeling better, and she wondered what had happened about Ernest's funeral.

When his sister's husband had died, it had been such a palaver, all that Jewish stuff. Over so quickly, all done and dusted in a day. And then the mourning, it seemed to go on and on. His sister wasn't allowed to wear make-up, she seemed to remember. But a suicide. Maybe the police would bury him; maybe they had already. She didn't know.

When he'd come back from the Isle of Man, they had both been pleased to see each other. It had surprised her. He had taken Desmond in his arms and gazed down on his face for the first time, and when Desmond had grinned his gummy grin, Ernest smiled back like the sun had come out. He could not father a baby, but his grin was the size of a banana. When Desmond's tiny fingers had clutched around Ernest's thumb like wee pink petals, she had felt a lurch deep in her belly. Guilt or relief, she couldn't decide.

Things had changed when she fell pregnant the second time. Graham had been home on leave, and they'd met twice in a boarding house at Earls Court. They'd drunk whisky from his hip flask and had a lark. When she told Ernest she was expecting again, he bent double as though she had punched him in the stomach, and then walked out of the room. He never really spoke to her properly or looked her in the eye again, even when Rebecca was born.

The three young nurses had finished gossiping, and began the rounding up and counting in for lunch. Agnes trudged back inside with the others. At the table, the auxiliary with the hunched back walked up and down handing out the spoons and forks, counting each one out. Plates of cabbage, pale green mashed potato and bully beef were slammed down in front of them all. Next to Aggie, old Maddie sneaked a pick at her meat. But the auxiliary saw her and slapped her hand away.

'Grace,' she hissed.

Old Maddie carried on picking, and the auxiliary twisted her arm behind her back.

'Wait, I said, or it'll be the pads,' she hissed again.

Charge Nurse Harrison strode to the top of the table and said grace. There was a quick ramshackle amen and then the clink of cutlery. The big fat women gulped their food down in seconds and looked round at the plates of the feeble ones. The food tasted of nothing. Agnes often yearned for a wee bit of sugar. Once, only once, when the nurses weren't looking, she'd managed to nab a couple of sugar cubes from their tea tray. She'd kept them up her sleeve until bedtime and then sucked on them for hours, feeling the grit and sweetness coat her teeth. She vowed to herself that if she ever got out of here, she would always have sugar.

The meal was over in five minutes, but the women had to stay sitting at the table until all the cutlery was washed and counted. Then it was rest time. Agnes lay back on her mattress and closed her eyes. A big bluebottle was buzzing against the window, but the nurses saw that the ward was quiet otherwise. She was warm and drifting off to sleep when the buzzing came close to her ear. She reached out to swat the juicy brute and her wrist was gripped hard by something bigger than a fly.

'Only me,' his singsong music-hall voice rang out in the quiet.

Agnes opened her eyes. Roger was crouching at the side of the bed. There was a small dark brown smear on the front of his porter's coat.

'Rise and shine,' he chimed. 'Fancy a little stroll?'

Agnes screwed up her eyes and gulped back a yawn. 'But it's rest time. The nurses—'

'Never mind the nurses, missus. Me and the nurses have got what you might call an arrangement,' he said. 'Come on, a little stroll around the grounds. Occupational therapy – isn't that what they're calling it?' He winked, as he rolled her out of the bed and shoved her shoes on.

He unlocked the metal gates in the courts and grasped her elbow with his hand, guiding her towards the grounds. The sun had come out. The sky was blue and the lawns and shrubberies were green. Agnes's eyes burnt at the colours.

'Nice out, ain't it?' he said. 'Oops, I'd better put it away then,' and he laughed like a donkey.

Agnes felt muzzy. Her legs were heavy and she didn't understand.

'Tired, are we, ay? Here we go, then.' He sat down on an old wooden bench and patted the seat next to him. 'Come on, park yourself here.'

Agnes sat and listened. A wood pigeon was calling in the trees above them, and in the distance a dog was barking.

'So, then, Ags, tell me a bit about yourself.'

Agnes looked at him. The back of her head throbbed. What did he want? The dog stopped barking.

'Joyce, you know, Nurse Slater on the insulin ward, she said you was married. What's he like then, your hubby?'

'Dead,' she said, and he laughed.

'Dead, ay? Good one, Ags. Dead.'

Suddenly she was hungry to talk about Ernest, to tell someone, anyone, what had happened. No dirty little secrets, no holds barred. How he'd been unable to do anything for months when he came back from the internment camp. How when the news came out about his family and the concentration camps he'd stopped sleeping completely. And then business was bad. Diamonds, he'd said, I thought you could always rely on diamonds. She even told Roger about Graham and Desmond and Rebecca. The whole sorry story, faster and faster until she finally ran out of steam. Until her mouth was dry and she couldn't talk any more.

Roger pulled his face back into his neck and shook his head slightly, wobbling like that wee duckling puppet Lucy gave Rebecca at Easter.

'Bloody hell, Ags, bit of a state, weren't he?' He raised his eyebrows, looked down at his hands and asked in a matter-of-fact voice, 'So what happened to his dosh?'

Agnes looked blank.

'His lucre, moolah – you know, his money?'

'Ach, mine, I suppose,' she said, watching the colour rise in his face.

'Right,' he said, 'enough of this jaw jaw. Time for a little action. Do you fancy getting out of here?'

'What do you mean?' Aggie's headache was back, and she wanted to lie down.

'Out of the bin. Home, you know.'

'But I don't understand. The doctors, and the other girls on the ward, they say—'

'Never you mind all that. You just listen to what your Roger says, and we'll have you out of here in no time. I know exactly what the doctors, God bless them, need to hear.'

Her eyelids kept closing as they walked back to the building. There were midges in the air and the chapel bells were ringing. Not everyone on the ward was allowed to go to church, and it was the only time they had a chance of seeing the men. Agnes had been last week. She'd have missed it today. She looked at Roger.

'I'll come and call for you tomorrow, then,' he said as they arrived back at the ward. He wiggled the right key from his belt and unlocked the door. 'Take you to meet some of my mates, maybe. Would you like that?'

Agnes nodded, and shuffled over to her bed. As he went, the women came back from church. Big Linda reckoned that one of the men had fancied her, but Renee said it was her he loved. Linda threw a punch. Renee ducked and kicked her in the shin. Linda bellowed and lashed her arms around like a windmill until the nurses took her off to the pads.

The next evening Roger came for her again. It was later, dusk, and he guided her down to the porters' lodge. Aggie was woozy and hungry; she'd been on coma treatment again. Roger was whistling that tune. They played it on a funny string instrument like a banjo, but not a banjo, in the film. What was it?

A paraffin heater was going, blue flames hissing at full blast in the corner. Otherwise the lodge was dark. Agnes could make out the shapes of three men sitting around a low table.

A layer of blue cigarette smoke hung down from the ceiling.

'Who's in, then?' said a high-pitched voice, taking a deep drag on his cig.

'What we playing?' said another, with a West Country accent.

'Poker. But let's have a bit of fun with it,' said the first voice, turning his head towards her. She couldn't make out his face, but could hear him smacking his lips.

Roger nudged Agnes. 'You up for that, Ags?' He turned to the men. 'Ags'll be up for a bit of fun. Likes a bit of the other, this one. Don't you, Ags?'

'You got the camera, Rog?' asked the high voice.

'Oh, yeh, got it,' said Roger. And he whistled again.

Orson Welles disappearing in the sewers and up a ferris wheel. Harry Lime, that was it – the 'Harry Lime Theme'.

She heard the cards being shuffled and dealt, and their dirty low laughs, and soon she closed her eyes and was back in the dark at the Gaumont watching *The Third Man* with Lucy and Desmond and Rebecca.

March 15–19 – Fat Padded Neon Creatures

I do sometimes think about my funeral. What songs I'm going to have, who'll be there. Doctor Hassani at the back, sobbing uncontrollably into his silk hankie. And June, although she'd probably bring a flip chart along and try and make it a learning experience for everyone. I can rely on Mum and Dad to make up the numbers, and maybe they'll track down Aunt Rebecca for the occasion. Not sure if Nan'll make it though, the rate she's going.

I want lots and lots of daffodils and *My Coo-Ca-Choo* by Alvin Stardust as the curtains close on my coffin. None of that Whitney or Sinatra drama for me – real English pop. Songs that matter.

Colin's funeral is all planned. Thumbs up to Colin. He was so disorganized in real life, it's a bit of a coup. Couldn't get his act together to get to the shops or laundrette, or even wash very much if the truth be told, but he's worked out poems and records and everything.

I'm sitting in between Cathy and Julia. The others from the day centre are in the rows in front. Cathy is rocking, just a little bit. Julia is nice and still, but Steve in front of her is muttering something over and over. Colin's brother, Ian, gets up and comes to the front. He looks like Colin, except he's older, clean and trim. He's wearing a black suit that is slightly too small.

'Colin left this letter with a request for me to read it here today.' He lifts his fist to his mouth, coughs a high cough and starts reading very fast.

*'I'm taking this message with me to all those who've gone on
ahead. It's a message from the living to the dead. Sometimes we
can't do it. We can't survive. Life is too hard. Life is too lonely.
The people you left behind do their best. Thanks to Ian, thanks,
Bruv . . .'*

Ian stops reading. He gulps. He's got a huge Adam's apple,
almost the size of a real apple, and it makes his collar and tie
wiggle. When he starts reading again his voice is squeaky and
tight. My throat is sore. Cathy is rocking harder.

*'Thanks to Ian, I can also send this message from the dead to the
living.'* Ian looks up. *'To all those who have been left behind. Do
your best. Carry on the struggle and be strong. See you when I see
you. Love, Colin.'*

Steve shouts out but I can't understand what he's saying. Cathy
is rubbing her arms, wafting the smell of lavender about. She
says it calms her. It's making my legs itch, but I won't scratch.
I run my fingers over my thumbnail. One two three thumb.
One two three thumb. I think about Timmy, dead. I think
about Natalie.

Ian looks down at the piece of paper. He turns it over and
then back again. Nothing more so he nods at a little old man
sitting at a table in the corner and then says, 'Colin also gave
instructions that we had to play these two songs and everyone has to listen.'

I expected something grand, opera, Queen, I don't know,
but the first song is *Boy Named Sue*. The Man in Black with
his lovely deep voice singing a funny, fighting song. Colin's
family sit with their heads staring down at their shoes. Water
drips onto the floor from the face of one woman with ironed

blonde hair. Us lot from the day centre look round at each other. I didn't know Colin liked Johnny Cash. There are a lot of things about Colin I don't know, and I never will now. I do know he's brave. I couldn't jump from twelve storeys. Cathy said he landed like a dollop of jam.

The sun shines in red and blue shafts through the tall thin stained-glass window, and the little old man fiddles with the CD player. My mum insisted on proper hymns at Timmy's funeral. And Vivaldi, for God's sake. Vivaldi – Timmy would have preferred a bit of Pet Shop Boys, but Mum wasn't having any of it.

The next song comes on. It is very quiet at first and he adjusts the volume. I hate the Eagles normally, but this song makes my chest go tight and my cheeks go red. It's so angry.

It's country-rock, but not as we know it Jim. A tinkling piano and the quietest strangulated voice singing through gritted teeth about paradise.

There's a small quiet jolt at the front of the hall. The conveyor belt starts.

About paradise, and kissing it goodbye.

Colin's coffin totters away into a hole in the wall.

The *Last Resort* plays on, the piano crashing and the strangulated Eagle bleeding his heart out until the music grinds to a halt, and the coffin's long gone.

Something brittle in my head cracks. I close my eyes and the big bright faces of Timmy and Natalie fill my vision.

Steve stands up and shouts, 'Bye Girl! Bye Girl, Bye Girl, Barbie Girl.'

There's a lot of uncomfortable coughing, and other people slowly stand up too. We shuffle our way out. Cathy is nuzzling up next to me, but I try to push her away. Outside it smells of bonfires. A flake of dirt falls on my arm. I flick it off but it smudges and I realize it is ash.

We had a big debate at the day centre about whether we should go to the reception after. In the end we decided that we should: camaraderie for Colin. His brother has hired a hall around the block from the crematorium, so we all troop across the zebra crossing like some twisted version of the *Abbey Road* cover. The sky is an unnatural colour, an electric yellow that's making my eyes hurt. There are three airplane trails high up, crossing each other. I wonder if it is a sign. My limp is worse and I don't feel right. My heart is beating fast. I need food.

The hall is very hot. It's got huge fuck-off-and-die industrial radiators and triple-glazed windows. Natalie's funeral was huge, so I heard. I was in hospital at the time. Smashed leg and not quite right in the head. Half the art school turned out, and her coffin was decorated with collages, mobiles and candles. I wondered if they'd put her crash helmet on top, like they do for soldiers, but never got the guts to ask. I couldn't ask her mum or dad. They wouldn't communicate with me after she died. I'm sure they blamed me for the crash, and it is true, if I hadn't nagged her to come out for a ride she'd be alive now.

I shrug off Cathy and, trying to keep it slow and casual, I make a beeline for the trestle tables running across the back wall. They're covered in green and red crepe paper tablecloths, too festive for a funeral. Must be left over from Christmas. There's a pile of white paper plates, each with a shiny hard paper napkin folded into a triangle on top. I pick one up and start piling. No one else has reached the food yet, so I've got a free rein. The coleslaw is runny, and I drip milky mayo down my front and on the dance floor. It is also seeping a soft grey circle through the Poundland plate, so I stick two more plates underneath to be secure.

People are wandering over to the tables, and forming an orderly queue for the quiche. I pile my plate up again and stand back against the wall, but I still feel very conspicuous. I look around for some support. Julia is standing with Steve way off by the front door, and I can't see Cathy anywhere. The woman with ironed blonde hair comes over. Very neat and restrained arrangement of food on her plate: one vol-au-vent, *one* mind, plus one tiny triangle sandwich and two silverskin onions. No coleslaw. She smiles at me. I wipe at my mayo stain, but it's just making a smeary mess on my favourite black T-shirt. She looks down at her vol-au-vent and picks up an onion. She has fingernails the colour of coral. I blow puff pastry flakes from my mouth.

'Were you a friend of Colin's?' she asks.

Her voice is gentle and calm, but I'm not feeling like talking. I close my eyes but she is still there when I open them, so I nod.

'What's your name?' she tries again.

I swallow a lump of quiche pastry and close my eyes again. I see Timmy in my head. 'Jodie,' I croak.

'I'm Eileen, Colin's sister,' she says. 'I'm glad Colin had such good friends.'

I wasn't a good friend of Colin's, for fuck's sake. He was a moody sod, drank a lot, so no one got very close to him. Plus he smelt. But I did like him – well, when I say liked him, I mean I felt for him. He was in a fucking terrible depression, tormented because he'd split up with his girlfriend and she wouldn't let him see their baby. I sat with him at the day centre canteen once or twice, but I wouldn't say that it qualifies me as a good friend. Besides which, as I said, I don't feel much like talking. My head is still brittle and full of that angry song and I want to concentrate on my food. In private, preferably.

I look around, but Colin's sister smiles at me, still thinking she can engage me in small talk. I can't do this. She's very nice but I can't do this right now. My stomach is churning and my legs are itching. I reach over to grab a couple more cream cheese rolls and some sausages on sticks. Put my head down and walk away.

The toilets will be private. They are out of the main hall and down a hot white corridor. I'm looking forward to sitting down, locking the cubicle and eating in private. The door pushes open with a swish and then a creak. It needs oil. Warm air blasts out with the smell of pine and piss. The door closes behind me. There's a row of sinks and two toilets behind short doors. A tap is dripping. I don't like the sound of taps dripping. Something moves next to my foot. Out of the corner of my eye I can see a small brown thing scuttling. I won't look down. I won't look down and see them. Something tugs at my head. Shifting sand. I'm alone and it's hot and it's dark. No one will help me. I'm all alone.

My heart is beating too fast. My face is suddenly covered in sweat. I feel green and sick and scared and I can see bugs moving everywhere. I drop my plate. I'm twitching and I hear myself shouting. I'm banging on the door and screaming to get out. I must get off the floor. I hurtle into a cubicle and stand on the toilet, waving my arms and shouting for help. After a while people come through the squeaky door. A man in a suit is asking me questions, but all I can see is his mouth moving up and down, up and down. He is asking me something again and again, but my sweaty head is too full of death and bugs to understand the words. I'm still twitching and jumping when the ambulance comes.

I'm a voluntary patient. Again. That's what they tell me. I sit in the day room and look at the telly. *Doctors* is on. The story is about an old woman with Alzheimer's. Her daughter is horrible and doesn't even try to listen to her. It's raining outside and my leg hurts. I really need a wee and I'm waving my leg side to side to try and force the wee back up. I don't like going to the toilets here. You can't lock the doors. Kate, who is thin as a syringe and can't have anyone within a metre of her face, is sitting way over by the back wall. She has pieces of J-cloth stuck to her cheeks with Sellotape. The two black lads are playing cards, but the tall one with long dreadlocks keeps getting up and pacing round in circles shouting to himself.

I've been here three days. My mouth is lined with sandpaper and my eyes feel like they're superglued shut. Last time I was in hospital, I was out after a fortnight. I've been in and out probably a dozen times, including this little jaunt. The first time nearly twenty years ago, a few months after the accident. My leg was healed; physically I was okay. I just couldn't cope with anything. Nothing made sense. I'd look out of the window and see Natalie's head looming over buildings. And my legs would give way whenever I heard a motorbike rev up. Post-traumatic shock – obvious, yes – but I knew it went deeper, that something inside had changed and got worse. Still, I got sympathy and a wodge of counselling that first time, although it was still a bit wham bam thank you mam and out you go.

The next time I lost it, there seemed to be a spot less of the old sympathy. More pills, less talking, I'd say. The time before last, mind you, the unit was full and they had to put me in a private clinic. It had flowers and new carpet. I was out of there pretty sharpish. But this time they just look sick and tired of the sight of me. But then maybe I'm being paranoid. I have seen a doctor. She asked me about my childhood and then said she'd talk to June about more support and some new practical therapy.

It's cold today and the air is grey and yellow. There's no one here I recognize this time. The old bloke sitting by the door is rolling another fag, but I'd say that overall there are fewer smokers. That health promotion malarkey must be working. Either that or they've all died of cancer or topped themselves.

Pork Pie Hat comes round with the medication. He's wearing his nylon navy-blue trousers with his huge bunch of keys hanging from the belt loop. He jangles them like an old-fashioned janitor. He always goes right up close to Kate's face. He trundles over towards me and hands me my little beaker with the pills in.

'Go on, down the hatch,' he grunts, giving the keys a jangle.

I swallow them. I'm feeling calmer, it's true. They must be working.

I watch *Miss Marple* and doze a bit even though my feet are stony cold. The nice nurse with the curly perm comes over and strokes me on the shoulder. My bladder is so full that it's burning. I squeeze myself tight.

'Jodie, love,' she smiles, 'you've got a visitor.'

It'll be my dad with a copy of the *Puzzler* and a bottle of Appletiser. Is that really Dick Van Dyke on the telly? It sounds just like him and that's his smile, but he's got white hair and glasses, plus a thick moustache.

'Jodie?' she says again, and hooks me under the arm to stand me up. I've got pins and needles in my foot and hobble a bit as I turn round.

It's not my dad. I can't not smile and a warm trickle of wee wets my pants. It's Owen. No *Puzzler*, no pop, just Owen wearing a leather jacket and a beret.

'How did you find me?' I manage.

'I've been searching for days. In the end I went to the day centre. They told me.' He takes off his beret and pulls up a chair. We sit down and he holds my hand.

'How you doing?' he asks.

'Oh, you know.' I shrug. He strokes my fingers and everything goes blurry. There are tears in my eyes. We sit there for ten minutes looking at each other but not saying anything. The children's telly programmes come on, and I half listen. All over the country there must be small children home from school watching fat padded neon creatures. *Postman Pat* starts and I hum the theme tune very quietly. Over on the other side of the day room a young bloke whose name I don't know starts pacing up and down. Outside a car or taxi pulls up. *Postman Pat* finishes.

'I am feeling better,' I say eventually.

'You look like shit,' says Owen.

'You silver tongued bastard, you.' I smile.

'What happened?' he says.

'I lost it. I lost it.'

'Why? What happened?'

I can't remember why. I remember the coleslaw and being in the toilets, but not why.

'I dunno,' I say.

The Eagles' song comes into my head and I start to cry. Owen holds me tight.

'It'll be alright,' he whispers, and I nuzzle his neck. 'We'll have you out of here in no time, back home, safe and sound,' he promises.

'It's all too hard.' I'm snivelling and I don't know if he's heard me. 'It's horrible out there. I can't do it.'

The *Blue Peter* theme starts up. Owen pulls away from me. He wipes my eyes.

'Yes you can,' he says. 'You're not on your own.'

1938

The apartment block was curved and white, large as a spanking brand-new cruise liner. The wooden floor in the lounge put her in mind of a dance hall, and there was a smooth shiny drinks cabinet and dark smart furniture. It was a man's flat, more like an office than somewhere cosy where you could let off and giggle. Agnes nipped her arm again, making another tiny bruise like a raisin to join the line of faint purple dots up her arm.

Whilst he was out at Hatton Garden, she wandered the shiny rooms, a feather duster in one hand, a glass in the other. One day she tried sherry, the next gin.

'No need for my wife to work,' Ernest said when she left Mr and Mr Walker's.

Agnes listened to the clock tick. She shimmied into the bedroom, and glanced out of the bay window and the metal balcony. Dusk was falling and the wind was picking up. Dozens of little orange leaves blew off the silver birch, landing on the front lawn. The caretaker would rake them up. The room had an underlying smell of bitter aftershave and cheese. No matter how much mouthwash, pomade, hair oils, aftershave and talcum Ernest used, his mouth smelt faintly of rotten vegetables and his feet mildly of cheese. Agnes swore that when she was forty-one she wouldn't smell.

The bed was high as a sacrificial altar, and the shiny plump purple counterpane didn't look right for sleeping under. Agnes perched on the side and took a swig of gin. Some liquid splashed into one of the stitched valleys of the counter-pane.

'Shiza,' she hissed through gritted teeth, in her best Marlene accent. 'Shiza, Shiza, Shiza,' as she crouched down and tried first to lick and then to suck the drink from the fabric. The shine had gone in a long dark patch. Maybe it wouldn't show when it dried.

She laid her forehead on the bed and breathed out deeply. After a small cough, she jumped up to standing on the bed. Slowly and gently at first, she bounced. The mattress dipped and the walnut headboard moved slightly from the wall. Agnes kicked off her slippers. She could feel the glossy soft material between her toes. She gripped her feet like a monkey, bent her knees and aimed for the ceiling. The bed creaked as she shot into the air. The headboard shifted at an alarming angle.

'Weeeee,' she laughed at the jerking wood, and started to sing as she bounced. '"I loo a sossie,"' bounce, '"a bonnie bonnie sossie,"' bounce, '"You can always tell it by the smeeeeelll."' She didn't hear the key turn in the front door. '"If you fry it wi an ingin, you can hear the sausage singing, Aggie, mah . . ."'

Ernest stepped into the room, coat and hat still on. Agnes's hair was down around her face, her cheeks were red and she was screaming at the top of her lungs: '". . . Scots bluebell."'

Ernest stood with his hands by his side. His hand and arm didn't move, but his black bag dropped straight down on the floor, making a soft thud. Agnes looked at him and her mouth twitched. His skin was blue, his forehead wrinkled, and above his soft brown eyes, his eyebrows were moving up and down like wee beetles.

'Are you alright, my dear?' he finally asked.

The twitch became a pout and Agnes snorted. A tiny bit

of snot shot out of her nostril making her snort again as she brought her hand up to her nose.

'I'm just dandy,' she said, laughing now like a steam train.

He walked slowly over to the bed and Agnes sat down.

'You'll ruin the springs,' he said slowly, but with the slightest hint of a smile about his thick lips.

'Ach, come on Ernie, I'm only having a wee bit of fun.' She swung her legs around and patted the counterpane. 'Sit down a while.'

Ernest put his hand on top of his bowler, lifted it and placed it carefully on the bedside cabinet. He shrugged his heavy blue wool coat off his shoulders, folded it over his arm and picked a small piece of lint from the sleeve before hanging it on the back of the chair.

Agnes watched him and patted the bed again.

Slowly he came and sat down next to her.

She took his hand and placed it on her left breast. 'All that jumping's made my heart beat so fast, feel here.'

His breath didn't smell so bad today. Slightly fishy. Sometimes he went out at lunchtime to a nearby café for gefilte fish balls. Before they married, he told Agnes that his sister kept a kosher kitchen, but he didn't expect it of her. One suppertime, though, he had produced a box of large square crackers, the size of face flannels. They had tiny spots – like the dots on Papa's brogues – in regular lines across them, and little dark burnt areas like muddy puddles.

'Matzos,' he said. 'Try.'

Agnes had nibbled a corner and it crumbled. It tasted of toasted sand.

'Not like that. Like this,' he said, and took a large snap. Half the matzo fell on the floor and he scrambled down after it like a puppy. Two years had passed since Ernest played pup.

He moved his other hand to Agnes's other breast. She tipped her head back and he kissed her neck. Small damp kisses. He used his finger to trace the edge of her scar. A shiny patch of skin in the exact shape of a star. The chimney fire and the clumps of burning soot seemed so long ago. It fascinated him. He traced it round and round, in a trance, until Agnes pulled his hand down to her lap.

Outside, the wind had dropped and darkness had fallen. Ernest undressed Agnes carefully and then stood up to undress himself. He shook his shirt out before dropping it to the floor. He glanced at the window before turning back to Agnes. His penis was poking ahead like a little pink cigar. The room was chilly, and the counterpane smooth and silky.

Agnes shivered, and wanted to snuggle under the blankets, but now Ernest was on top of her. He was warm, and she wanted heat. She shuffled her bottom down, and tried to reach out to touch his cock. Ernest grunted and sighed. She stroked it a few times and lifted her knees. The little cigar had deflated again. She pushed her groin up to meet it, and Ernest thrust at the same time. But it was soft like tripe, and wasn't going anywhere. Agnes lifted her knees again and kissed his neck. Ernest ground his teeth and pushed once more, before cursing and rolling off her.

He lay with his back to her. Agnes was covered in goosebumps. She felt under the pillow for her flannelette nightdress with the powder-blue roses and pulled it on. She tried to push her feet down inside the bed, but Ernest's weight was pinning the counterpane and blankets down.

They lay in the dark.

'Are you not cold?' she asked.

Ernest turned his head towards her. She leant over him to switch on the bedside lamp. Electric. It still impressed her.

'No need for light,' he whispered as he switched it off again, but not before she saw the lines of tears down his cheeks.

'Sorry,' he said.

'It's every time now. What about me?' she whispered. 'What am I supposed to do?'

'In Germany, bad things are happening,' he said quietly.

'I'm here all day, just waiting. A bit of fun – that's not too much to ask now, is it?'

'I met a man at lunchtime, just off the boat. Kristallnacht, they're calling it. God help them.'

'I thought London would be exciting. Lights and music . . .'

'And work, everything's gone. It's not like the old days. I'm sorry.'

Outside, a man walked by, his shoes clipping along slowly. A church bell in the distance chimed the hour.

'You must do what you must do to be happy,' Ernest said quietly, his head turned away from Agnes.

Agnes looked up at the ceiling. There was a thin crack she hadn't noticed before, and a tiny spider was walking alongside it. It had a plump black body and two of its front legs were unusually long, more like fangs than legs. It walked in lopsided steps and stopped at the end of the crack. She waited for Ernest to start snoring. He was still and quiet for a long time, but when she looked at him in the gloom his eyes were open. He was looking up at the ceiling, but she didn't know if he'd seen the crack or the spider. She didn't ask.

At the end of the following spring, a letter came from Lucy. Dolly was to be married. She'd bagged one of Arthur's pals, a farmhand. Papa was much the same and there was no news of Mama. Lucy wanted to visit, to see the sights and go shopping. She needed an outfit to wear to the wedding. Agnes found a postcard of the Tower of London. 'Come as soon as you can,' she wrote. 'Shops, cafés, clubs, laughs and a bit of life, come soon.'

Agnes met Lucy at Euston Station. She was wearing the most enormous hat: jewel blue with an unlikely bent peacock feather drooping down her collar. Her coat, though, was a modest navy buttoned affair. She'd been made manageress at Madame Florence's. She'd not managed to marry. Her face was powdery and pale, and the fine hairs running along her jawline were new. Agnes kissed Lucy's cheek. Lucy kissed first one, then the other of Agnes's cheeks.

'You're looking bonny,' said Agnes. 'A fine hat.'

'You're looking fine yourself. Have you put on a pound or two?'

Agnes patted her stomach. 'No, I don't think so. Still flat as a pancake.'

'Married life suits you then?'

A group of pigeons flew loudly and low overhead and a dollop of bird dropping splashed on the ground in front of them. It was white as clean linen against the greasy grey pavement. The smoke and oil caught in Agnes's throat. She nodded and quickly took Lucy's arm to lead her out into the sunshine. They passed a fat old woman on the flower stall, selling bunches of pink hyacinths. A weedy little man in a flat cap with a ciggie poking out of the corner of his mouth was holding up rolled-up papers and shouting about Mussolini.

'Papa well?' said Agnes as they reached the taxi rank.

'Quiet, you ken. Sleeping more and more. And Ernest?'

Agnes paused. She lifted her hands and waved them in two quick short circles. 'Oui, c'est bon, ma chérie. Ja, gut.'

The sisters looked at each other. Lucy smiled with half of

her mouth and then nodded her head again and again in a rhythm that they both knew. The peacock feather bounced up and down, and the hat slipped down over her left eyebrow. She looked more squiffy than continental.

'You remember, zen, non?'

The old tram foreign tongues game. The two of them were back in Edinburgh. It was a sunny day and they were young and silly, speaking in preposterous accents.

'Let's have some fun,' said Agnes.

The noise was deafening. Children were rushing around splashing. It was a hazy day, and groups of mothers sat on red and green tartan rugs on the clipped grass, laughing like gannets, drinking cups of tea and eating sandwiches. Egg and potted meat, by the smell of them. Small gangs of young people were lounging about, and every now and again, a youth would suddenly stand up, launch himself across the concrete path and jump very boldly into the water, waving and shouting as he went. Trim, muscly men and women were queuing at the steps for the diving boards, and there were regular big splashes followed by the occasional tinkle of applause.

Agnes came out of the cubicle breathing in deeply. It smelt of water and sunshine. She tucked the last bits of hair into her swimming hat, and the newly painted yellow wooden door clunked shut behind her.

'Come on, Loose,' she said to the red door next to it.

There was a raucous round of laughter from the grass and she turned round to see. A couple of men were lying on their fronts, booming jokes at each other. The sun suddenly shone hard on her neck. Agnes smiled. Ernest didn't like this sort of thing. He shivered at the idea; said, 'If God had meant us to swim . . .' and muttered about the League of Health and

Beauty and the Nazis. Truth was, he would look ridiculous in a bathing costume.

'Come on Lucy,' she shouted directly at the door.

There were small gasps and grunts coming from inside. Agnes stood on her tiptoes and peered over the top into the gloom. Lucy was poking about with her tight black rubber hat.

'What you doing?'

'My hair's pulling. Coming.' Lucy's eyes were bright and watery.

Aggie sighed and spun back round again, with her arms stretched out to capture the sunshine. One of the young men on the grass looked over at her, and muttered something to his friend, staring at her all the time. He had thick blond eyebrows.

The red door swung open and Lucy came out, still poking at her hair, and pulling the edges of her bathing suit down.

They stepped across the concrete and through the puddles to the pool. Agnes braced herself for the cold and walked down the steps backwards, like a ladder, into the water.

Lucy stayed on the side.

'What's it like?' she said, tugging at her costume.

Agnes ducked down to her shoulders, waiting for the freezing water to take her breath away. It didn't.

'It's no' bad, you know.'

Lucy rolled her eyes and clucked, but started to climb in.

Agnes lay back in the water and looked up at the sky. It wasn't bad. Warmer than the sea and the tidal pools they went to in summer before Mama was ill. A white cloud in the shape of a Scottie dog's face floated in front of the sun. A crow flew high in the sky, followed by another, flying lower with something lumpy in its beak. The leaves and new little pompoms on huge plane trees swayed as a breeze chopped across the water. Her toes and face felt the draught, but her back stayed lovely and warm.

'It's not cold, I swear,' she shouted up.

Suddenly her face was covered in water and she was tipped over by a huge splash. Bubbles of bleachy water burnt inside her nose and she thrashed about to standing.

'What in God's name are you doing, you fool!' she shouted, rubbing the water out of her eyes. But it wasn't Lucy. It was the young man with the thick eyebrows and he was smiling at her.

'It's heated, that's why,' he said, flicking water at her. 'One of the only lidos in the world that is, this is.'

Agnes stood and stared at him. His eyebrows were like one long caterpillar.

'Graham,' he said, and he clicked the corner of his mouth. He had a broad brown chest, and there was curly hair showing at the top of his bathing suit.

'I'm called Graham. What's your name?'

'The bare-faced cheek of it,' she said.

'Irish, are you?'

'Scottish.'

'Even better,' he said. 'I like foreign girls. And who's this?'

Lucy had sidled over to Agnes, walking on tiptoes and still dry above her waist. 'Don't tell me, you're sisters. Two lovely Scottish lassies. Lovely.'

Lucy looked down at the water, blushing like a wee ninny.

'See up there,' Graham pointed over to the grass. His arm was thick and bumpy with muscles, and the hair in his armpit was wet and thick. 'That there's my mate, Tobe.'

A skinny man with ginger hair and freckles was sitting on a stripy towel, reading a newspaper and smoking a ciggie.

Graham pulled his mouth wide with his thumb and finger and whistled. The shriek of it made Agnes's ears tickle.

'Oy, Tobe, here,' he yelled.

The ginger man looked over and waved. He shrugged at Graham, smiled at Lucy, stood up and walked over.

Graham suddenly duck-dived. He swam underwater, weaving around scores of other bathers' bodies, and burst through the surface again gleaming like an otter. Aggie moved her hands behind her back, and covered her wedding ring with her fingers.

They spent most of the afternoon sitting in the fountain. When they got hot, they sat on the wedding-cake tiers with the water cascading down onto their backs and shoulders. Agnes peeled off her swimming hat and threw it on the ground. When they got too wet, they moved to sit on the low hexagonal wall surrounding the fountain, with their feet in the blue-tiled paddling pool.

At half-past three Graham strode across to the swish low brick building and bought ice creams sandwiched in wafers for the four of them. Agnes watched his neat hard bottom as he walked away, and then his lumpy crotch when he came back, vanilla dripping down his front. He handed them out, took a long lick of the soft white middle with his fleshy tongue and leant back to catch more sun. Agnes's shoulders were getting very red.

'Well, say what you like, but this is the life,' he said.

'Better make the most of it, ay?' Tobe chipped in. He finished his ice cream in very small quick nibbles. 'War on its way and all that.'

'Ach, don't let's talk about the war. That's all you hear. War this, war that,' Agnes said. She shook her head to loosen up her hair.

Graham looked at her neck and chest. 'No, no. Fair play to Tobe,' he said slowly. 'It's coming, whether we like it or not. In fact, I'm signing up next week. Get in there first. Beats pushing a barrow around town.'

He lifted a pretend rifle, closed one eye and pointed at the diving boards. He made a couple of bullet noises as a large man dropped from the top board like a dumpling.

'Shot, my son,' said Tobe, clapping his freckly hands.

'Come on, then,' Graham said, pulling Agnes up and over towards the main pool. 'Time to cool off.'

Aggie swam nearly a length underwater. There were slow-moving bloated leaves and lumps of fluff at the bottom of the pool, and misty shafts of sunlight cutting through the surface. She sang a slow Al Bowlly song to herself and her ears were filled with humming. She shivered as she bumped into other people's bodies and thought again about Graham in his bathing costume.

When they got out of the pool, there was hardly anyone left on the grass. The sun was still shining, but the shadows were long. Tobe and Lucy were nowhere to be seen.

Graham looked at her. Her skin prickled as the water dried on her burnt shoulders.

'Coming?' he said, moving towards the trees and bushes.

She felt a rush of heat to her groin and nodded.

It was dank and dark and the ground was lumpy. Graham pulled her bathing costume down in one go, roughly. He was heavy and damp, and his mouth smelt of vanilla and tobacco. Bits of dirt and twigs stuck to her back and bottom. But she was warm and breathing fast. Her arms and hands pulled at his fleshy back and he tugged and squeezed her bosoms. He went into her like a battering ram. They pushed together for only a minute until he clenched his jaw and snorted. Aggie was thumping inside. Her head was light and woozy. Graham rolled off and let out a sigh followed by a rippling fart. Aggie sniggered. Ernest would have said sorry.

Tobe and Lucy were dressed, and sitting at a table outside the café, drinking cups of tea. Lucy ran over to them like a wee vexed goblin.

'Where have you been? I was so worried,' she said. 'Toby and me called out for you and searched about, but couldn't find you anywhere.' She looked at Agnes queerly and pulled a twig from her hair.

'Are you all right?' she said.

Agnes smiled. 'We went for a stroll. Had a bit of a chin-wag. I'm a bit chilly now. I'm going to get dressed.'

Tobe looked at Graham. 'Chelsea bun, matey?'

'Don't mind if I do.' He sat down at the table, and Aggie headed off for the cubicles, damp, sore and smiling.

When they got back to the flat, Ernest was waiting. He was twitching with excitement and holding a large black-and-white-checked hatbox on the dining-room table. It was tied together with a big lavender silk ribbon but the lid kept popping up and down. There was a puddle of liquid on the shiny table, and a dark stain at the bottom of the box.

'Inside, look. For you,' he rasped.

Aggie tugged impatiently at the bow.

'The sun has caught you,' he said.

'In English, we say, "You've caught the sun",' she said as two tiny fluffy grey heads with triangular ears and green eyes poked out of the box.

'You like?' he said, anxious as a schoolboy. His forehead was ruffled and his eyes narrow.

Lucy squealed and ran over. 'Ooooh, kittens, so adorable. Let me, let me.'

Aggie lifted one out of the box and held it out in front of her, her thumbs under its front legs. She stared at the wide flat face and rosebud nose. Its bottom legs and tail flailed about in the air and it let out a series of high-pitched mewls.

'You like?' Ernest said again.

She smiled. 'They'll remind me of this day. Yes, I like.'

Ernest beamed.

She named them Mister Bowlly and Fluff, and vowed to always have cats.

Lucy asked about Graham time and time again, and Agnes refused to talk. But she wouldn't let it lie, pestering like an irritating bluebottle, until Agnes had to cuff her, like the old days. Lucy went out for tea with Tobe two more times before returning to Edinburgh. They planned to keep in touch by letter, so she said.

The day war was declared, three months had passed without the curse. Agnes's nipples were brown as cocoa, and a thin beige line ran down from her navel. Her belly was round and plump like a cushion. The day war was declared, the police came for Ernest. Four beefy uniformed men banged at the door and demanded to see his papers.

'But I'm Jewish,' he said as they pushed him towards the door. 'I fled the Nazis six years ago.'

'You are Ernest Ledermann and this is a German passport, en't it?' said the biggest and beefiest, waving the book close to his face.

'Ja, well, technically, but this is crazy . . .'

'Well, German is German, and I'm arresting you,' he said, pulling Ernest's arms behind him to fit the handcuffs.

'You can't take him,' Agnes screamed, thrusting her belly out. 'Can't you see – I'm having a baby.'

Ernest stopped thrashing about and looked at her. 'You are what?' he said. His face was the colour of chalk with pinpricks of pink in the centre of his cheeks. His eyes filled with water.

'A baby,' she said.

'But . . .'

The police bundled him out of the door and down the stairs.

He was taken to Liverpool by train, and then over to the Isle of Man. By Christmas time, there was no hiding it. Her skirts and petticoats needed letting out, and corsets were no good at all. Papa and Lucy sent money. Papa wrote to say that Mama had died. She wrote to the internment camp, but heard nothing back. Mister Bowlly and Fluff took it in turns to sit on her belly, pushing and purring and digging their pinprick claws into her as the baby swooped and swam about inside.

She gave birth to Desmond on a glorious late winter day, six weeks after rationing was introduced. Papa paid for a hospital birth, as there were complications with Agnes's pelvis. Not capacious enough, were the doctor's exact words. The hospital provided Desmond with a special baby gas mask. It was like a small rubber and steel goldfish diving suit, with metal studs running around a wide glass visor. He slept inside for long stretches, and she could hardly hear him crying at all.

April 20 – Baywatch

I was in for just over a week, and I've been out for a month. My medication is still a bit on the high side, but overall I'm feeling better. Things are improving. Owen has been over to mine most days. His flat is two bus rides away and I've not had the courage yet to visit. But right now – well, I'm really not sure about this. How can plopping into a pool of pale blue chlorine be as good as popping pills? According to Doctor Hassani, as he wrote me my prescription for health, exercise is all part of the picture.

Owen would have come but he had a meeting. He thought it was a good idea, though. Try it, he said, what harm can come of it? And the pool is only down the road. He convinced me at the time, but I'm not so sure. I loved swimming at school, but that was then and this is now. I didn't sleep very well last night, worrying about it all, so this morning has been a struggle so far. I take a deep breath. It's got to be better than repeats of *Bargain Hunt*.

Also: my legs are better. I've not been scratching them so much and the scabs have nearly all gone. Plus I've got my favourite, lucky pink towel with the see-through bald patches. It's wrapped most of the way around my waist, but I'm not going out there yet.

The cubicles run alongside the pool. Each one is numbered and has a dark blue plastic shower curtain. Coming in, I walked behind the regulars and I think I looked like I knew what I was doing. But there's not enough room to turn around in this poky little hole, so as I pulled my top off, I elbowed the poxy curtain open and exposed myself. Luckily the only person out there was a bored-looking attendant sweeping bleach around the lumpy beige floor tiles with a wide broom, and she just coughed and carried on sweeping.

I'm changed and shivery, and I don't want to go out. I got my swimming costume from Help the Aged. There was only the one in my size, but it's not too bad, plain enough. It is red and has special pointy bra cups. The shoulder straps are wide and sensible and stay up even if you shrug your shoulders very hard. I tried it on in the shop, over my knickers and bra. I tried on a swimming hat there too, pixie pointy with rows of rubber scales, but that was plain ridiculous. Even I could see that. It made my eyes water when I pulled it off and anyway, my hair could do with a bit of water. I didn't even bother trying on the other hat, the one with the large floppy pink and blue flowers. According to the woman in the shop, I was lucky, spoilt for choice. Swimming hats are a thing of the past, she said, and more's the pity. She went on to explain how the lack of swimming hats went hand in hand with the rise in drug abusers and violent criminals, but I just paid her my £2.95, took the recycled Sainsburys bag and backed out of the shop slowly.

I pull the shower curtain back to peek out. It swishes across my leg and leaves a clammy trail of black mould on my thigh. I lean my head out and breathe in. The air is foggy and warm. Everything is echoey, muffled, and in slow motion. On the opposite wall the words Drowning Alarm are painted in big black paint above a large round white button that reminds me of something. A light switch, a timer light switch, like the one Nan used to have in the hallway outside her flat. Pressing it was always a strange sensation, because the click never came. It started ticking immediately, beginning its twenty-second journey to coming back out again and switching the hall light off again. Just enough time to get to her front door and knock the brass door knocker shaped like a fox. Nan was always slow answering the door, shuffling about and peeking through the letter box, saying, 'Who is it?' in a tremulous voice even though you'd phoned a bit earlier to let her know you were coming. I'd have to press the timer light switch at least one more time before she eventually opened up.

I'd like to go and push that Drowning Alarm, to see if it is a proper click button or a slow sludgy timer press. What do you do if it goes off? Do we have to evacuate the water? I look around for someone to ask, but all I can see is a bloke sitting in a tall white plastic chair on stilts, like some monstrous fairy-tale highchair. He is wearing a blue polo shirt and shorts, his feet are bare and he looks so bored it would be rude to interrupt him. *Baywatch* this pool is not.

There are other notices on the wall. Lots of large red circles with diagonal slashes running through them. The blobby black drawings inside the circles are what is being prohibited, and I can just about make them out if I concentrate for long enough and squint my eyes. No Diving, No Running. One of the red circles is shaped like a love heart. The black blob is shaped like a pair of lips. No Petting. Very funny that one; knight the graphic designer.

I could have been a graphic designer if I wanted. But I preferred the freer wackier ways of fine art. Natalie said we'd be wasted on graphics, and once, when we were in the college toilets, she got her nail scissors out of her bag and cut us both in the tip of opposite index fingers. We had to solemnly swear that we would never squander our talents on the squalid world of commerce. I can't remember the exact wording of the oath now, but when I rub the tip of my finger I can just feel the tiny shiny scar. She cut us deep, and the blood sat like fat little ladybirds until we squished them together. Natalie's blood was slightly lighter than mine, even though her skin was five shades darker. It was only afterwards that I worried about HIV, but Timmy said that was all blown out of all proportion and not to worry. And he was the one to know.

I sometimes wonder what I'd be doing now if I had a career. Maybe graphics. Even though my blood sister is dead and gone at the side of a motorbike, my fingertip pulses at the disloyal thought. Nat always had style: very Jimmy Dean; very live fast, die young. But it left me without her.

I like signs, though – always have. I've spent lots of happy hours looking at signs, wondering who thinks them up, who actually makes them. There have been times, of course, when I've been absolutely convinced that signs are saying more than they should, that some of them are up there to give me and a few other chosen people special messages. But not at the moment. These are health and safety signs in a local municipal swimming pool. No more, no less. Nothing to do with a new world order or how to save yourself, all to do with not drowning. Has anyone drowned in there?

People have begun to emerge from their cubicles. They are drawn to the pool like zombies in nylon, in a rush to get the best swimming spot. Positions near the sides are popular.

I stand up. I have to do this now, if I'm going to do this. I hold my towel around my waist and walk towards the shallow end, keeping my eyes on the plastic weeping fig in the white tub in the corner. A scrawny man with skin like pinhead porridge brushes past me in his rush, and I am overtaken by three more people before I reach the side. Slow lane on the motorway every time, that's me. I look around, but the sides are empty now. The pool is awash with activity, arms, legs flapping about in the same general direction, up and down, up and down. The lifeguard is looking at his fingernails. I unwrap my towel from my waist and quickly chuck it against the back wall where it lands like roadkill. I turn round and grab the metal handles sticking up above the steps. They're slippy and hard. I lean one foot back down, and scrape my shin finding the first step.

I brace myself for a shock of cold, but the water is warm like soup. My legs itch a tiny bit. I stand still, with the bleachy liquid lapping around my waist. This isn't bad, it's going to be alright. I don't need to do my finger pressing. I watch the other swimmers go up and down, up and down. There are a couple of women who are doing lengths that finish where I'm standing. One of them is about sixty with tight curly dyed black hair and very thin eyebrows. She's got perfect make-up, and is swimming a really still breaststroke so her face never goes underwater. The other woman is big and blousy in a pink checked costume and, yes, a swimming hat. She looks like a plump Mekon matron, so Christ alone knows what I'd have looked like in that one from Help the Aged. Good call. They arrive at the side near me at different times, but they are both huffy that I am standing there, and give me dirty looks.

I prepare for take-off several times, but each time I duck down to my shoulders in the water and take a deep breath, my window of opportunity, my yard of clear water disappears in a sea of blobbing bodies. I'm beginning to get cold. A pale old bloke with a white moustache, barrel belly, thin blue legs and stripy green trunks climbs down the steps and nearly drops his arse on top of my head.

'Scuse I,' he says in a gargle.

I close my eyes and push off from the side.

Water swooshes in my ears and I rush along at a fine pace.

The woman with the make-up stops and stands up to wipe her face. She gives me a filthy look before bobbing down to continue, but I'm well away, halfway up to the deep end. My body has never felt so light and in control. I flip round onto my back and send the air hissing out of my lips as I narrow my eyes and look at the rainbow patterns on the lights on the ceiling. The sun is coming out and Hand of God shafts of light are shining through the windows. They light up millions of water droplets and dust motes. I'm so busy looking at all this useless beauty that when I reach the other end, I bang my head on the wall. The shock sends me under the water where I flail about for a second before resurfacing the right way, right in front of the old bloke. He has tiny eyes and his white moustache is very thick. He gives me a small smile before continuing back the other way in his blubbery lolloping sidestroke with his belly dangling half in the water. Walrus, he is exactly like a walrus.

I try a length of backstroke on my return length. I smack someone in the head when I raise my arm, so after that I swim like I'm in a coffin, arms crossed over my chest. I'm about two-thirds up the length when I feel something soft and slow swipe over my right thigh. I crane my neck, look around and catch sight of green stripes, but everywhere is awash with pensioners' limbs.

I spend some time at the deep end, pretending to be a mermaid when no one is around. I haven't had such fun in years. So I'm in a happy mood as I set off for another length. Halfway down again I feel a rub, this time up the length of my left leg, ending with a bit of a slap. Not an accident. I stop swimming and stand up. Water runs right into my sinuses and burns behind my nose. As I turn round I see the back of the walrus man's head and his stripy trunks heading towards the deep end.

I feel sick and want to cry. I fold my arms around my chest and wade down to the safety of the wall at the shallow end. As I haul myself up the steps, the walrus man is just below me, treading water and looking up. I turn my head right round and frown at him. My mouth won't form words. He wrinkles his mouth up and his moustache quivers. You Dirty Leering Old Bastard, I want to shout, but he is off again in his lolloping sidestroke through the blue ripples.

My mouth is full of mucus and bleach. I pick up my towel from the side and try to cover my arse as I skid over to the cubicles. I dry myself too quickly and my legs are so clammy that I can't pull my leggings up. I sit down on the wooden slats to do my socks, and catch something small and brown out of the corner of my eye. I feel the sweaty panic coming over me. I close my eyes and lift my feet up onto the bench. I nearly totter over, but blow slow and deep through my nose the way Owen showed me. After a minute, I open my eyes, turn my head and look. A piece of mud from my trainers is on the floor. I put my feet down carefully and prod it just to be sure. There's just a blade of grass poking out of it.

I go out to the machine in the lobby. I put in fifteen 10p pieces and press the buttons for three Mars bars and a packet of Quavers. I eat one of the Mars bars and shiver. I'm starting to open the second one when a lifeguard walks by. I think about the dirty old man touching me. It wasn't right. Perhaps it's the endorphins created by the exercise, just like Doctor Hassani said; or perhaps it's just that I've had enough, but I go up and tap him on the shoulder.

'Excuse me,' I say.

It's the David Hasselhoff one from the poolside highchair.

'Yes madam,' he says in a voice like Ken Livingstone.

'I'd like to report an incident.'

'Oh yes? What kind of incident?'

I know it will sound weird, but I have to say it very quickly all in one breath, just to get it out of my system, otherwise I won't say it at all.

'A horrible dirty old walrus man touched me and slapped me on the leg he was wearing green stripy trunks and had a big white moustache and I didn't want him to and it made me feel sick.' I take in a huge breath and wait for his response.

David Hasselhoff doesn't laugh, he doesn't sneer. He folds his arms and shakes his head slowly. 'Not again,' he mutters.

I look behind me to see if he is talking to someone else.

'Thank you very much for reporting this, madam. I am sorry that the incident has spoilt your visit, but can I assure you that the matter will be taken very seriously.' And with that he produces a voucher for a free swim.

Being believed makes me glow.

I open the door to my flat. Darth Vadar is in humming mode.

'Hello, Darth,' I say, but I don't open his door. I go over to my little table and get out my best green gel pen and some paper. I take off my parka, dump my carrier of wet swimming things and sit on the edge of the bed. Owen says that writing things down can help. Like a diary, but not a diary. This is what I write.

The day started badly (lack of sleep) but overall result. Swim (not done for twenty years); only ate two (out of three) Mars bars; not scared of bugs, plus took action on Dirty Leering Man. I'm definitely on the up.

I think about going over to Owen's flat.

1934

The only brother who survived was Arthur. And he was shot down and killed in France less than a decade later. First wee Matty, then baby Jimmy, and finally Robbie joined Frank in the family plot at Joppa. Matty and the baby were strangled by diphtheria, and Robbie smothered by pneumonia three years on.

After Robbie died, Mama wouldn't get out of bed. The heavy maroon brocade curtains were closed for weeks. The house was quiet, and Agnes took care of Arthur, Lucy and Dolly, fetching them meals, ordering them about and keeping the place clean and tidy. She took porridge, soups, neeps and tatties up to Mama too, but she barely ate a thing.

In the afternoons, Agnes would walk across the Meadows to the upstairs office of Walker and Walker. Old Mr Walker had met Papa when he'd visited the Customs and Excise office. He'd needed a clerk for filing and basic bookkeeping duties and Papa had jumped at the opportunity for Agnes.

'Not for the income, you understand, Jack, but the lass needs to get out and make the most of herself,' Papa had said, fingering his wallet inside his pocket, as she stood in front of the old Mr Walker a few days later.

The old man was sitting on a straight-backed chair, and stared intently at her chest all the while. The office was bitterly cold and the work was numbingly dull.

One December morning, after she'd pushed Papa to work, Agnes went upstairs with bread and dripping and a cup of tea, and Mama was up. She was looking out of the window, wearing her big brown cloak with the shiny silver feather brooch. Agnes stopped by the door. She was taller than Mama. She'd not grown that much: more likely Mama had shrunk whilst she was lying in bed.

Mama turned round. Her face was the colour of cheese, and there were dark fish-skin rings under her eyes. In the middle of her watery blue eyes, her pupils were black like raisins. They flickered around the room. She only filled half the cloak now, which hung limply round her ankles. Mama's mouth was opening up and down, but no sound was coming out.

'Mama?' Agnes said, staying by the door.

Mama smiled.

Agnes took a step into the room.

'Good to see you up, Mama. Are you feeling all better now?' Agnes gulped.

Mama's mouth began to open and close again, and Agnes could catch the sound of words. She had a book open in front of her: Mama, who couldn't read. Mama turned round to the window again, and the talking was louder. Agnes took a breath and walked over. She tapped Mama on the shoulder and the old family Bible dropped to the floor with a dusty thud.

'And the blood shall be to you for a token upon the houses where ye are, and when I see the blood, I will pass over you,' Mama rasped. She waved out of the window with sweeping arms, her cloak opening like a bishop's cape.

Agnes touched Mama's cheek and eased her head away from the window. She looked down to see who Mama was talking to, but the street was empty aside from two fat grey pigeons and a wandering Jack Russell.

'Mama? Mama, what's wrong wi you?'

Mama's eyes flicked over Agnes's head and she turned back to the window and spoke much much louder: 'And the plague shall not be upon you to destroy you, when I smite the land of Egypt.' She began to sing, a low mournful hymn with words that Agnes didn't recognize.

'Mama, Mama, do you know who I am?'

But Mama closed her eyes and was lost in the dirge.

Agnes didn't know what to do. She tried sitting Mama down on the bed, but she was stiff as yew and wouldn't move.

All of a sudden, Mama rushed right up close to the glass. She pressed her cheek against the pane and pushed up at the sash, grunting like a sow. At first it didn't move. She grunted more and it shifted. Outside the pigeons had gone, but the doggie was still sniffing the gutter. Mama leant down to peek her head through the gap. She snorted in the fresh air, humming the dirge all the while, her lips flapping and vibrating. She pressed the window higher, swung round and hoiked herself up to sitting on the sill, facing Agnes.

A noise like a frightened lamb made its way out of Agnes's mouth. For a moment, she couldn't move, but when Mama shifted her backside down way over the edge, babbling about babbies and her eyes glittering like fire, Agnes grabbed her by the cloak. The silver feather brooch flew off and landed in a dustball under the bed.

Mama fell forward in a tumble on the floor, and was finally quiet.

Whilst Mama snored and snuffled, Agnes paced the room. Lucy would be home from her new job at the milliner's shop for her lunch soon. Then she could leave Mama and get help. She'd run straight up the hill, all the way to Princes Street without stopping. It'd take a quarter of the time without Papa's wheelchair to push. He'd be cross with her for bothering him at work, but would understand when he saw Mama's flickering watery raisin eyes.

The asylum was in Morningside. It used to be the workhouse. They didn't visit. Papa said it was best not to. But occasionally – holidays or sometimes Saturdays – Agnes and Lucy would take a tram ride across town. If the tram neared the gentle Morningside hill with its grey slated villas, Agnes became hot and sick. She would feel prickles in her fingertips, and her knees had a pressure inside them that made her judder her legs up and down. Lucy would prattle on louder and faster when Agnes juddered, and they had an unspoken agreement never to get off near Morningside.

The girls' favourite tram game was pretending to be continental. Agnes didn't quite have the nerve to do her full and unadulterated Marlene in trousers, but she would often pull her beret across her hair in a dramatic slash, and rub her lips fiercely in the hopes they'd look redder. One day Lucy came home from Madame Florence's with an Oxblood lipstick. Cherie, one of the hat makers, had given it to her. Agnes had that straight away.

'You're much too young for that,' she'd said, snatching the pot and holding it tight in her hand. 'Besides, it's far, far too dark for your milky complexion.' She drawled the phrase in the weedy voice that made Lucy mad. Lucy was easy pickings. She'd cried and pulled and pummelled at her to get it back, of course, but Agnes just held her hand up high and laughed.

Lucy's tram continental look was more peasant-like. She wrapped a scarf around her head, nodded vigorously and would make lots of hand gestures, whilst Agnes mouthed exotic words from glossy red lips.

Whitsun that year was mild. Papa stayed in bed because it was a holiday. Dolly wanted to come but Lucy smacked her and told her to go play with her dollies. Arthur was out with his pals, up to no good. One of the lads had a shotgun from his uncle, who was a farmer, and they spent days shooting at small animals and birds. Sometimes Arthur would come back smeared in blood, but smiling. He didn't smile much otherwise.

Agnes and Lucy slammed the front door behind them and ran out to the road, squealing like piglets. Lucy pounded her feet up and down on the pavement in a frenzy, whilst Agnes opened her arms wide and breathed in so hard that her backbone made a cracking noise.

The breeze was warm. They could hear a baby giggling through an upstairs window, and the smell of lamb roasting in lard snaked up their nostrils as they passed the house on the corner. They said very little to each other as they strode up to town. There were a lot of folk out in the sunshine. A large shiny man in a bowler hat with a tiny tan dog on a lead walked towards them.

'Fine morning,' he said, and he tipped his hat.

The girls looked at the doggie and smirked.

'Bon jo-ur,' said Agnes. Lucy opened her hands and tipped her head sideways but didn't speak.

A pair of old women with faces caked in white powder passed them. They were both carrying umbrellas and walked in step with each other.

'Good morning, lassies.' They spoke in identical creaky voices.

'Madames,' said Agnes, curtsying, and Lucy snorted.

The old women smiled at the girls and walked on.

'Ze people round 'ere, zey are, 'ow you say, so common,'

Agnes hissed at Lucy as they approached the tram stop. 'Zey leeve in a small world wiz ze tiny weeny small-world ideas.' She poked Lucy in time with the words, until she was tickling her and Lucy was chuckling and trying to get away. Agnes carried on, reaching under Lucy's armpits and wiggling and pinching. Lucy's face was red, and her eyes watered.

'Stop, stop.' She was having trouble breathing, but Aggie didn't stop.

Then Lucy rolled her eyes, gasped for air several times and sneezed, spraying snot out in a huge arc.

'Gesundheit, mein leetle seester,' said Agnes.

Lucy lunged forward to get Agnes back, and Agnes jumped out of the way, knocking into a man waiting at the tram stop.

'Pardon, Herr, mein mistake,' she said as she straightened up.

Lucy wiped her face, smirking and laughing.

'Nicht, think nothing of it.' He spoke clearly and without irony, and his voice was deep and liquidy.

Agnes stood still and gulped.

'You speak German?' he continued. He was quite old, slightly shorter than Agnes, and on the stout side. He was carrying a bulky briefcase, holding it very tightly in his paw. His head was bald, completely bald. His boots were of an unusual continental style. Rather high and tight. Agnes thought of Erich Von Stroheim. But this man wore a long blue coat, and although it fitted well, Erich would never wear blue. Besides, his face was podgy, like clootie dumpling, and he was confused.

'Ja, mein Fräulein?' he said again, and a dimple appeared on his left cheek.

He had a large nose and his eyes were brown. The colour of polished walnut. Agnes had never seen brown eyes before.

Blue, grey and green, with and without flecks, but never brown.

'No, not really. Just messing around,' she said, in her ordinary voice.

The dimple disappeared and the brown eyes lost their glint.

'Are you German?' Agnes asked. Lucy nudged Agnes.

'My family are from there. I had to leave.' His mouth made unusual smacking noises between phrases.

'Why?'

'Trouble brewing for our people. No place to be.'

The tram came. The man bowed to Agnes, picked up his bulky bag and turned to get on it. Five other people at the stop followed him on. One red-headed bearded man stood out of his way and scowled. The tram was going to Morningside. Agnes watched the solid little man with the salivary voice find his way to a seat. No one sat down next to him. He looked out of the window and she saw his brown eyes again.

Life at home was boring and drudgy. Lucy got on Agnes's nerves with her wittering ways. A good smack put paid to her tormenting Agnes about the plump Jew-boy, as she called him, but she continued to flounce around the house like a mayfly.

Papa hardly spoke. After work he'd eat his meal and settle down to an evening of drinking whisky. He fell asleep in his chair and would still be there in the morning. The house had a permanent smell of malt and biscuits.

It was worse at Walker and Walker's. Old Mr Walker still looked at Agnes's chest too often, whilst young Mr Walker took every opportunity to humiliate her and tell her off. She called him the Weasel, but only to herself. The office was usually bitterly cold and damp, and Agnes took to wearing her muffler all day. One day after Whitsun, there was a late snap of evil snow. Mr Lindsey, the clerk, had spoken to the Mr Walkers and they relented, allowing Agnes to light a fire in the grate of the main office. She laid wood and kindling and soon had it roaring away. The red and yellow flames were the only bright thing in the paper-filled room. She loved fires. When she had her own house and her own husband, she was going to have a fire going all the time, even in summer.

Later Agnes was sent out as usual to buy teacakes for everyone in the office. She ducked into an icy closie on the way back from the bakers and opened the warm bag. She lifted the lids of two of the teacakes and spat in them, as was her habit.

'One for the father, one for the son,' she chanted under her breath.

She put them back in the bag and twisted the corners. The paper looked rather crumpled, but nobody ever noticed. She headed back down the street to the office.

A short man in a big coat went in the door and up the stairs before her. The stairway was darker than usual, and smoky like a kipper house. The smoke was worse at the top of the stairs, and it smelt queer, like factories, not like woodsmoke at all. The man was standing in the smoke, and when he turned round, Agnes saw his large nose and brown eyes.

'Ernest Ledermann. Come to see Mr Walker,' he said in his ripe voice. Then he jerked his head back like a chicken. 'Thetrolleybusgesundheitgirl,' he said, as the young Mr Walker's door flew open and he raced out, not seeing the man.

'What the hell is all this smoke, girl?' he shouted.

Agnes shrugged. Shrugging always made him mad. He lunged towards her with his teeth gritted, and his hand in the air.

'Well I suggest you find out, you imbecile. Why on earth we had to waste decent wood at this time of the year in the first place, I—'

The man coughed. The Weasel jumped straight up in the air, his hand still raised. With his floppy hair and his wee moustache, he put Agnes in mind of Adolf Hitler and she giggled. The man snorted too.

'Mr Walker, this is Mr Layda . . . Laydaman.'

Mr Ledermann nodded and thrust his hand out. Mr Walker quickly lowered his arm, flattened his fringe and shook his hand.

'An appointment I have, with Mr Walker at 3 p.m.,' he said.

'Please, please, do come this way. And may I apologize for the . . . the . . . atmospheric condition in here.'

Mr Walker ushered Mr Ledermann into his room.

'How long are you staying in the city?' he asked in a high light voice.

'One week only.'

'You must find Edinburgh quiet compared with London?'

Agnes didn't hear the answer. She thought she'd got away with it.

But the Weasel turned back and hissed, waving his hand through the smoke, 'Clear this up.'

The smoke was getting thicker. No doubt about it. The flames were still bonny. More than bonny really. Reaching up very, very high. Agnes put the teacakes on her desk and knelt in front of the grate. She peeked up the flue. The chimney was aglow. It was gorgeous. She stared up with her mouth open, and a huge clump of burning orange and white soot fell down. She pulled her head out of the way, but the clump landed on her muffler. It burnt through the grey wool into her neck before bouncing onto the rug in front of the fire.

Agnes screamed. The smouldering wool smelt sour. She'd never felt such pain. She pulled the muffler off and touched her neck. She screamed again and sat back on the floor. Young Mr Walker's door opened again.

'What the hell is going on in here?' he shouted. His voice was not high and light now. He spotted the smouldering rug and let out a squeal. 'It's on fire! It's on fire! What have you done, you stupid girl?'

Mr Ledermann plodded out behind him, walked over to the rug and trod the fire out.

'A chimney fire. You must put this fire out with a bucket of water,' he said, crouching down to look at Agnes.

'Agnes, girl, fetch a bucket,' boomed Mr Walker.

Mr Ledermann stood up. 'The girl is hurt. You get the bucket, ja?'

Her neck was throbbing, and she felt sick. The smoke was dark and thick. The tickle in her throat became a full-throttled cough and she couldn't stop shaking.

Mr Walker didn't move.

'The bucket. Get the bucket now,' Mr Ledermann said slowly and carefully.

Mr Walker huffed and headed off downstairs. Mr Ledermann patted Agnes on the back gently until she gradually stopped coughing. Up this close, even through the smoke, she could smell cigars and a heavy cologne on his coat.

'Water, you need also,' he said, lifting her by the arm whilst waving the smoke away with a large handkerchief in his other hand. 'To drink, and for your neck.'

'But what about all this?' Agnes hissed. Her eyes were watering and all she could see was grey.

'Leave it to the shmok,' he said.

'I beg your pardon?'

'Don't beg, sell matches,' he said as they passed the Weasel, dragging a full bucket up the stairs. Water sloshed down his legs and he cursed all the way up. Agnes, raw eyes, burnt neck and no voice, laughed. Weasel. Shmok. She could just see his pale eyes narrowing at her through the gloom.

Ernest Ledermann, she thought. Brown eyes, funny words and foreign smells. London. That would do.

April 22–May 6 – Funny Old Bird

I went out with a few boys at college every now and then, but I didn't have a lot of sex. Not like Nat. The two of us would go down to the student bar and drink snakebites until we could hardly stand up. Nat had two squirts of blackcurrant in hers, to look like blood, but I always had plain cider and lager. More sophisticated, we'd say, taking the piss, although underneath we did really think we were sophisticated. There were a couple of punky boys who we'd meet up with down there in the dark, smelly bar with its loud thrashing music. They looked alarming – well, that was the idea – but they were public school-boys and very polite. Edward and Rupert, they were called. Edward had short bleached spiky hair and a cobweb tattoo on his face. Rupert had an eighteen-inch cerise mohican.

One time the four of us ended up in the stairwell behind the bar for the night. I don't remember how we got there, but I remember waking up with a terrible stiff neck and a mouth so dry it felt like all the saliva had been extracted by a dentist's sucker. There was a big dent in my temple from where my head had been leaning against the corner of a step whilst I was sleeping. My arse was dead and cold. The lights were out and the stairwell stank of Jeyes Fluid and piss. The other three were in a pile a flight above me. My knickers and jeans were intact.

Since the accident and hospital and everything, I've never really met anyone that I liked, or anyone that liked me. Not until Owen. So I do it, I only bloody go and do it. Right money, two buses, on my own and I'm here in his flat. He met me at the bus stop.

One wall of the sitting room is completely made up of window. This town is full of blocks of retirement flats, with proper balconies covered with garden furniture. Owen's little ledge is streaked white and grey; a family of pigeons lives on it. His former flatmate took a shovel to some pigeon eggs once, and Owen chucked him out.

'No, goodness me, no. Not literally chucked him out,' he says, screwing his face up on the word 'literally' like Malcolm Muggeridge. 'No, I threw him out, told him to get on his way, on his bike, find somewhere else to lay his hat. I wasn't going to live with a murdering cycle-path. That's what I told him. There's enough violence in this world, I said, without you going all spare with a shovel on some innocent pigeons. And him a vegan. Frankly, I'm amazed that Maisie stayed with her eggs after seeing him towering over her like that.' He pauses for breath and purses his lips.

'Anyway, he used to smother himself in Lynx, and he never did the washing-up.' He looks at me again.

This is the great thing about being with Owen. I don't actually have to say very much, but he takes my views into account.

'Oh, alright then, he was leaving anyway. He was getting a flat with his boyfriend. But I did tell him that threatening innocent pigeons was unacceptable behaviour.'

The view from Owen's flat is monumental. It is on the seventeenth floor, so you can see an entire stretch of coastline, flat like a map. The waves are still from this height, and the strings of lights along the street and on the pier are just coming on. I can see the toytown cars and lorries along the coast road, but they are quiet and rumbling compared with the purring and juddering of the pigeons.

'Are you alright then, lovee? Enough to eat?' Owen takes my plate and puts it on the breakfast bar that separates the kitchen from the sitting room.

I nod and smile.

I rub my stomach and lean back on the leopard-skin cushions. Owen changes the CD. We'd been laughing at Spandau Ballet. It was hard to laugh at Ella Fitzgerald. He comes and sits down beside me. I gulp. He looks into my left eye and then my right eye.

'You know I really like you,' he says.

'Yes.'

I lean up to kiss him on his cushiony lips but he moves his head at the same time, and I kiss his chin instead. We try again. It's like coming home after a bad day at school.

We kiss for a long time, the kisses getting harder, more complicated and turning to licking. We move on from faces to necks, shoulders, chests and nipples. Owen has got a pierced nipple, and when I fiddle with the silver ring, his pink-tipped flesh goes wrinkly and pinker.

We are panting. My legs are like water and I am shivery all over.

'You've got goosebumps,' he whispers. His voice is low and hoarse. 'Shall I put on the fire? Make it hot in here?'

The tap in the kitchen is dripping loudly. The shivers turn to shakes. My jaw rams shut, and my tongue turns from fluid to cardboard.

'No. Don't put on the fire,' I hiss. I don't want to be in a hot room and left all alone with a dripping tap.

'What is it? What's wrong?'

But I don't know. I can't say. I can't remember.

Owen is patient. He says he doesn't mind, and I believe him. 'I haven't had a shag for eight years, so a wait isn't going to do me any harm,' he says, bringing me coffee in a bright yellow *Simpsons* mug. It is made with beans that have been flavoured with rum and topped with spray-can whipped cream.

'I want to,' is all I can say.

'Then we shall,' he says, like he's talking about going to Tesco. 'But only when the time is right.'

The room is cold, and I have got the fake-fur throw off the sofa wrapped around my shoulders.

'You look like Boadicea,' he says.

I lift my hand, batting the palm against my mouth as I make the noise of a playground Red Indian. 'Ah whah whah whah whah whah whah whah.'

'What happened, Jodie?' he says.

I shake my head. He waits.

'Something to do with Roger, I think.'

'Who's Roger?'

'My nan's second husband. He looked like a gnome.' I remember the feeling of being abandoned. Of darkness and being alone. My mouth feels hungry. I can't remember any more. I screw my eyes up and think of pigeons instead. I won't think about what happened.

I stay the night. Owen has a king-size mattress on the floor in the bedroom, and we huddle together, listening to the faraway traffic and the family of birds on the ledge. I drift in and out of sleep. I'm warm at last.

In the morning, I am hungry, really properly hungry, not just mouth hungry. My stomach is growling. Owen makes us sandwiches of sardines and chopped egg in slices of economy white bread.

'It's the closest I can get to doing smoked salmon and croissants on a budget.'

I eat mine slowly, tasting it properly and feeling all the lumps and chunks go down. I only need one. Owen is very quiet this morning, looking at me and holding my hand but keeping that little mouth shut most of the time.

Eventually he coughs and says, 'Is he still alive?'

'No, he died. Lung cancer, I think.'

'What about your nan?'

'Yes, she is.'

'Was he bad to her?'

'Well, she divorced him.'

Owen goes to his tiny minibar of a fridge, and pulls out two cartons. He mixes us semi-skimmed milk and orange juice smoothies, frowning like a TV chef. He brings over two tall glasses, topped with glacé cherries.

Then he shimmies over to a 1950s kitchen dresser in the far corner of the sitting room. It is painted bright orange, with purple drawers. He opens the drop-leaf work surface, rustles around inside and pulls out a photo frame.

'This is my lot,' he says. 'Handsome bunch.'

It is a family grouping. About twenty-five people all holding up glasses, squinting into the sunlight and smiling. In the middle, sitting on a fancy garden bench, is a smug-looking man. He is stocky, wearing a tight blue blazer, and has the most unlikely eyebrows. Or should I say eyebrow – it is like one great big blond caterpillar.

'My Granddad Gray's seventieth. The last time we all got together.'

'He looks . . . interesting,' I say. I discover a little chunk of chopped egg lodged between a front incisor and my gum, and use my tongue to move it to the back of my mouth for swallowing.

'Well, you could say that,' he smirks.

'Why's he called Gray? He looks more white to me.'

'Short for Graham,' Owen explains.

He slurps his smoothie up through a black bendy cocktail straw, making a noise like a pneumatic drill, frowning again.

'You could go and see her.'

'I did.'

He stops drinking and looks at me like I'm Mother Theresa or someone really important. Naked admiration. My face goes red and I lean down and take a sip of my drink. It is a disgusting grey with flecks of beige, and tastes sweet and cheesy at the same time. Owen is still gawping at me.

'Not to ask her about . . . you know. But that day when you and me first met on the coach, I was going to see her.'

'Well, Lordy, Lordy, there's a thing,' he smiles, before wiping the bottom of his glass with the end of the straw and licking the drips off.

'Would you come with me, if I go again?' I ask.

'Of course,' he says, without blinking. 'Don't you want the rest of that?'

I try to smile but it ends up a weird scowl and he laughs.

'It's okay, they're an acquired taste,' he says, sliding the glass over and sucking hungrily on my straw.

Two weeks later we do the coach trip again. This time, the bluebells are out in force, like armies of aliens huddled in front gardens and along embankments, waiting for their marching orders. Owen just raises an eyebrow when I say this to him, and then carries on with his planning and paperwork for the rally next month.

When we reach Mildred Mayfield House, Nurse Christine isn't there and the day room is empty. We follow a young male nurse down an echoey corridor, leaving the modern part of the building behind us. The old block is like another world. The floors are covered in lino and the temperature drops about twenty degrees. The walls are painted two colours: dark sludgy green below the dado, and pale piss yellow above.

We end up in a long conservatory, which is mainly used for storing furniture: plastic stacking chairs, a huge old television and a couple of filing cabinets. An old man is snoring and muttering in a wheelchair, parked next to a wicker table with a high pile of magazines. Long beige dry leaves hang down from a half-dead spider plant in a wrought-iron flowerpot holder above his head. When his nose whistles, a baby plantlet on a manky tendril moves in and out in time with his breathing.

'It's such a lovely day,' the nurse suddenly says. It is the first time he has spoken to us and he has a sweet quiet Irish voice. He takes us to a pair of glass doors. 'And the garden is so lovely at this time of year,' he says, walking out into the sunshine.

I stop still at the sight of the garden. Never mind garden, it is more like the grounds of a stately home. I can see the huge lawn running downhill from the conservatory, with the ancient cedar tree in the middle. Chuck in a few lions and a couple of fountains, and you could be at Longleat. The low branches of the tree have shaded the grass underneath it into a big brown circle. Four or five more people in wheelchairs are dotted around the thick tree trunk, facing outwards. A couple of old women are sitting on a bench near a flowerbed stuffed with dark bushy shrubs. The sun bouncing off their Zimmer frames blinds me so I have to screw up my eyes.

'God, look at it,' I say.

'I know,' says the nurse, standing with his hands on his hips, looking down. 'It's being sold off and redeveloped in the summer,' he says, walking away towards a sprouting pampas grass, so we can't hear the rest of his sentence. He pushes some of the tall spiky leaves aside with the back of his arm and there's another wheelchair just behind the flowerbed. She is sleeping, wheezing away like a kettle about to boil. Her head is bent over onto her left shoulder and her mouth is open. There is a line of dribble running out of her mouth like a snail's trail, and bruises on her neck.

'How did she get them?' I ask.

'Ah, those. She's a funny old bird, is Agnes,' says the nurse, gently rocking her shoulder and talking into her ear.

'You did them yourself, didn't you, Agnes, ay?' He raises his voice a bit. 'Agnes, you've got visitors, time to wake up, now, there's a good girl.'

'What on earth do you mean, she did them herself?' says Owen.

The nurse stops rocking Nan, and stands up. He talks quietly, with his palms in front of him.

'Look, I know it sounds unlikely, but she really is a funny old bird. You must know that already. Last week, she got upset. We don't know what precipitated it, but she was found in her room, trying to strangle herself.'

'You can't give yourself bruises. It's impossible,' says Owen with authority.

Something inside my head pings. I look up at the sun. Nan snorts and opens one eye. Her nose is red. She dips her bumpy arthritic fingers into the cuff of her thin lavender top, circling them around, concentrating and feeling for something. Eventually, she pulls out a hard grey ball of tissue. She puts it in her lap and uses both hands to gradually pick it open, slowly plucking and pulling until it's a flat wrinkly square, covered in yellow snotty streaks. It's like watching a flower open in time-lapse photography. She strokes it flat and looks up at us.

'It's all been recorded and dealt with. The doctor has seen her and we've upped her medication,' the nurse continues.

'You're a lot calmer now, aren't you, Agnes?' he says loudly. 'Feeling a bit happier, aren't you?'

She looks at him and then turns her head to the pampas grass, looking up and down the long fluffy spears. A black bumble bee the size of a wine gum flies by. She raises her hand.

'Joos boot,' she says, following it with her eyes, until they settle on my face.

'Hello, Nan,' I say.

She opens her mouth and takes in a long gasping breath; her chest rattles. She sneezes so hard the pampas grass shakes. Strings of see-through snot run down into her mouth. The nurse reaches down and quickly gives her a clean fresh tissue from his pocket. Must have been a boy scout. Nan looks at the new tissue and smiles but she slowly collects the snot into her mouth with her tongue.

'Oh, Aggie, what are you doing?' he says. He snatches the tissue from her lap and wipes her nose hard. She closes her eyes.

'Well, I'll leave you to it,' the nurse says, more singsong than before. He strides off towards the cedar tree.

Me and Owen sit on the grass. Nan sighs and opens her eyes again. She looks at me for a while and leans over and feels the material of my new turquoise Hawaii shirt between her finger and thumb, like a tailor feeling for quality.

'Nice,' she says, 'pretty.'

'Thanks.'

She looks at Owen and shakes her head. 'It's no good. Don't

tell him about the money. Him, him. Such a mess, such a mess. And all that clearing up.'

I say what we practised.

'Nan?'

'I'll have them, all of them,' she says, rubbing her neck.

I look at Owen, and he nods.

'Nan? Do you remember Roger?'

She stops talking and purses her lips. 'And he was no better than he should have been. Did you know that? All that drink, but no feet. He had no feet.'

'Roger? Your second husband? Can you remember him?'

'Hummph. Sausages indeed.'

'Nan, do you remember when I used to come over for tea? When I was a girl. Do you remember?'

'A little girl, such a sweet little girl. Lovely hair, like beautiful clouds, ribbons and bows, loose loose, that's what we said.'

'If Mum was busy or going out, I'd come over to your house, and Roger was there.'

But she's twirling tufts of brittle white hair around her fingers and looking up at the sky with her mouth open. She starts humming an old tune. She used to sing it all the time. A big tear is collecting in the corner of her right eye. She slowly closes her lids, and the teardrop rolls out of her eye onto her cheek.

My stomach tightens and I get on my knees so I can use the side of my hand to wipe it. I'm gentle as I can be, my pink sausage fingers curled against her pale crinkly skin, but she flinches. I wait a minute. A bird is twittering in the tree above, bees and flies buzz around. A plane drones across the sky.

'Nan? Do you remember him?'

She doesn't open her eyes, but she shakes her head. It is a small shake, just a bit more than a twitch really, but it is an answer. Then she is shaking her head over and over again and moaning.

I open my mouth to ask again, but Owen touches my shoulder.

'Enough,' he says.

He's right, of course. But it's not nearly enough for me. My stomach is bubbling and my jaw is tight. My legs are itching like mad. We sit and hold hands for a while, looking around at the gardens and up at the cloudless sky. Nan quietens down, but somewhere on the other side of the lawn another old woman is mewing for her mother.

'It's not right,' I say.

He shrugs and nods at the same time, like a caricature of an East End Jewish tailor. A what-can-you-do type shrug.

'We must be able to do something,' I say.

Owen just gives a smaller shrug, but I'm on a roll. I stand up.

'You know and I know what it's like to be locked up. You need help, that's what you need,' I whisper in a hiss, eyeing up all the exits and judging the staff-to-patient ratio. 'Help, and a plan.'

1932

As the years went on, Papa got better. It was Agnes's job to push him to work at the Customs and Excise office on Princes Street. Day in, day out, he sat in his Bath chair with the green tartan rug across his lap, and the neighbours would wave and greet him, paying not one bit of attention to Agnes as she huffed and puffed. But over time it gave her fine broad shoulders and arm muscles like seed potatoes. She was far stronger than any of the lads, even Arthur, who was much taller than her now, and twice as wide. She could always push over his big lardy arm during their daily arm-wrestling matches. Quite often he cried, which was even better. Frank was too weedy to bother with, and usually in bed anyway, and Robbie, Matty and the baby didn't count. Not that she'd hurt Matty, even if he was big enough. Matty was a wee tubby bear. Everybody loved Matty.

Sometimes she would sneak into Papa's parlour bedroom and put on a pair of his trousers. They smelt of Papa, a mix of cigar smoke and shitty pants, and were made of scratchy grey material. He still went to Mr Travis the tailor to be measured and fitted, and for some reason, Mr Travis made his trousers full length. When she was little, Agnes thought that Mr Travis hadn't noticed the bottom halves of Papa's legs were missing, but now she supposed he was just being polite. The jackets always fitted beautifully, but Mama had to lay the trousers out flat on the kitchen table and chop off the bottom two feet. Later, she'd sit in front of the range, silver thistle thimble on her index finger, pins sticking out of the side of her mouth like whiskers, and carefully hem them up.

They were wide, of course; Agnes could have probably fitted two or three of her own legs in each side, and her legs weren't as skinny as Lucy's, but they were a great length. They swung down neat and straight just to the top of her feet and if she belted the waist with her ribbon she could believe they had been made for her. It was a shame that the jackets were too big. She needed to roll the sleeves up and clothes-peg the back so that it started to pull across her breasts. But if she pulled her navy-blue beret at a severe angle down the side of her face, plonked her left foot up on a couple of thick books until the knee turned out, and thrust her hand into the right trouser pocket like a man, she looked like Marlene Dietrich. Especially if she smiled a wee cat's smile, and squinted her eyes to blur the image in the mirror inside the door of Papa's big press.

She based the look on a newspaper story she had cut out with pinking shears from Papa's newspaper. She'd quite lost her breath when she saw the picture. Marlene was getting into a big black shiny car – right leg up inside the door, knee turned out, hand in other pocket. Erich Von Stroheim was holding the door open for her, standing to attention in a long black leather belted coat and with a blank adoring stare on his face. Marlene was looking straight at Agnes. Her cheekbones were sharp as razor blades and her nostrils flared like an angry horse. The story read that she had visited Paris wearing a man's suit in defiance of French laws against women wearing men's clothing in public. It was shameless. It was bloody marvellous.

'What you doing, Aggie?' Lucy and Dolly came skipping in, giggling and wearing their little white pinafores that fluffed around them like puffy clouds.

Marlene narrowed her eyes and flared her nostrils.

'Vye are you here, you cheeldren?' she drawled, rolling her eyes and giving an arch knowing look to Erich, standing cold and erect behind her.

Dolly plonked herself down on the bed, and giggled like a silly kitten.

'Frank's taken poorly, and everything's late. Arthur's gone to get the doctor,' Lucy said, standing still and looking at Agnes from head to foot.

Frank was always ill. Agnes thought his head was much too big for his sticky body. His nose and eyes were forever pink and his skin was pale blue because he didn't like playing outside.

The three girls stopped to listen. They could hear his funny breathing all the way from the bedroom: shrill and loud, and then quiet in between breaths. Just under the noise of Frank was Mama singing slow and deep.

'Oh, that boy, 'e is soo sensitive.' Agnes shook her head gravely. 'You like vhat you see, no?'

This set Dolly off snuffling with chuckles, rolling onto her back and kicking her legs in the air.

Lucy was unmoved. 'Why are you talking funny, Aggie? And what do you keep looking behind you for?'

Agnes snorted and jolted her head to the side. She took a pencil from her satchel on the floor and held it casually between two fingers of her upturned hand before ramming it in her mouth for a suck.

'Why have you got Papa's troos on?'

'Qvestions, qvestions, alvays soo many qvestions, ha.'

'He'll swing for you if he finds out.'

'No, he won't.' Dolly was running the edge of the counter-pane over her face, muffling her voice. 'Remember that time she let his chair roll halfway down the hill? He just laughed. If it had been me or you or one of the boys he wouldn't have laughed.'

'You shallow wee ninny, how could you pawsibbly understand?' Aggie smiled as mysteriously as she could.

She caught sight of herself again in the tall smeary mirror and scowled at her long wavy red hair bursting out of the nice tight beret.

'Fetch me the scissors,' she ordered Dolly, 'and I'll make us all into film stars.'

Mama never went out in the day. If she did go out it was after dark and she wore her big brown cloak. She'd wrap it around herself, pulling it carefully across her thighs, covering her large belly and digging her shiny silver feather brooch in at the shoulder to keep it in place. When she walked, she held tight to the bottom so it didn't flap open. None of them asked her why she didn't go out, but for quite a long time Arthur believed she was a vampire. *Dracula* had been playing at the Gaumont, and there had been a lot of talk of cloaks and darkness. Arthur had taken to wearing matchsticks for fangs and walking about in a tall stiff manner, jumping out from behind doors and scaring Frank witless at every opportunity. Robbie copied Arthur, and poor little Matty didn't understand and just cried and fell over.

Agnes knew that the cloak was to cover Mama's shyness. When the milkman came to the door, she couldn't look him in the eye. She would shuffle off for her purse, leaving the girls to chat about the weather and the horse. Most of all, she didn't like folk to see her pregnant. Papa said she was of good fecund peasant stock, and should walk tall, preferably in the light, but Mama would just go red and snuffle off to the kitchen like a miserable farmyard pig.

The back of Agnes's neck felt chilly; she'd finished her own hair first. Now her brow was creased in concentration, and the tip of her tongue poked out of the side of her mouth. She held a big clump of Lucy's thick brown hair up high.

'Ow, that hurts,' said Lucy.

'Nearly done,' said Agnes.

'You're crying,' said Dolly.

'No, I am not. My eyes are watering.'

'Cry baby, cry baby.'

'I'm not crying.' Lucy lunged at Dolly, and the scissors in Agnes's hand scratched her forehead. A thin drop of blood dripped down towards her eyebrow.

'Now look what you've done,' she wailed, catching Dolly and thumping her hard until she cried.

'Will you just stop that, you wee ninnies? How can I be expected to create beauty when you are acting like beasties?' said Agnes, not a trace of German left. But Lucy was still thumping Dolly, who was curled up like a baby to protect herself. Agnes strode over and pulled the two fluff-balls apart, giving Lucy a good slap on the cheek to calm her down. The room was loud with the sound of weeping and sniffing, and only the noise of the front door slamming shut shocked them into silence.

A strong bleachy smell, like the smell of the school nurse, wafted in. They heard Arthur clump up the staircase followed by lighter swishing footsteps taking the stairs two at a time. Mama's bedroom door opened briefly and Frank's piercing trill filled the house.

'Silly Frankie,' said Dolly, but the others ignored her.

'Is it the doctor?' asked Lucy.

Agnes nodded and all three looked up to the ceiling, listening for a whole minute until it got boring and Agnes picked up the scissors again.

'Your turn.' She gave Dolly a stern look. 'Wipe your eyes now, and sit still.'

Dolly's curls were like sweet chunky bedsprings. Strangers would stop her in the street to stroke her head, although she was getting a bit old for all that now.

Dolly gulped. 'Do I have to?'

Agnes nodded serenely and started chopping.

'Can I see it yet?' Dolly said, after a short while. She tried to lean forwards from the bed to open the wardrobe door.

Agnes pushed her back up straight by the shoulder. 'No, you have to wait till I've finished.'

'I want to see it.'

'You'll just have to wait. We'll all look together at the same time.'

'How long, how long will it be, Aggie?'

'She looks like a boy,' said Lucy, chewing her lip.

'She does not.'

'Why is it all lumpy, Aggie?'

'It's supposed to be like that,' said Agnes, scissors snapping faster and harder.

Lucy snorted.

'There,' Agnes said a minute later, 'finished.'

It was quiet overhead now. Agnes shut the door on the little girls and craned her neck to look upstairs. She could see Arthur, sitting outside Mama's bedroom door. His long hairy legs were pulled up to his chest, with his arms wrapped around them, but they still jiggled. His grey bristly jumper was too short in the arms and blue hard veins ran along his forearms. He knew nothing about style. Agnes walked slowly up the stairs, holding the banister and checking her deportment. When she reached the top, Arthur looked up at her. His eyes were dark and watery, and she thought of Greyfriars Bobby.

She forgot about Marlene briefly, and sat down next to him. His bare legs and shorts pressed against Papa's scratchy grey trousers. Arthur leant his cheek against the front of his thighs and they listened.

Downstairs, Dolly and Lucy were galloping about. There was a mixture of giggling and high whining. Behind the door, Mama had stopped singing and the doctor was talking in a deep, slow murmur. They heard Mama cry out, and the doctor make a funny shushing noise. After another minute, a chair scraped across the floor, followed by an even click of footsteps. The door opened and they looked up at the doctor with his long dark coat and humped leather bag.

They knew that they were forbidden to speak to important folk like the doctor, but Marlene had given Agnes courage.

'Excuse me, Doctor, but when will our brother be better?' she asked.

He looked down at them for a moment, put his hand up to his mouth and coughed a sharp healthy cough. Frank's shrill breathing rang out from Mama's bed. Arthur and Frank didn't normally look like twins, but Arthur was so pale and quiet that the resemblance was clear as glass. The doctor bent down and patted Arthur on the head.

'I'm sorry, laddie, but there is nothing I can do,' he said.

Arthur shook his head and looked at Aggie, his face open like a question. 'Frankie willnae die, will he, Aggie? He'll be right as rain, won't he, Aggie?' he pleaded.

Aggie looked at the doctor and he shook his head. 'I'm very sorry.'

He paused a moment longer and then set off down the stairs, taking a white handkerchief out from his pocket and methodically wiping his hands as he went, taking the steps two at a time.

Agnes looked in through the open door. Frank was a small bump in the big bed; she couldn't see his face. Mama was sitting next to him, with Matty and Robbie playing at her feet. She was half rocking the baby, with her head sunk into the beige counterpane. There was a muffled noise, halfway between singing and sniffing, and the smell of lavender water. Agnes had pins and needles in her left calf. Arthur was standing in the doorway now. He was rubbing his mouth up and down against the inside of his elbow. He sat down again, and they listened for a long time as Frank's high piercing breaths grew more and more frantic. Eventually they stopped altogether, and Mama let out a quiet low sob.

Arthur pelted down the stairs. He rushed out of the front door into the rain. Agnes couldn't keep up with him. She went back down into Papa's room and watched her brother through the window: his arms swinging in the air, and his head shaking from side to side. A ginger tom leapt down off the wall and into next door's garden. Arthur turned his face to the sky and yowled.

'No no no no noooo.'

The rain was slowing to a feeble patter, and strong rays of sunshine shot out from behind a big black cloud.

'There's a rainbow,' said Lucy, bolting over to the window. Dolly got up and followed her. They stood next to each other, cooing. Agnes looked at the fuzzy arch of colour and felt a slow sick feeling in her stomach.

Arthur was off down the street, running fast and hard, his arms still swinging.

Mama's face was still, plump and blank as she stood at the door. She was holding the baby, and Matty and Robbie were clutching her skirt. Matty rubbed his eyes and Robbie sucked his thumb. Mama looked down at the hair on the floor and the bed. There was an awful lot of it. Red waves, brown chunks, mousy curls. She stared and stared at it. The girls stood very still, waiting for the shouting and the hitting to begin. But Mama just got down on her knees, holding the baby in the crook of one arm. With her free hand, she started stroking the layers of hair, and then scooped big handfuls up. She pushed her face down into her hand, smelling and feeling the hair close up.

Agnes needed to pee very badly. When Mama looked up, her cheeks were hairy. She was making no noise, but her eyes were full of water, and the hairs had stuck to her tears.

'Clean this up,' she said, quietly at first so that none of them could hear her. 'Agnes, I said clean this up,' she growled, shaking her head, so sprinkles of hair fell to the floor. 'All of this, right away, clear it up, I said.' She was rigid and clenching her fists. The baby began to whimper.

'You stupid, stupid, stupid . . .' Mama looked at the three of them, crunching up her red, hairy face, 'stupid girls.'

The bedroom was damp and cheesy. It was very quiet; the window was closed and the curtains were drawn. There was still no sign of Arthur, and the other three laddies were asleep. No more shrill breathing, no more mewing, no more Frank.

Agnes walked over to the bed. She hadn't seen a dead body before. There had been Mama's two dead babbies, of course, one between the twins and Robbie, and another between Matty and Jimmy. But that was years ago now, and the old woman from Cragwell Street had bundled them up with the rest of her things and taken them away. Anyway, babbies that young didn't really count. Arthur and Frank, though, they were twelve. She couldn't remember them not being there.

The counterpane was pulled up to his shoulders. His eyes were closed. She could smell lavender. His skin was yellow, his lips the palest blue, and the corners of his mouth a scabby pink. His neck was so swollen and puffy that the bottom half of his face was a different shape to living Frank's. Diphtheria choked you round the throat till you popped, that's what they said in the playground. It was like being drowned and hanged at the same time and they'd all cheerfully try to act out swimming and swinging in one movement.

Mama had combed his thin hair back off his face but she hadn't lifted his head up properly. Some of the strands were flat on the crumpled pillow round his head like a messy halo. As Agnes looked at him, wondering whether or not to lift his head and smooth the hair back properly, she was suddenly sure that he was going to sit up. The more she looked at his neck and his hair, the surer she became that they would move.

'Sorry, Frank.' If she spoke to him, he would stay still. 'I didnae mean the things I said. You were a good boy, a fine brother. I couldn't have wanted a finer brother.'

She kept talking as she backed out of the room slowly, staring at his misshapen neck the whole time.

'And don't you worry, we'll look after Arthur, we'll see that he's alright. You just go now, and tek care of yourself.'

She was whispering, burbling, saying anything to keep him from sitting up.

'Wrap yourself up warm, you know how you suffer with the cold. Don't forget your muffler. Wrap it round you, nice and snug. Snug as a bug.'

She made it safely outside and pulled the door quietly shut.

During the night Agnes heard Frank's choking breathing again. In and out. Loud and then quiet, shrill and then low.

It was coming from Mama's bedroom. When she did sleep, she dreamt that Frank was in bed with her, his great big yellow head sinking into a huge red blanket of a neck. He had fangs dripping blood, and all his hair was chopped off. Agnes cuddled Lucy close to her. In the morning Matty was wheezing and mewing, drowning and hanging, wee tubby bear Matty.

May 30–June 14 – Blatta Orientalis

At the time it is like some kind of Ealing Comedy. The Lavender Hill Mob on a bad day. More Eric and Ernie than Bonnie and Clyde. Owen in the phone box across the road clutching his 2ops and a scrap of lined paper, and me meandering around the grounds, sticking my nose deep into the roses and pretending to appreciate the scent. I can't smell a thing. Fear usually concentrates the sense of smell, but maybe those roses just don't whiff. I sniff and sniff, bent over different bushes at different flowerbeds, working myself nearer and nearer to the fence at the top. I am pushing Nan in her wheelchair and if I see a nurse out of the corner of my eye, I stop, dip down and gulp at a flower with my eyes closed. Nan is muttering to herself.

Owen comes out of the phone box and gives me the thumbs-up. A bus passes in front of him, so he does it again. He leans against a lamppost, but he is stiff and nervous. Eventually, hundreds of flowerbeds later, the taxi honks its horn three times and I wheel her out across the asphalt drive, past the big white minibus and through the open metal double gates. I don't look round. I've been practising looking straight ahead. My hands are busy pushing the wheelchair so I can't press my thumbs, but I can hum, very quietly. It helps my breathing and it seems to soothe Nan.

She comes alive in the cab, presses her face right up against the window and leaves a dollop of saliva and steam on it. Owen and the driver finish folding the wheelchair into the front, and the driver knocks on the outside of the window as he walks around to his door. Nan shrivels back into her seat and puts her fingers to her ears. Owen slams the door as he gets in the back and I squeeze even closer to her. I take hold of her hand.

'It's alright, Nan. We're going home.'

She looks out of the window. The driver turns on the radio. Heavy reggae fills the back of the cab. Owen clicks his fingers, slightly out of beat. I'm humming, but Nan is humming louder. The driver twists his head round. He tuts his tongue against the roof of his mouth and shakes his head, but he is smiling. He turns up the music. A fire engine goes by on the other side of the road and Nan's tune starts to mimic the noise of the siren, sliding into *Somewhere Over the Rainbow*. Then she is shuffling forward in the seat, but the seat belt is keeping her back in place. She frowns and looks down at it.

'Wass this? Wassis bloody thin? Gerrit orff.'

'What are you doing, Nan?'

'Ma grand finale, on ma knees. On ma knees.' She is snorting like a horse.

'It's okay,' I say, trying to stroke her arm, but she narrows her eyes and spits at me. The bubbles of spittle sit on top of the sleeve of my leather jacket before sliding down onto the seat.

The driver turns round. 'I don't want any trouble, you know.'

Nan is suddenly looking out of the window again, staring intently at the lampposts and turning her head each time we pass one. There's a lot of jerking but she is quiet.

All that planning. Days and days of working out the fine detail, and in the end it was just a walk across a drive and a taxi ride to the coach station. The getaway car was a black cab, Owen was the lookout; and I was Fingers Ledermann, criminal mastermind, safe-cracker extraordinaire. Only there was no safe to crack. Just a wizened old woman in a wheelchair to spring to freedom, to bounce out of the home where the nurses drugged her and called her the wrong name, and she ended up with mysterious bruises on her neck. It wasn't right. I'd been inside places like that and I knew that something had to be done.

I was Jack Nicholson in *One Flew Over the Cuckoo's Nest*. I was McMurphy. I even resurrected my old leather jacket. It was wrapped in carrier bags next to my helmet in the little loft space above my bed. It was stiff and crinkly and smelt of mould. I opened it out flat on the bed, laying the arms out wide like a group therapist starting a group hug. Where it had been folded and creased up, there were ridges of flaky leather. The left arm was scuffed up from forearm to shoulder, and there were lumps and chunks of black gunk still clinging to it. When I scraped them off with my thumb, they were crumbly and very slightly sticky. On the leather they looked black, inside my thumbnail I realized they'd been dark red once. They smelt faintly of meat and petrol.

Rubbing the jacket down with oil was lovely. It slurped it up, like a baby taking a bottle. Three times I had to do it, to get it back to its glory days, but three times I rubbed it in, round and round with an old stripy sock till it was healthy and glossy and smooth again. From a faded grey rag to a shiny black beetle shell. Doing the zip up was nigh on impossible. I lay on my mattress, sucked in hard all the flesh I could and pulled the two sides together. It cut into my waist but I hauled the zip up in stages. Breathing was hard. I rolled off the bed and crawled into the bathroom on my hands and knees. I managed to get a glance in the mirror before I felt so faint that I had to undo it. What a sight for sore eyes: big woman in a tiny slick jacket. My face was red as a beetroot, and the sleeves were too short. You don't think that your arms will grow more once you are an adult, but mine must have been at least four inches longer over twenty years. I looked like a nightmare caddis fly – hard taut torso pulling a flouncy lumpy arse and legs in my paisley pyjama bottoms.

Last time I wore it I was nineteen. Last time I wore it my best friend died. Last time I wore it I was well. I pulled the zip down and let out a sigh like the air going out of a Zeppelin. I stood up and ran my oily hands through my scalp. I liked the way the grease made my hair go backwards, and I smiled an Elvis smile. A-ha-har. The jacket actually looked quite stylish undone. Shiny and confident. It would be my lucky jacket now. I'd wear it with my lucky watch and ditch the travelling parka. I was ready.

Owen, as usual, went over the top. When I got to his flat, he was parading around the sitting room with nothing on except a beautifully brushed fedora. He'd got it off a bloke called Gerard, so he said. As he pranced around, his prick jiggled about in little swings. I got giddy watching him. When he leapt over the sofa, it whipped right up in the air. Then he stood still and tipped the hat forward so it covered the top of his face. He hunched up his shoulders like Jimmy Cagney.

'What do you think then, Doll? Like the titfer?'

I looked down at his dick. 'Very nice.'

'Ooh you are awful,' he said, giving my shoulder a shove, 'but I like you.' And he minced off into the bedroom to put on some clothes and take off the hat.

We went over and over the plan. Everything was ready. Nan could have Owen's spare room. His flat was best because no one would come looking for us here. We'd got some furniture from the mental action furniture store – a new bed and a kidney-shaped dressing table. It had a mirror and everything. I'd bought her a fancy hairbrush. We knew the coach times, the taxi firm numbers and the route back. We were on a mission and we did it. We only bloody did it.

We have a kind of a routine already, and it's only been a fortnight. In the mornings she is very quiet, so we all sleep. At lunchtime, we have something to eat. Nan can't eat solids so we make her porridge and mash and gooey food. Owen makes a good root-vegetable mix that he blends up all smooth. Me and Owen sit with her in the afternoons. We are like her parents. The bruises on her neck have just about gone.

The first couple of days she hardly moved or said a word; they were easy. Then she started waking up in the nights, singing and shouting. The tranqs are out of her system now. Owen sleeps through it, but I can't stand it. Her cough has got much worse. We thought about taking her to the doctor's but we don't know how safe it is, so Owen bought her some bronchial balsam and Strepsils, which she just spits out. We're running out of money very quickly. All that planning, and the things we didn't think of. Incontinence pads, moisturizing cream, food. What the hell did we think we were taking on?

Owen is good with her. He is so patient. She growls like a dog when she sees him, and yesterday she bit his arm when he was trying to feed her. I try to comfort her but she pushes me away.

Her bedroom smells of old digestive biscuits, shit and sour milk. It's a slog changing her clothes and bedding. But both of us like the trips to the laundrette. It's a relief to get out and sit somewhere different. The holiday season is cranking up into full swing and there is a constant drip of mothers dropping off bags of kids' clothes for service washes. Owen says that he and his mates used to take cans of Special Brew down with them in the good old days. Slurp it back and stick their heads in the dryers for a hot groggy thrill. But we haven't got the money for the tumble-dryers, let alone beer, so we dry the sheets over the bath and on a clotheshorse in the sitting room.

This morning I think she's dead when I go in. She is lying on her side with her hands held up to her neck, all hooked like claws. Her head is back on the pillow with her chin in the air. I can't see her chest moving. I go up close and put my ear in front of her face. Then she splutters and wheezes and a spray of spit covers my cheek. She coughs until her blue face is red and then her breathing isn't very regular.

I come back before lunch to give her a wash. I put the big pillow behind her, and shuffle her up to sitting. I've got a red plastic basin of warm bubbly water and a sponge and I start gently on her arms. She has rows of thin pink scars running up the front of them, that I don't think I've seen before. There are more marks on her neck and throat. They remind me of something. Her hair is as limp as a tea towel. She's got a receding widow's peak but it's long and straggly at the back.

'Would you like a haircut?'

She gets a devilish look in her eyes. Good result: a reaction. Then she starts singing in a cracked deep voice with a strange Eastern European accent. The words are mainly all a slur, apart from the last phrase.

'I can't 'elp eeet.'

She is smiling, so I go to the kitchen and fetch the scissors. When I come back in she is snoring again; her nose is blocked up and whistling. I get the hairbrush and run it over her skull, flattening out all the white Shredded Wheat strands. I use my hand to tip her head forward and she wakes with a jolt. She looks at the scissors and licks her lips. I start snipping at the sides first, and a mini snowstorm flutters down onto her lap. She picks up a wisp of hair and rubs it between her thumb and forefinger. She is frowning and poking out her lower lip, just like a toddler. She holds the hair up right in front of her eyes and stares at it.

'No no no no no no, but I don't know,' she is crying.

'What's the matter, Nan?'

'But it can't be, it's no' right. Ha, Mama didnae want us to, no no no.'

She stuffs the hair into her mouth and starts to chew and cough at the same time. She picks up more hair and rubs it into her face. It goes deep inside the long wrinkles running down the side of her nose, it goes up her nostrils and into her eyes. She is sobbing now and big tears and snot are dribbling down her face, flushing little white hairs down towards her mouth and jowls.

'Aach, the babby, weematty, weematty,' she is crying over and over.

Owen comes in and we try to shoosh and talk to her in low quiet voices. I hold her back on the pillow whilst he washes her face carefully with the sponge, changing the water a couple of times to get rid of the hairs. She rattles to a halt and then coughs again for ages. She isn't well.

When he has finished her face and the hair has gone, he gives her a spoon of the dark brown medicine. It smells of chloroform. Then I carry on and wash under her arms, breasts and around her arse and fanny. She doesn't struggle at all. When we've dressed her, we hoik her up into the wheelchair. Owen walks slowly across the room, pulls up the bamboo blind and opens the window. A warm breeze blows in, rattling the blind. An ice-cream van is tinkling *The Blue Danube*. We both look at her, then stare at each other across the room. He is very pale.

'We can't go on like this.'

The ice-cream van parks right below us, followed by children squabbling and laughing.

'I'll take her out. Get some fresh air.' I pause. 'Give you a bit of your own . . . space,' I say, balking at myself for using day-centre speak.

Owen nods. 'Don't go out for too long, though. Be careful, wear the hat.'

'We've still got no idea how hard they're looking for us. I haven't been home, but Dad must be trying to find me.

My Vidal Sassoon attempts have left Nan with a lop-sided hairstyle. Well, style is too grand a word for the state her hair is in now. I look through Owen's extensive hat collection – pausing for a second at the fedora – and find a simple soft navy-blue beret. I show it to her, and she shrugs. I don't know what the shrug means, so I put it on top of her head gingerly. She doesn't cry or anything, so I pull it down on a jaunty angle and actually it looks okay. Intentional almost. I put on my baseball cap and my lucky purple summer jacket. Too hot for my lucky leather jacket today.

Thank God the lift is working. Nan mutters and quakes when I wheel her in, rocking gently backwards and forwards until we come out into the light again on the ground floor. The pavement is in the shadow of the tower block and there is a sharp breeze whipping round the block. My nipples are hard and achy and my jaw clamps shut. I push her a few steps away from the flats, and the sun comes out from a big grey cloud at the same time. The sunshine sinks down through my head and face into my chest. I go soft at the warmth, and I exhale loudly, blowing my cheeks out like balloons and letting the air out in little bursts. Nan claps her hands. A woman with a small girl in a bright pink T-shirt glances over before hurrying her across to the other side of the road. What does she think I'll do – eat her? They cross back over further down the road to get to the ice-cream van.

A police car turns into the road. I turn the wheelchair towards a gate, crouch down and look busy with Nan's blanket. It drives by. Every time I hear a siren I stop breathing and start sweating big time.

The funfair is only ten minutes away. It is packed with kids. They're running all over the place, round in circles, thumping each other, squealing and stuffing their faces with candyfloss and chips. Nan is snoozing again, but all that activity unnerves me. I wheel her into the amusement arcade, but the jangling and jingling and pops and kapows make me jump more than the kids. A little boy is standing in front of a machine with a margarine tub stuffed with coppers, at least a fiver's worth. He shovels them into the slot without any kind of strategy, a glazed expression on his face like he's eating his tea in front of the telly. I think I'd quite enjoy that if it wasn't so noisy in here. A thick layer of blue-grey smoke is hanging a couple of feet down from the ceiling. Someone is smoking a cigar. The smell tugs at my memory and makes my stomach lurch. I light up a fag and Nan starts jiggling to go outside through the other door.

She is pointing at one of the kiddies' rides. Not the giant plastic brown soup bowls that go round and round. There are children in some of them, looking lost, and ringing the bells that are attached to the great big soup handles without very much enthusiasm. The bells are clanging and Busted is blaring out from the speakers, so I don't hear her at first. I'm busy worrying about what it would be like to really sit in a giant bowl of hot oxtail, when her voice starts to cut in on my thoughts.

'Srod, isrod,' she is wheezing.

The sun is blazing down now, and the top of my head is beginning to prickle. The tops of my ears are getting very hot. I drop my dog-end on the ground, lean against a wall and close my eyes. Everything is orange and red behind my eyelids. As I open them, a seagull flies right over my head. I can feel the air move and hear its wings swishing. A big white dollop of bird shit splats down in front of me, just missing my fag end and a half-eaten burger.

'Good luck, that is,' I say to Nan.

The wheelchair is rocking like mad.

'Srod, srod,' she is saying and coughing and pointing.

I look.

It's just another funfair ride. Eight brightly coloured plastic minicars going round a tiny weeny circle. So what? Each car is driven by a giant plastic gnome with a tall pointy hat and a bell on top. They've got pointy ears the size of handbags and white chunks of plastic hair. Each one has a sun-bed brown plastic face with a lumpy nose, thin purple lips and a huge maniacal grin. White beard, no moustache. One has a fishing rod. Rod.

Rod.

Out of the speakers, a chipmunk version of *The Laughing Gnome* plays over and over as they go round and round. I stand still and stop breathing. The faces come and go, come and go, again and again.

'See see see,' Nan is squealing.

I push her forwards in a daze, her arms are reaching out towards them. The chirpy chipmunks are louder.

The wind blows and something scuttles under my feet. Bottle tops. I jump out of the way of a couple of bottle tops. Nan is laughing and wheezing hard. She is squirming. She is stamping her feet and shaking her head. She says something that I can't quite hear through the clanging bells and the chipmunks.

'Rudgeno,' she says. 'Rudgeno.'

I bend down next to her and look her in the face.

'Rudgersnomes,' she is saying, 'Roger's gnomes.'

There's a waft of grease from the burger van, the smell of frying sausages, and, woomph, I'm back there.

Skipping down the garden path on a cold and frosty morning, wearing my favourite Eskimo coat, holding Daddy's hand and then running off to see Uncle Roger's funny gnomes. There was a new one with a fishing rod.

Nanny Aggie's house was smelly, but Daddy said it was rude to say it. It smelt of medicine and smoke and sometimes fish. What I did like about Nanny Aggie's house was her red tartan biscuit tin. She always had chocolate fingers. I did painting that day. I painted Timmy and the gnomes. Nanny came into the kitchen with the big white bogies up her nose. I laughed, I remember, but she was strict and scared me so I stopped laughing.

I watched the great big telly inside a wooden cupboard. I watched Bizzy Lizzy and Little Mo, my favourites, and I ran in to tell Nanny Aggie. The paint water spilt and she got red in the face and cried like she had fallen over and really hurt herself. Then she took my yellow cutting scissors, and she cut herself, all up her arms until they were bleeding. From under the table, I could see drops of blood falling from her arms onto the black-and-white floor squares. I didn't want Nanny near me with my scissors. She would cut me and make blood drip from me onto the floor too.

And then she was down under the table and pulling at me. I tried to get out of her way, but the wall was behind me, and the table legs trapped me. She got me and took me upstairs.

A pussycat runs out. It is hot in the room. There is a tap making a drip, drip noise. The room smells like poo and there are little things in there. Some of them don't move, like musical statues. Then, as the room gets dark, alive ones come out. My tummy hurts because I am hungry. The things are the colour of my brown paint. I think about the biscuits and cakes Mummy made for my birthday party. And the jam sandwiches in triangles with all the crusts cut off. The things have sticks that came out of their heads. They move fast and make a clicky noise. Later, when it gets darker, they come out from behind the pink stripy wallpaper. They run over to the cat's sick on the red rug and click at it like it is a feast. My tummy makes a big rumbling noise. It is empty. I still believe that someone will save me.

I call and I bang on the door, but no one comes. Later, much later, I hear the front door closing. I am so hungry that my tummy and my mouth ache. I hear a loud scrapy noise from downstairs. Maybe my daddy has come to save me. I bang on the door again, stepping round the things on tippy-toes. I cry every time I think one is going to touch me. Then I hear a voice coming up the stairs. A man is coming. But it's not Daddy, so I lie down on the rug and pretend to be asleep.

The door opens. I keep my eyes closed. Uncle Roger puts me in the bed. He is coughing and bits of spit go on my arms. The sheets are so tight that I can't move my legs. I open my eyes and see Nanny Aggie looking down at me. She has a big fat brown cigarette in her hand.

Then they go out again. I know the things are still there, running about on the floor. I lift my head to see if I can hear them getting closer. The bed makes me sneeze. There is a plate of four sausages on the bedside table. I eat them very very very fast. I can't hear the things then; all I can hear is my mouth eating the sausages. I lie there all night as still as I can, listening to them moving on the floor and dreaming of chocolate fingers and party rings. Whole ones, half ones, broken ones. My stomach hurts and I know then that the world is a scary place.

The noise of the fair fills my ears again. I look up from the ground. My eyes feel stretched open and raw. My chest is light and loose.

I never stopped at Nanny's again after that. Every time my mum and dad tried to get me to visit I would scream and shout and throw such a tantrum that eventually they gave up. I never told them why. They didn't ask. I wouldn't think about it.

A few years later I came across a picture of *Blatta orientalis* – oriental cockroaches – in the A–D section of Daddy's *Encyclopaedia Britannica* when I was doing my homework. The line-drawing made me scream and drop the big heavy book, but I didn't know why.

I think about it again, rewinding the new images in my head. It's like a slap. I know it was only one night. I know that nobody actually hurt me. I know other kids get beaten and raped. But I can see now that that night has always been there at the back of my mind. Before then I thought the world was safe and lovely and full of flowers and teddies. That feeling went away. Grown-ups did very scary things, and they didn't come to save me. The hollow shifting sand feeling deep in my tummy started when I was four and stayed with me all my life: one more thing that's made me the woman I am today. Multiple bereavement, accidents, heredity all helped. A night alone in the dark, clicking beetles and the need for food to calm myself clinched it.

Nan is still stamping in her chair. I look down at her hands. They are red around the knuckles; the rest of the skin is pale and baggy. The nails are jagged. They were buffed to a gleam in their heyday. She looks up at me, straight in the eye. Gloating, I think she is gloating. There's a surge of blood and energy shooting down my shoulders to my hands. I am breathing in rough little gasps. I am chewing the inside of my mouth. My fingers are splayed out so hard that the tendons are raised and white. I don't know what to do with them. I move each finger in turn, counting them to empty my head of the pictures and memories. I am holding on, rocking. Then I throw my head back and I'm howling like a dog.

The shouting and laughing stop. The bells and music get louder. All around people and children are frozen, mouths open and ice creams in hand, staring at me. I have to get out of here.

Head down, I grip the wheelchair handles and push full pelt back to the flat. I don't stop to look for cars. I bump up and down kerbs and thud over drain covers, getting faster and faster till my face and back are soaked and my chest hurts. Cars toot, people shout. She is still.

I leave her on the landing. She has conked out. I burst through the front door. Owen is hoovering the sitting room, singing and dancing as he goes. I stand in front of him, dripping and shaking.

'She locked me up,' I shout over the sucking drone.

He shakes his head and puts his foot on the off switch. He walks towards me.

'She locked me up,' I shout again, even though the flat is ringing with silence now. 'With cockroaches.'

I know it sounds lame, but Owen smiles. Wrong thing to do. He comes nearer but I don't want him to. I don't want comfort. I want hot and cold and sweet. I want the world to be a safe place again. I don't know what I want. I turn and run out of the flat, pushing the wheelchair into the wall. I stumble down the stairs, holding the shiny banister with one hand and swinging round the bends faster each time. Round and round the cold concrete steps, splashing through puddles of piss, so fast that I'm giddy at the bottom. I have no sense of direction, I don't know in from out, up from down, left from right.

I can smell the sea and I run towards the salt. There are people on the beach. Clusters and groups and gangs and cliques of Lucky Lucky Fuckers living lives. Stripy windbreaks, buckets and spades, towels and deck chairs. Food, warmth, love. Eating sandwiches, fiddling with radios, rubbing in sun cream, flicking through newspapers, laughing, eating, breathing.

It is dark and cool under the pier. I am like a wounded fox cub. I slump down next to rusty beer cans and a vodka bottle, a third full of green water. My brain is on fire. Nan. Roger. Natalie. Mum. Timmy. Owen. Their faces and voices move around inside my head like a nasty home movie. I listen to the sea breathe in and out. Eventually, when it's dark, the faces fade and the voices stop.

1920

Her first memory was of Papa. He was sitting in bed wearing a shiny jacket covered in purple and blue peacocks. Perched on top of his head was a funny round hat with a fat rope tassel that hung between his eyes, all the way down his long hooked nose. A thick stick made of dark brown paper and burning on the end poked out of his mouth, and his legs stopped just above his knees.

'Why'f you got no feet, Papa?' she asked, pressing the beige braided counterpane up and down, her hands in the flat space in front of him. If she pushed hard enough, the mattress bounced up and down and made a good squeaking noise.

He smiled and breathed in a big breath so the brown stick went a sharp red on the end and puffy blue clouds floated in front of his eyes. When the clouds cleared, his eyes were watery.

'Blown off,' he said.

'Oh,' said Agnes, bouncing extra hard, the bedsprings sounding like mice, and his tassel swinging like the pendulum on the clock over the fire. 'Where did they go then, Papa?'

'Somewhere in a green field in France, there is a leg that is forever Scotland's,' he chuckled, quietly like a steam train at first, but then harder and harder until his body was shaking and the burning smelly stick fell out of his mouth onto the floor.

Mama bustled into the room, with the big chipped white bucket, shushing and nudging Agnes out of the way. She bent down and picked up the cigar, stubbing it out on the side of the bucket.

'It's alright dear, alright.' She rubbed his back, but his coughing had become a racking machine, and the shaking mattress made the mice squeak again, crazy and loud. Bubbles of pale yellow dribbled out of the side of his mouth, and Mama used the hem of her apron to wipe them away. The rich smoky smell had gone cold, and Agnes felt sick. Outside the room, the babies were crying.

'Agnes, go see to the twins.'

'Aye, Mama,' she said, but she was stuck looking at him, and the flat counterpane, and the bubbles. 'Mama, when are Papa's feet going to come back?'

Mama didn't answer. Papa's coughing was quieter now, and Mama was humming a lullaby to him. His eyes were closed, and she brushed the tassel away from his face. Looking up, she repeated her instructions to Agnes, but this time to the tune of the lullaby, softly, so as not to disturb him.

'Agnes, Agnes, go to see to the babies, will you go now, will you go now, before I get mad?' She narrowed her eyes at the last few words, and lifted her plump arm, making her hand into a fist.

Agnes ran out of the door and followed the noise of squawking and crying across the hall and into the kitchen. It was cosy and warm, and Mama had been baking. But the twins smelt bad. They were bundled up tight in yellow and grey blankets, side by side in a big brown box, a drawer from Papa's clothes press, on top of the sandy wooden table that Mama was always scrubbing. Their faces were as red as tomatoes, and crumpled up like paper. Peas in a pod, Mama called them, but it was easy to tell the difference. Arthur was double the size of little Frank. Lucy was sleeping on the chair in front of the range, her thumb in her mouth, despite being told. Tibs was curled up against her in a tabby ball, taking up most of the chair.

'Shush now, little ones,' Agnes crooned. 'You'll wake up Lucy.'

The crying got angrier, and their faces redder. Agnes tried to rock the box, like Mama did, but it was heavy and it would not budge very much.

They wouldn't stop crying, even when she sang as loud as she could. She didn't know all the words to the song, but knew it was from that funny man in the tam-o'-shanter and crooked walking stick that Papa hated but Mama loved. Mama played the big black record on the gramophone when she was feeling blue. It was about when the boys come home after winning the war and Agnes thought it must have been written about Papa.

The twins gradually quietened, Arthur first, then Frank, their cries turning to funny hiccups as they wore themselves out. The smell of dirty nappies was stronger. They must both need changing now. If she stopped touching the box for even a second, Arthur screwed his tomato face up again, so she carried on. By now she was bored with the song. She wanted to dance, but was stuck with the box.

Wisps of smoke began to wheedle their way out around the edges of the range door, and soon the smell of burning bread covered the smell of Arthur and Frank.

Across the hall in the back parlour, Papa's coughing had stopped and the mice were squeaking again, but this time with a steady tune of their own.

Squeak squeak squeak squeak.

They made Agnes laugh. She imagined a whole party of mice sitting on the end of Papa's bed, each with a very wee crooked walking stick and a tiny tam on top of its head.

They were squeaking much faster now and Agnes could see them again dancing a funny dance in little gillie-shoes made specially for them by elf shoemakers. Then all of a sudden she heard Papa shout out, the mice stopped and it was quiet.

Lucy opened one eye and looked over at Agnes.

'Tek your thumb out of your mouth, you big babby,' said Agnes, trying to sound as much like Mama as she could bluster.

But Lucy just closed her eye again and sucked harder.

Mama was late kissing them good night. Agnes lay under the covers with her eyes shut, listening to the creaks and settling of the house. The others were snoring and snuffling. But she knew she would come: she always did.

She kissed them in order of size. Sugar in the morning for Frank, sugar in the morning for Arthur and sugar in the morning for Lucy, she whispered.

She always finished with Aggie. 'My big girl,' she said, a soft kiss on her cheek. She stroked the hair off Aggie's cheek. 'Sugar in the morning.'

June 15 – Just Like That

There is cold water touching my heel. Then it's gone. Here again. Gone. I open my eyes. I am stiff and lumpy. Cold right through. There is a pale yellow crack in the grey clouds, and fluffy purple pompom clouds over on the horizon. The hotel lights and streetlights are still on. I watch the sun come up. The beach starts filling up. It is going to be a hot day.

Something bright on a piece of driftwood a few yards away, outside the shadow of the pier, catches my eye. I crawl over on my elbows and knees and pick up a red dummy. The rubber teat has rotted, but the plastic has survived the sea. A helicopter is phutting across the horizon and there is a light warm breeze. I stand up and sniff the sea. It is salty and rotten and exciting, with a tang of sludgy seaweed. I pull my arm back and chuck the dummy out as far as I can, hoping it will skim like a flat stone and then bob off into dummy freedom. It sits on top of a wave and gradually works its way back to land again.

The sun is getting stronger and glinting down on a paint tin lid. I squat down and wipe it with my forearm till it works like a murky mirror. My hair is sticking up on one side, and there is a Bride of Frankenstein streak of seaweed running down the other. The grey skin under my eyes is like fish skin, my eyes are red and darting all over the place.

I feel in my tracksuit bottom pockets for my fags. Still there. My new rainbow lighter is inside, nestling next to the bent white sticks. Owen bought me it, to cheer me up, he said.

Five for a pound at the market. I run my thumb down the
flint wheel three times but nothing happens. It's damp. I pat
my jacket pockets and find a little black folded book of
matches from the pub, battered and bent up at the corners.
Damp too, of course. So I snort in some more sea air instead
of smoke. My head clears.

I am going to kill her. I am going to go back and get a
pillow from the bedroom. I am going to take that pillow and
place it over her face. I am going to lean down on the pillow
with all my weight and squash the life out of her. It'll take
me one, maybe two minutes. She won't struggle that much,
and if she does, I'll just lean harder.

My fingers are twitching. I look down at my hands. Fuck
the pillow, I'm going to strangle her. She deserves it. Locking
me up. I am going to kill her, and who will know? I curl my
hands around a pretend neck and begin shaking them in the
air, when there is a crunch on the pebbles behind me. A young
bloke is hauling a pile of deck chairs down. He's got a bulging
black bum-bag, and a joke white captain's hat with a strip of
navy-blue cord and plastic peak is perched on top of his big
bristling head. His face is very pink. I've seen him somewhere
before. He stops and looks me up and down.

'Nice jacket,' he says.

My mouth is open and I pat my pockets again for the black
match book.

'What's the matter with you, ay?'

I find the matches and stare at them, remembering the pub
and the three men. I rub my eye. He smiles at me.

'Look fuck off out of it, will you freak? You'll put my punters
off.'

I think about it. I think about fucking off, I really do. But
enough is enough. I drop the matches and look him in the eye.

'Fuck off yourself. It's my beach too.'

He drops the deck chairs. They clatter on the pebbles. He pulls his shoulders back and walks over to me.

'What did you say?' He pauses and then hisses, 'Freak.'

I stand up tall myself. I walk up the pebble bank until I'm towering over him. I speak quietly and firmly. No humming, no scratching, no monkey business with my fingers. 'I said: it is my beach too and I have a right to be here.'

He looks me in the eye. I stare straight back. A huddle of pensioners with carrier bags is heading our way. He takes a step backwards, waits a nanosecond and then quickly leans down to pick up his deck chairs.

'Alright, alright. Don't get overheated. I was just saying.' And he walks off towards the pensioners. Just like that.

'Just like that,' I say to myself when he is well gone, and I put my hands out like Tommy Cooper. I do the funny laugh through my teeth. I used to have a fez.

I walk up to the prom. The little blue benches and shelters are all clean and fresh in the sunshine. LLFs are strolling along with pushchairs and toddlers. On the main road a bunch of people are gathered outside the Grand Hotel. There must be about thirty of them, complete with placards and banners and an awful lot of yellow. A big man with a bulbous pot belly, square institution glasses and a greasy baseball cap is walking towards the crowd. He has a key around his neck, hanging on manky rope. I recognize him from that first meeting with Owen. He shakes hands with a skinny man with a scruffy white dog. As I pass them, the dog looks up at me and barks.

'Hey, it's Owen's friend, isn't it?' says the man with the dog. Bob, I remember now. Both men smile and wave.

'Hiya, what's your name? You come to join us?' says the other man, taking off his cap to scratch his bald patch. Friar Tuck.

'Look, look,' says Bob, reaching down to a pile of long sticks on the ground. He fiddles with them and suddenly opens a huge yellow umbrella. 'We used Fablon in the end,' he says, 'just in case it rains.'

He twirls it round in the air like Gene Kelly. My eyes are sore, my head hurts and my mouth is dry, but the yellow plastic is like immediate sunshine in my face. They did it. I look around at the other people. I realize I recognize most of them. Cathy and Julia from the day centre are fiddling with a large banner, but they don't notice me. I unclench my hands.

'The rally's starting at eleven. Should be good. You coming? Is Owen coming?' asks Tuck.

Owen. The flat. Nan.

I shake my head. The dog whimpers. I bend down and pat him.

'Another time,' I say.

Bob pulls a sheet of stickers out of his jacket. He peels one off and sticks it on my chest. 'Glad to be mad.' Plus the logo, of course. Purple line-drawing of a strait-jacket. Not sure about that. Not sure at all.

It's deadly quiet inside the flat. Quiet and dingy. I can hear the pigeons purring on the ledge. The medicine-and-biscuit smell hits me as I walk through the hall, past the closed bedroom door and over to the sitting-room window. I pull it wide open and breathe in the salty fumes. The sea and the town are laid out like a tablecloth. The sea is glassy blue and sun glints into my eyes from the red and yellow cars pootling along the main road. The bright colours make my head spin. The bedroom door closes softly. I turn around and look back into the gloom. My eyes take a while to adjust and I can just about make out Owen's figure.

'You're back,' he whispers.

I nod. I expect him to come over to see me, to check I'm okay, to give me a hug, but he stays just outside the bedroom door. I don't want to think about Nan.

'I saw Bob and the others. They were meeting for the rally,' I say.

'Yeh?' he says.

'It's today.'

I wait for him to shout and scream and run out of the door, but he stays standing still. A seagull cackles as it flies by the window. I can hear its wings cutting through the air.

'Jodie . . .' he starts.

I don't want to hear what he has to say. I turn and look out at the clear blue sky again.

'She's very ill. I think we fucked up.'

I want to put my fingers in my ears, I want to go la la la not listening, but I have to hear his voice. I clear my throat.

'I wanted to kill her,' I say. 'Not at first. I think what we did was right. She didn't like it there. They weren't treating her right. But then when I remembered what she did to me, I wanted to strangle her.'

There's a strange noise from the bedroom, like a screech owl.

'I don't think you understand. She's really not well. I think we should call an ambulance.'

I take a couple of steps towards Owen. He is very pale, pale as cheese spread. I reach out to touch him but he moves back.

'Jodie, I think you need to come and see her.'

The room is dark and hot. It stinks of sweat and piss. But the noise is the worst thing. Huge ratchety squeals followed by long long silences. Nan is lying in the fetal position with her hands clawed up like a praying mantis. Her eyes are closed. She is still for the moment.

'I'm going out to the phone box,' says Owen. 'We should have got help days ago.'

And with that he's gone and I'm alone in the room with her. She is tiny and flat under the duvet. I'm sure she's halved in size since yesterday. She breathes in hard again. The squealing starts as her whole body struggles to get air. I don't know what to do. I pull the chair up to the bed and lower my face close to hers. Her face is screwed up with the effort of breathing. Her mouth fills with liquid and it dribbles onto the pillow as she sighs out again. She is still and quiet for a long time. I rub her arms with their bumpy scars. I smooth her damp, badly cut hair off her face. She is hot and clammy. I stroke the funny star-shaped scar on her neck. She breathes in, and the noise and the pain and dragging up of her lungs starts over again.

It seems to go on for ever. The wrenching in-breaths followed by quiet. Each time I think she's died. I'm useless. There's a bowl of water and a flannel on the bedside table. I wring the flannel out and wipe her face. She flinches at first, and I hum an old musical tune until she is still again.

'What happened to you?' I whisper. I look at her scarred arms. 'Why did you hurt yourself?'

The next breath is the worst yet. Her chest rises up from the mattress and her face scrunches like a boxer. I can't stand to see her this way. I pull a pillow out from under her head and get up. It is soft and damp. Nan is quiet again. I lean down. Suddenly she opens her eyes. Not just slits, but really wide. I've never noticed how blue they are, like shiny blue marbles.

'Ach. Girlie. Chick.' She turns her head to look at me. A

hissing noise comes out of her throat. 'Sssooooorry,' it sounds like to me.

Then she closes her eyes and the hissing stops.

I sit in the dark on the hard chair with the pillow on my lap. I'm not crying. I'm not really feeling anything. Sorry, she said sorry to me for that night in the dark. It's over now. I think about Nan and her life. How can this skinny Roswell alien with the hooky claws have been a living breathing woman? It just doesn't make sense.

The front door opens, and then the bedroom door. Owen looks at me, and then at the bed. He walks over to Nan and puts the back of his hand up to her mouth.

'She's dead,' I say.

He looks at the pillow in my lap.

'It wasn't me. She just died.'

'Shit.'

He stares at me. He takes the pillow and puts it back under her head.

'The ambulance will be here any minute,' he says. 'You'd better get up.'

But I can't move. I'm stuck. In the end, Owen pulls me up and half pushes me into the sitting room.

'We're going to get done, you know,' he says. 'How could we be so stupid? One way or another, we're going to get done.'

I can hear singing. I really can. I can hear cheering and whistles and horns honking. I walk over to the window. Over by the beach, the Glad to be Mad rally is in full swing. There are a few police in day-glo jackets stewarding the hundred people meandering along the prom with their banners, flags and yellow umbrellas. A couple are dancing in the street. The cars are slowing down to have a look. I close my eyes and smile. My eyelids are flickering like butterflies. I tilt my head towards the window. I can hear something else. A siren. It starts quietly like a wasp buzzing, but builds very quickly until it is screaming outside the flats. I open my eyes. The ambulance pulls up, followed by a couple of police cars. I look down as men in green and blue uniforms head for the stairs.

Owen is still staring at me.

'I didn't do it,' I say, but he looks over to the front door and we wait for them to knock.

I glance down out of the window again. Parked in his little red car is my dad. He is leaning his head against the steering wheel.

Three Years Later

The café was scruffy and warm. There were piles of news-
letters, flyers and postcards stacked on the windowsills, and
Stop the War posters and kids' drawings of lollypop trees and
smiling suns all over the walls. A plump woman with red wavy
hair sat on a wooden bench drinking rosehip tea out of an
earthenware mug. The window was open and the city farm
smell of goats, chicken shit and damp hay mixed with the
fried veggie sausages.

A teenager with a buggy came in.

'Alright there, Chloe?' said the woman. 'Cup of splash?'

The girl nodded and pulled up a chair.

The woman got up, groaned and pushed her hand into the
small of her back. A navy-blue butcher's apron was tied around
her bulging belly. She smoothed the stripes with her other
hand and smiled. She looked at the table and wiped the crumbs
and trails of granulated sugar onto her eggy plate with the
back of her hand. She picked it up with the mug.

'You got any flapjacks?' said Chloe.

The woman waddled round to the back of the counter and
put the crockery on the draining board. She bent down and
then sideways to briefly scratch her legs, humming a snatch
of an old Kylie Minogue song.

'Yes. With cherries? Anything for Mikey?'

'Nah, he's still sleeping.'

The woman took the flapjack and mug of tea over.

'What you up to today then, Jodes?' the teenager asked.

She'd been volunteering at the city farm for nearly a year now. The hours suited and she got free food.

'I'm only on here till half-three. Then I think I'll pop across to the allotment. Do a bit of weeding, see how me beetroot's doing.'

Chloe picked at her flapjack. The door opened and a crowd of six-year-old Pakistani boys bundled in with a couple of teachers. Jodie went back behind the counter to sort out beakers of apple juice and Panda bars.

She gardened nearly every day at the moment. There was dirt under her fingernails most of the time, except when she scrubbed them for the café. She tottered down the stepping stones to the bottom of the allotment and the drills of lettuces, carrots and beetroot. There were some nasty little dandelions that needed seeing to. She got down on her knees and started pulling.

She often thought about Nan, especially when she was weeding. After she'd died, hell broke loose. Police, doctors, lawyers and talk of manslaughter. She'd been back in hospital, and so had Owen. They'd let her out for the funeral, but then she'd done another stretch before things calmed down. The funeral was a muzz, apart from Aunt Rebecca turning up. She hadn't seen her since she was a little girl, and when the big woman with curly grey hair had strolled down the aisle, she was smitten. Her mother didn't approve, of course. Her dad, on the other hand, had surprised her by rushing over and hugging her.

Rebecca came to see Jodie in the hospital and brought her freesias, Twiglets and eau-de-Cologne. She travelled down from Manchester again when Jodie got out. She came back to the bedsit and cooked her spaghetti with a Quorn bolognese sauce. They talked for hours and hours and looked through all the photo albums. Rebecca didn't have any photos herself.

She answered lots of questions about Nan. She explained about Granddad Ernest's suicide and Nan's spell away in hospital, and Roger and what a pig he was. But she wouldn't talk about her own childhood at first.

When Jodie moved to the new housing association flat, Rebecca came down again. She and Owen helped with the decorating. They'd bickered about the colour. Owen wanted lime green; Rebecca wanted olive green, and in the end Jodie decided on buttercup yellow. Owen had his new flat a couple of streets away; he could have lime green there: it would go with his lava lamp.

Then one night Rebecca had turned up in a state with a bottle of brandy. It was raining and she looked more like a yeti standing on the doorstep than a teacher. She said all the talking had dragged up the past. She wanted to know about Agnes's last years, and Jodie told her what she knew. She made her tea and biscuits and listened as Rebecca talked about her mother knocking her over, scrubbing her red raw with a bristle brush and screaming about demons. She'd thought she was going to kill her. Jodie remembered her own night in the dark and they were both quiet.

'She never said sorry,' Rebecca eventually said. 'That's all I wanted.'

Jodie had nodded and taken another sip of tepid tea. She remembered Nan's deathbed. She'd certainly said sorry to her.

The sun was hot, but the elder tree from next door's allotment shaded her. Jodie looked at the pile of weeds and leant back on her heels. She took in a deep breath. Warm creosote and leaf mould filled her nostrils. A light breeze rattled the CDs and milk cartons on the bamboo poles. Owen was low at the moment, and she was pulling up a couple of lettuces to take over to his flat for tea, when she felt the first pain.

She'd struggled long and hard with the question of medication during pregnancy. Owen said she should point-blank stop taking them. She was scared about what would happen, and it was Rebecca who had suggested cutting the dosage to see. Dr Hassani had gone along with it. So far, it was okay. She had bad days, but it was okay. She took in another deep breath and the contraction eased.

She lay down on the ground out of the shade, on her back with her arms stretched out, and looked up at the sky. Tiny transparent shapes floated down in front of her vision. She followed them down, and when she rolled her eyes, they shot back up to the top again. The sky was blue and hazy. The baby shifted and pushed on her bladder. School must be out because she could hear children shouting and squealing off in the distance. She closed her eyes. She was going to have a boy.

She couldn't be sure that there wouldn't be hard times ahead. Owen was flaky as ever, and she knew she was still up and down. But at this moment, lying there in the sunshine with the CDs rattling and the wood pigeons cooing, she was content. She wasn't lonely. She was happy.

Acknowledgements

Thanks to Paul, Sean and Michael for your love and support. Thanks for suggestions and encouragement to Juliet Annan, Carly Cook, Sue Cook, Sara Gowen, Bill Hamilton, Lucille Kaye, Clodagh Phelan and Jane Rogers.

Plus, of course, my mum.

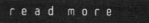

MARINA LEWYCKA

A SHORT HISTORY OF TRACTORS IN UKRAINIAN

'Two years after my mother died, my father fell in love with a glamorous blonde Ukrainian divorcee. He was eighty-four and she was thirty-six. She exploded into our lives like a fluffy pink grenade, churning up the murky water, bringing to the surface a sludge of sloughed-off memories, giving the family ghosts a kick up the backside.'

Sisters Vera and Nadezhda must put aside a lifetime of feuding to save their émigré engineer father from voluptuous gold-digger Valentina. With her proclivity for green satin underwear and boil-in-the-bag cuisine, she will stop at nothing in her pursuit of Western wealth.

But the sisters' campaign to oust Valentina unearths family secrets, uncovers fifty years of Europe's darkest history and sends them back to roots they'd much rather forget...

'Hugely enjoyable...yields a golden harvest of family truths' *Daily Telegraph*

'Thought-provoking, uproariously funny, a comic feast. A riotous oil painting of senility, lust and greed' *Economist*

'Delightful, funny, touching' *Spectator*

'Extremely funny' *The Times*

ZOË HELLER

NOTES ON A SCANDAL

'Superbly gripping. One of the most compelling books I've read in ages'
Daily Telegraph

From the first day that the beguiling Sheba Hart joins the staff of St George's, history teacher Barbara Covett is convinced that she has found a kindred spirit. Barbara's loyalty to her new friend is passionate and unstinting and when Sheba is discovered to be having an illicit affair with one of her young pupils, Barbara quickly elects herself as Sheba's chief defender. But all is not as it first seems in this dark story and, as Sheba will soon discover, a friend can be just as treacherous as any lover.

'Excellent. An undercurrent of subtle malice, cleverly controlled by Heller'
Evening Standard

'Fascinating, brilliant, horribly addictive' *Guardian*

'The most gripping book I have read so far this year' *Independent on Sunday*

'Deliciously sinister' *Daily Mail*

He just wanted a decent book to read ...

Not too much to ask, is it? It was in 1935 when Allen Lane, Managing Director of Bodley Head Publishers, stood on a platform at Exeter railway station looking for something good to read on his journey back to London. His choice was limited to popular magazines and poor-quality paperbacks – the same choice faced every day by the vast majority of readers, few of whom could afford hardbacks. Lane's disappointment and subsequent anger at the range of books generally available led him to found a company – and change the world.

'We believed in the existence in this country of a vast reading public for intelligent books at a low price, and staked everything on it'
Sir Allen Lane, 1902–1970, founder of Penguin Books

The quality paperback had arrived – and not just in bookshops. Lane was adamant that his Penguins should appear in chain stores and tobacconists, and should cost no more than a packet of cigarettes.

Reading habits (and cigarette prices) have changed since 1935, but Penguin still believes in publishing the best books for everybody to enjoy. We still believe that good design costs no more than bad design, and we still believe that quality books published passionately and responsibly make the world a better place.

So wherever you see the little bird – whether it's on a piece of prize-winning literary fiction or a celebrity autobiography, political tour de force or historical masterpiece, a serial-killer thriller, reference book, world classic or a piece of pure escapism – you can bet that it represents the very best that the genre has to offer.

Whatever you like to read – trust Penguin.